# Can't Stop Believing

Center Point
Large Print

Also by Jodi Thomas and available from
Center Point Large Print:

*Chance of a Lifetime*
*Just Down the Road*
*The Comforts of Home*
*Wild Texas Rose*
*Texas Blue*
*The Lone Texan*
*The Tender Texan*

**This Large Print Book carries the
Seal of Approval of N.A.V.H.**

# Can't Stop Believing

## JODI THOMAS

CENTER POINT LARGE PRINT
THORNDIKE, MAINE

This Center Point Large Print edition is published in the year 2013 by arrangement with The Berkley Publishing Group, a member of Penguin Group (USA) Inc.

The text of this Large Print edition is unabridged.
In other aspects, this book may vary
from the original edition.
Printed in the United States of America
on permanent paper.
Set in 16-point Times New Roman type.

ISBN: 978-1-61173-858-2

Library of Congress Cataloging-in-Publication Data

Thomas, Jodi.
  Can't Stop Believing : a Harmony Novel / Jodi Thomas. —
  Center Point Large Print edition.
    pages cm
  ISBN 978-1-61173-858-2 (Library binding : alk. paper)
  1. Vendetta—Fiction.  2. Arranged marriage—Fiction.
    3. Texas—Fiction.  4. Large type books.  I. Title.
    II. Title: Cannot stop believing.
  PS3570.H5643C36 2013
  813'.54—dc23
                                                      2013020266

For Sally Cottrell.
A woman whose bravery
will always make her a hero in my heart.

# Chapter 1

March 2012
Harmony, Texas

Cord McDowell felt sweat trickling down his back as he worked in the pit beneath the semi-truck's engine. He ignored the heat along with all the sounds and smells around him. His hands were black with oil and dirt, but he didn't dare take a break. Old Man Whitaker had been itching for a reason to fire him since the day he'd come to work three years ago.

Tannon Parker might own the trucking company, but Whitaker ran the shop. The old ex-Marine had told the boss he'd take Cord McDowell on, but he'd also fire the convict the first time he messed up. Like a vulture, he'd been waiting and watching for his chance. Cord made a habit of being early to work and last to leave. He ignored jabs from the other mechanics and never talked to anyone unless he had reason. Cord worked alone, here and on his farm.

As long as he worked here he had a chance of keeping his farm, and as long as he had his farm, he held on to one dream. The last dream.

When Cord had been arrested nine years ago, his folks had a couple hundred thousand in reserve to cover bad years of farming, but when he got out of prison there was no seed money in any account and they'd both been buried long enough for weeds to grow up around their graves.

"McDowell!" Whitaker yelled from above. "You dead down there?" He barked a laugh. " 'Cause if you're dead, we might as well just fill in the hole with dirt and move on. No one will waste time trying to haul that big body of yours out."

Cord fought down a curse and pulled himself up. "I'm about finished. Another two hours if I work through lunch." He knew that would make the old man happy. He liked having his men work the noon hour without an extra hour's pay, and Cord didn't really mind. The work was easier than sitting in the box of a break room while men talked around him but rarely to him.

"Never mind the truck, McDowell. There's a lady out front who wants you to work on her Jeep. Says she won't have another man even open the hood."

Cord wiped his hands on a rag almost as dirty. "Since when do we work on anything but Parker trucks?"

Whitaker looked like he was irritated to even have to talk to Cord, but for once he didn't sound angry when he answered, "That's what I told Mr. Parker when he called saying he was sending her over, but Parker isn't a man to argue with. If he wants his shop to work on a Jeep, we'll work on a Jeep, even if the damn thing looks like it should have been scrapped twenty years ago."

Cord remembered how quiet he'd been when he'd met the owner of Parker Trucking. Cord had just stood in front of the massive desk and waited for Tannon Parker to read his application. The trucking company was the fifth place he'd applied that day. Every other shop had taken one look at where he'd learned his skills, Huntsville Prison, and said they'd call if they had an opening. One guy had glanced up at Cord and simply said their business hadn't had anything stolen in five years and he planned to keep it that way.

Parker, however, had studied Cord's application for a few minutes, then walked around the table and offered his hand like the part about Cord being in prison for six years hadn't mattered.

"We need good mechanics," Tannon Parker said. "Welcome to the company, McDowell."

Parker was the first person who'd treated him like an equal in years. Cord had been so shocked he barely remembered how to shake hands. He'd made up his mind that day that when he earned enough money to quit, he'd go back into Parker's office, shake hands with him again, and thank the owner for giving him a chance.

As he followed Old Man Whitaker through the maze of hallways toward the front office, Cord reminded himself he worked for Tannon Parker and not for Whitaker.

The sun almost blinded Cord as he stepped out the front door and into the cool morning air. There was a March chill, but he could feel spring coming. In another few weeks he'd need to have seed in the ground.

"Over there." Whitaker pointed with his head.

When Cord raised his gaze toward a beat-up old Jeep parked at the end of the drive, Whitaker swore, mumbling something about wasting time.

Cord pulled his worn baseball cap from his back pocket, combed his sandy blond hair back with one rake of his hand, and crammed the hat on his head. He followed the foreman over to a woman leaning against a piece of junk that looked like it had seen its best days thirty years ago.

As he neared, he recognized Nevada Britain. His farm bordered her huge ranch. He'd watched her from a distance riding her horses full out across her land or driving down the county road past his place at twice the speed limit, but it had been years since he'd seen her up close. If possible she was even more beautiful than she'd been at sixteen.

Only today, she was stone cold sober, a far cry from the wild, drunk teen he'd once watched.

Whitaker took on his official role as shop

manager. "What seems to be the problem, little lady?"

Cord hung back, staring at Nevada Britain beneath the shadow of his cap. A smile twitched at the corner of his mouth as he saw that she hadn't liked being called "little lady." Whitaker didn't pick up on it and was therefore destined to make the mistake again.

She was taller than Whitaker's five feet six inches and looked like she was dressed for a funeral in her expensive charcoal suit and high heels. Only her white blouse was unbuttoned just enough to show a hint of lace when she straightened.

Maybe the wild teen hadn't completely vanished, Cord thought.

No, she wasn't quite funeral proper, and she knew it. From all he'd read, Nevada Britain hadn't been proper in years. If Harmony, Texas, had a tabloid, she'd be the centerfold.

She was beautiful, he'd give her that. Darn near perfect as far as he could tell from looking, but from what he'd heard, she was no lady. Some said she had her mother's beauty and her father's ruthlessness. Cord had never figured Nevada Britain out. She looked like she'd always gotten everything she wanted, but it never seemed enough. She'd even called the sheriff on him once for flying too low over her horses. People like her even thought they owned the air.

Harmony was a small town, and he'd heard about her wild parties and parade of loser husbands. Apparently she fought to outdo her three crazy brothers.

Technically, he was her neighbor, but she didn't even wave when she passed him. She lived five miles down from him, but it might as well have been another planet. The Britains called themselves ranchers, but mostly they were from old oil money. When he was in prison, his mother used to send him clippings of their court battles and wild ways. He'd seen pictures of her in the Founders Day parade and riding one of her fine horses at some big horse show. Like all the other pictures of her, she wasn't smiling, so it didn't surprise him that she didn't smile now.

When he went to prison there had been four Britain children, all sent to private school back east after they aged into double digits. By the time he got out of Huntsville, two were dead. One from an overdose and one from a drunken boating accident.

Nevada was the youngest, and probably the only person in the county disliked more than he was. Folks said, to the Britains' way of thinking, there was only one way—their way. Like pit bulls, they were bred to be hot-tempered scrappers and all the money in the world couldn't wash away heredity.

"How can I help you, Miss Britain?" Cord asked as Whitaker moved aside. He'd seen Parker Trucking's rigs going onto her land and could guess why Tannon Parker had said yes to having his men look at her little Jeep. Business was business. Parker probably shipped all the cattle they raised.

She frowned at him. "Is that you, Cord McDowell, under all that dirt and grease?"

"It's me." He was surprised she remembered him. They hadn't talked since he'd been arrested ten years ago, and they hadn't been friends then. Cord braced himself for the insult or questions to come. Something about how he had liked prison or how he was wasting his life.

"I heard you were working here." She leaned her head sideways as if studying him. "Tannon says you're the best mechanic he's got."

Looking surprised that Cord and Nevada were talking, Old Man Whitaker said something about getting back before the whole damn shop fell apart and left the two of them to work things out.

"I don't work on Jeeps much." Cord kept his voice low. Nevada wasn't afraid of him, which was more than he could say about most women in town. They all seemed to think that since he'd been in prison, he might go ballistic any minute and murder the whole town.

"I know," she pouted, like the spoiled woman

13

she probably was. "I've been to every garage in town. Nobody knows how to fix it. Half of them wouldn't even take a look."

"You could take it into Amarillo. There'd probably be someone there." He couldn't help but wonder if the other shops didn't want to deal with her, or the Jeep. He'd heard that her father had bankrupted the company who'd sold his son the speedboat years ago.

She pulled off her sunglasses and looked up at him with tears in her beautiful blue eyes. Cord had no trouble seeing why she'd had three husbands and wasn't out of her twenties. Any man would have trouble saying no to her.

"Please take a look at it, Cord," she said, as if she knew him well. She patted the old piece of junk as if it were her pet. "She was my grandfather's, and if she gives out, I'll lose the last part of him."

Cord knew how she felt. Sometimes things get attached to the love left behind when someone dies. Maybe that happens to leftover love when there's no one to pass it along to. He had one of those "things" taking up half of the old barn on his farm. His grandfather had loved the old biplane, and he couldn't bear to junk it.

"All right," he said. "If you'll leave it with me for a few hours, I'll see what I can do."

She handed him her keys. "You'll handle her with care?"

Her hand touched his for a moment as he answered, "As if she were my own."

He stood next to the Jeep watching Nevada walk away. For the first time in longer than he could remember, he wished for more than he had.

# Chapter 2

Martha Q Patterson drove away from Parker Trucking with the image of Cord McDowell and Nevada Britain stuck in her mind. Like she always did on her morning errands, she watched people, and those two were saying more with their body language in a few minutes than most people say aloud in a week.

For a few blocks she let the plot of a steamy novel play out in her thoughts. Tough guy in working clothes talking to society girl who'd been wild since she started wearing a bra. The lines from a song about a man not fitting into her highbrow world drifted through the imagined scene. Martha Q might be older than the two of them put together, but she could remember romantic times she'd once had in a garage with her fourth husband.

Or maybe it was her second. It was hard to keep

track, but the smell of motor oil still turned her on even though her engine never got a chance to run these days.

Everyone in town knew Nevada Britain. The girl was on her way to breaking Martha Q's record for number of husbands. Just seeing her standing beside Cord, good-looking trouble that he was, made Martha Q start writing love scenes in her head as she drove. Ever since she'd signed up for the creative writing class at the library, Martha Q couldn't stop building backstories in her mind. The habit was getting so dominant that she sometimes confused what was real and what she'd made up.

Occupational habit, she decided. All great writers have the same problem. Or at least she thought they did. Take George Hatcher, owner of the used bookstore; she'd provided him with a far more interesting past than he'd probably ever manage on his own. Martha Q waved at him as she made the square on Main and headed toward her huge old house that she'd turned into a bed-and-breakfast after her last husband died.

Once she'd made up a story about dear old George Hatcher being a time traveler come back a hundred years to collect period pieces for the History Channel. Martha Q couldn't seem to be completely truthful with the man who smelled like mildewed old paperbacks. She even left out one of the ingredients to her apricot scones just in case he planned to take it back to the future someday.

As she turned into the oldest neighborhood in Harmony, Texas, Martha Q let her mind drift back to the way Cord McDowell had tipped his greasy ball cap like it was a top hat when he'd said good-bye to Nevada in her tailored suit and she'd tried to look him in the eye. He was a gentleman, Martha Q decided, beneath all that dirt. It didn't matter what folks said about him.

Some claimed he'd gone wild one night and almost killed a deputy, but Martha Q figured there was more to the story. She considered herself an expert on crime because she had a pen pal in prison who grew more handsome in her eyes with every letter.

A moment later she was ripped from her fantasy when she almost slammed into the black hearse parked in her driveway.

Martha Q opened her door and wiggled out of her boat of a car before the engine finished its usual death rattle. As always, she'd parked too far to the left of the thin sliver of concrete and had to fight the budding elm branches to move around her car. "I'm going to cut that thing down before . . ."

She stopped when she noticed someone was listening to her talk to herself. Martha Q never minded the habit, but she hated others eavesdropping.

"Tyler Wright," she yelled at the man on the

17

porch as she waddled toward him. "I told you not to come before eleven. I get my nails done on Mondays and I need time for them to dry before I can have a proper conversation." She waved her fingers in the air while her purse, looped to her elbow, battered her ample breast.

The chubby funeral director just smiled as he watched her heading toward him. "It *is* eleven, but I'll be happy to come back if you like." He bowed slightly. In his black suit he looked funeral ready.

She frowned. Agreeable men always bothered her. She'd preferred the yellers and fighters. They made the best lovers, that was a fact. Course, they always turned into ex-husbands who either cried or stalked her. She'd figured out one fact about men years ago: Most couldn't do two things at once. It didn't matter if they were having sex or yelling, they didn't seem to be able to think at the same time.

Tyler Wright smiled as she neared, obviously having no idea what she was thinking, thank goodness.

"No, don't leave." Martha Q grabbed the railing and pulled herself onto the porch. "I need to talk to you, Tyler, and it has to be before noon. The widows will be back as soon as they finish the early-bird lunch at the Mexican Hat."

She motioned for him to take one of the wicker chairs on the wide porch of the Winter's Inn Bed-and-Breakfast. "I don't want you coming back, or staying too long for that matter. The neighbors will get the idea I've died and rush over to start picking at my bones."

"Now, Martha Q." Tyler sat beside her. "You know they'd do no such thing."

"I *don't* know." Strike two, she thought. She didn't like being corrected even when they both knew she was wrong. To argue her case, she added, "I think one of them stole my new rake. It was here, right by the porch, all last fall and then one day it was gone. Thought about turning it in to the sheriff, but she sometimes pats my hand. I decided rake theft was probably a hand-patting crime."

When Tyler laughed, Martha Q huffed up. "Just you wait about twenty years, Mr. Wright. Once you're into your sixties, folks start patting on you like they're testing to see if you bite before they step closer."

He rocked back in his chair. "I'm feeling older every day. Too old to be a father for the first time. Kate and I will both be forty-six by the time this baby comes in a few months. We'll be signing up for Medicare about the same time he enrolls in college."

"He?"

Tyler grinned. "He. Doc says for sure. I'm going to have a son."

Martha Q couldn't resist reaching over and patting his hand. "The next generation to run the

Wright Funeral Home. He'll be the fifth. Think of the history."

Tyler shook his head. "Kate and I have both promised we won't push him that direction. She says all her family has been career military. He might pick that road instead."

They both rocked in silence for a few minutes, Tyler lost in his future and Martha Q lost in fiction. She'd made a rule to never live in the past and did her best to stay out of problems in the present, but one was bothering her and it was time she got down to business.

"Tyler, I asked you here because you're Joni Rosen's friend. She and the two other widows you sent over last month seemed to think they can homestead here at my place."

The funeral director straightened, knowing the visiting was over. "Is something wrong with Mrs. Rosen? Has she been ill? Has she caused problems?"

"No, but she ain't right. Her husband died four months ago, and everyone understood when she stayed at my place after the funeral, but I'm not a boardinghouse. She needs to go home. Her place is so close she could walk, but instead, she's now entertaining the other two widows. I swear if they stay much longer I'll have to rename the place Widows' Inn. They play cards and watch movies until almost midnight, then wake me before nine tromping up and down the stairs."

"I wouldn't have thought she'd tromp," he whispered to himself. As always, Tyler looked concerned. Martha Q wasn't sure whether he felt it or had just developed a habit over twenty years in the burying business.

"Does she still pay her bill?" he finally said. "Her husband left her a nice insurance policy and she has her teacher retirement."

"Yes, but that's not the point. I'm used to folks coming and going, not coming and staying. I've had to get up and put on my makeup every morning for four months and now, with three of them, I'm running to the store more often for food and having to wake up the housekeeper regularly to keep the place clean. I only got two more rooms to rent and honeymooners aren't likely to book with three women in black sitting on the front porch knitting like happy Halloween decorations."

Tyler smiled.

"Don't you dare laugh. Being this beautiful at my age takes a lot of time and money. I'd like to sleep in, put on my oldest jogging suit, and read all day, but no, I have to be the innkeeper." When he didn't offer an answer, she prodded. "You got to talk to her about getting on with her life. She's young, not even fifty-five yet. At that age I still had two or three good tries at marriage in me."

Tyler stood. "When will she be back?"

"I never know. I have to stay dressed all day

just in case. She sometimes goes the ten blocks over to her place to do her laundry on Mondays. I keep thinking she'll just decide to stay, but she doesn't."

"I'll talk to her," Tyler frowned. "I have to anyway about her husband's headstone."

Martha Q stood. "Good." She was halfway to the door when she remembered her car still parked behind Tyler's hearse. "Thanks for coming over. I'll drive back out so you can leave."

Tyler walked beside her to his car. "I'll let you know when the baby comes."

"You won't have to. Everyone in town will be talking about it. It wouldn't surprise me if the hospital sold tickets to the waiting room. Give Kate a hug if you can still get your arms around her."

He nodded as he climbed in his long black car and waited for her to back out.

"Babies." Martha Q shook her head, and then an idea of adding a secret baby to her romance plot came to her and she couldn't wait to get back to her study and write. She might go thirty, maybe even forty minutes before her lunch break. Long writing spells always made her hungry.

# Chapter 3

## McDowell Farm

From the shade of his porch, Cord McDowell watched the road with mounting anger. His neighbor, Nevada Britain, was driving up his dirt drive like she was drag racing. The little Jeep he'd spent hours working on left a half-mile trail of dirt behind as it roared toward him.

He knew the second she spotted him. She slowed and he wondered if she was surprised to see him home before dark. There were always a dozen chores on the farm he needed to get to even after he stopped plowing. Only tomorrow morning he wanted to be at the bank when it opened, so he'd come in early. After three years of saving every dime he could, he was still five thousand short on paying off the loan he'd gotten the week he'd walked out of prison. Some said no one would give a convict a loan, but the bank hadn't hesitated when he put up his farm as collateral. If he couldn't pay, they'd make twenty to one on their money.

He'd dress in his best jeans and head for town

at first light, hoping they'd give him three more months to pay. One more season. Then, if it rained and the bugs didn't find his spring crop and the tractor held out, he might be able to come up with the money. Swearing under his breath, he watched Nevada come closer, feeling like he was Moses waiting for the next plague to strike.

Cord shoved what money he planned to pay on the loan deeper into his pocket and watched his beautiful, spoiled, selfish neighbor approach. Whitaker had been the one to hand her the keys after the Jeep had been repaired, and she hadn't even bothered to walk to where Cord worked in the garage to thank him.

There was little hope that she'd driven over after three days to say thanks, so Cord figured he must have done something wrong. Hell, she'd probably come to threaten to sue him for stirring up too much dirt while he plowed too near her fence line.

He watched her stop halfway between his barn and his parents' old house and look around as she climbed out. He hadn't had the time or the money to fix up the place, but right now it seemed to look worse than he thought. Imagining his farm through her eyes made him wish for more hours in the day, more days in the week, more time, period. Then he could have painted the barn, fixed up the fence, replaced the steps.

Only it was too late to worry about it now.

She was dressed western from her red boots to

her leather vest. If some women are shiny-penny pretty, Nevada was silver-dollar beautiful.

Near as he could remember, he'd watched her every chance he'd gotten since the day she was born. They'd gone to school together, ridden the same bus home a few times when her mom didn't pick her up, and then in the fifth grade she'd disappeared. She'd gone away to school and he'd only seen her riding her horses now and then during vacations. When her dad let her start driving, even though she was a year away from being legal, everyone on Sunset Road tried to stay out of her way.

Fighting down a grin, Cord remembered the half dozen cars she'd wrecked before she got driving down pat. One she'd rolled in the drainage ditch. Her parents had left it there a month, probably just to make her pass it every time she went to town. He doubted the lesson had taken.

Pulling off her sunglasses, she tossed her long blond hair back like it was a mane and she was ready to run. He liked the way she moved, all fast and headstrong, like she owned the world—and, as near as he could tell, her family did. Talk was that when her parents died her brother, Barrett Britain, cleaned out the family bank accounts and bought a villa in France. He left her with the ranch and the oil business, saying the next time he came to Texas he'd be in a pine box. She'd taken over everything, and as she walked toward

Cord, he realized he didn't even know how to talk to her.

"You're home," she said, as she stormed the porch with a large envelope in one hand and her hat in the other.

"Yep," he said without explaining, knowing it would irritate her. He wasn't disappointed.

She glared at him, as if considering turning around and leaving.

If he wanted her to stay, even a minute, he'd better think of something. "Why are you here, Nevada? Looks like the Jeep is still running."

She surprised him by saying, "I was in a hurry the other day or I would have stopped in to say thanks. You got it running better than I ever remember."

"Guess I should be glad you didn't bring the sheriff." She'd called in a complaint two years ago and he'd almost been fined. If the sheriff had sent deputies, he'd have been cuffed and hauled in before they even bothered to ask questions. Every lawman in the county except Sheriff Alexandra Matheson had dropped by to warn Cord that they'd be watching him. Alexandra wasn't friendly, but he guessed she was fair. She'd asked questions first.

"I can't believe you're still upset about that. If I hadn't sent the sheriff, you know you wouldn't have listened to me, Cord. I left three messages on your phone before I called Sheriff Matheson.

You can't just go flying that old plane around over my land. It stampeded my horses."

"I don't answer my phone." He shrugged, accepting an ounce of the blame.

Before he could step back into their two-year-old feud, she stopped him with an open palm like she was a crossing guard for his front porch.

"I didn't drive out here to talk about that. I came to ask a favor."

Every drop of anger and frustration went out of him even though he didn't move an inch. "A favor?" The Britains had never asked the McDowells for anything in three generations. His grandfather said once that they started out with bad blood over the boundary between the two ranches, and the wound it left would take a hundred years to heal.

"I'm not selling," he said, the first thought that came to his mind. She could probably already smell blood in the water, but he'd lose to the bank before he'd sell to her.

"I'm not asking," she snapped, none too friendly for a woman asking for a favor.

He remembered a time when she'd been home for Christmas break when they were in high school. He asked her for a date and she'd turned him down so fast it took him several heartbeats for his mind to catch up with his ears. They'd both changed a great deal in ten years. She'd grown from a skinny girl to a beautiful woman, and he'd turned into stone. Even now, if he'd been brave or wild enough to pull her against him, she'd feel no heart. Any kindness, any caring, had been beat out of him in Huntsville.

She straightened, all proper. "What I'm offering is a business deal that could benefit us both."

"I'm not interested in doing business with a Britain, and I'm fresh out of favors." He looked down at her and was surprised to find that she wasn't looking at him. He'd always pictured her as straightforward and demanding, a queen in her realm. Now he wasn't so sure. He didn't know her well enough to be able to tell if she was being shy or simply taking a moment to plan her strategy.

He'd watched her drive past his land. He'd seen her in town a few times, but they'd never been close enough to speak. Two years ago she'd called the sheriff on him. She hadn't even given him time to tell her he'd been having engine trouble and was flying low, praying he'd make it to his land before he crashed the plane.

Her hands tightened into fists, and she slowly raised her head. "I knew I'd be wasting my time coming over here. Since you went to prison, everyone says you've been nothing but mean. You don't have a friend in this world, Cord McDowell, and as near as I can see, you never will. You live out on this dry, worthless land and work all day seven days a week and for what? So you can die alone? I'll probably be the one who finds the body and has to see about the funeral, and I don't like you, either. If you weren't my last choice, I wouldn't be here, so you're going to have to listen to me for a minute before I leave and never step on your land again."

Cord felt a lecture coming on, so he sat down in one of the metal chairs that had been spray-painted a dozen times. While she paced, planning her next attack, he studied her. Watching Nevada storm was better than watching anything on TV.

Finally, she stopped and placed the envelope she'd carried onto the porch railing. "I came all this way and I'd like you to at least consider my offer. What I have to say is too important to give up on."

"All right," he said, knowing he wasn't buying or selling, but listening he could afford.

She stared out at the open land as she lowered her voice to almost a whisper. "I can't explain any of the why, so don't ask. Just hear me out and then say yes or no."

"Fair enough." He propped his long legs on the railing beside the manila envelope. "Tell me, Miss Britain, why'd you come out here?"

"I'm prepared to offer you the three hundred acres of my land that borders your land."

"In exchange for what?" Cord knew, as well as she did probably, that she was offering him the same plot of land their great-grandfathers had fought over. "I fear the price may be more than I can afford." The rich land was worth more than his farm, and he doubted the five hundred in his pocket would buy more than a few rocks.

For the first time she didn't look sure of herself, but she plowed forward. "I can't tell you why, but I promise you there will be no disadvantage to you. I'll sign the deed over to you when we're at the courthouse and our bargain is sealed. The land will be yours free and clear from that time on."

He frowned as he rocked back in his chair. "What's my part of the bargain?"

"Your name," she said simply. "The land is yours if you'll marry me and agree to live on my ranch for as long as we're married. I think eight months should about do it. That should be enough time to get a crop in, increase the herd and stock for winter."

The front two legs of his chair hit the floor. "I'm sorry; I thought I just heard you ask me to marry you?"

She looked down. "I told you I can't explain, but I've had my lawyer draw up a prenuptial agreement. Your land will remain yours, along with the three hundred acres, when we separate. Mine will remain mine, along with all Britain holdings." She squared her shoulders as if preparing to fight. "All I'm asking for is eight months. From now until the first hard freeze should do it. After that either of us can file for divorce and, as stated in the prenup, we both agree not to contest the divorce. All profits from both ranches will be combined for the length of the marriage and split evenly when we separate."

Cord felt like laughing out loud for the first time in years. Ideas this crazy only appear in jokes, or con schemes. Just for the hell of it, he asked, "What makes you think we'll separate?"

"I've been married three times before, and all three cost me dearly. This time I'll know the price going in. If you want, you can have total control of the farming and ranching on both places, but anything dealing with the horses or the oil business is mine. It's part of the agreement. I'll hand over the ranch business and accounts to you and trust you to run them wisely, since half of the profit for the term we're married will be yours. The horses are not part of the bargain, and no one can sell them or move them without my permission. I've seen the way you work, the way you run this place, and I think you'd be able to handle both my land and yours."

"What else?" He knew she was either crazy or trying to pull one over on him, but he'd hear her out.

"You'll have to quit your day job at Parker Trucking, but when we split, half of my ranch's income should compensate you for the loss of wages."

"What does your spread pull down?"

"A quarter million in profit on a down year when the ranch is worked. Since my dad got sick and died it hasn't been worked. If all goes well, we clear over half a million on a good year. The ranch is in my name only, so I can bargain with it and I've got enough funds to make it work."

He would have tried to look disappointed, but his jaw was open too far to fake it. She'd just offered him nearly a quarter of a million to stay married to her for eight months.

This had to be some kind of sick joke. She was playing a game, probably. "Why should I believe a word you've said?"

"Look at the agreement," she said as her fingers tapped the envelope. "Talk to your lawyers, then let me know what you decide. The only thing I ask is that we keep this agreement to ourselves. As far as everyone knows, you're just the next man I fell in love with and brought home. Most folks won't ask any questions."

"Are you crazy, lady?" He had to ask, though it occurred to him that either way she'd answer no.

"Don't call me lady or honey, or darling, or babe—"

"Got it." He stopped her before she went on. "You're not dying, are you?" It was the only reason he could think of that a woman like her would want to marry him. She might still die, but maybe she figured being married to him would make the time she had left seem longer.

"I said I wasn't answering questions, Cord, so don't bother asking. It's yes or no." She turned to leave. "I'll be at the courthouse all morning. If you show up before noon, the deal is on; if not, don't bother ever speaking to me again."

"If I say yes, I want one thing added." He figured he'd push a little to see how far she was willing to take this prank.

"What?" She looked back at him.

"If I play your husband, I want you sleeping beside me every night until it's over." He guessed sleeping next to him would shock her out of this game she seemed to be playing.

"Why?"

He smiled. "No questions why. Do we agree or not?"

He thought she'd keep walking, but as always, she surprised him. She turned and walked back until she stood a foot in front of him, her boot almost touching his.

"I've married and slept with three men I thought I knew and didn't. One more added to the list won't matter. I agree. Only, I warn you, if you ever hit me, I'll shoot first and wait for an apology later."

He studied her cold blue eyes and wondered if she'd been hit in the past. He'd bet on it.

"Just look over the papers, Cord. I swear I'm not trying to pull anything over on you."

"All right. I'll look at them." He doubted he'd have the time.

"As soon as possible," she added, pushing just a little.

"As soon as possible," he agreed.

She was doing a good job of acting like this mattered to her. If this was real, maybe he was just the lesser of two evils she had to pick between.

She straightened and took a long breath. "I'll make plans to meet you at the courthouse. My lawyer's office number is on the envelope. If you show up, we'll sign everything there and the three hundred acres will be yours."

He nodded once. "I'll be there by eleven if I come."

She gave him a jerky nod. A fighter realizing the fight was over.

For a moment he thought he saw fear in her eyes. Not of him, but of something beyond tomorrow if he didn't come. "Are you sure about this?" he said in little more than a whisper.

"No," she whispered back, "but it's the only plan I have."

Without another word, she walked away. No good-bye, no hello-next-husband kiss. To her this was a business deal, and he had no idea why she needed him. He'd be signing away eight months of his life if he showed up tomorrow, but he'd given away time before. Six years in fact.

This time, no matter how bad it was, if he took her offer, he could be walking away a rich man. He could farm the three hundred acres for a good profit alone this summer and, with just eight months of her farm income, he could afford the right equipment to make his land pay when he moved back home.

Cord picked up the envelope and began to read. Somehow this was too good to be true. She'd even included bank statements. He wouldn't be taking over a rundown ranch with everything falling apart. The account could easily buy whatever he'd need to get started. He'd driven by her land, and most of it that he could see from the road wasn't being used as farm or ranchland.

The sun was down by the time he finished reading every line twice. All the facts were there, except for the sleeping arrangements. Even if she planned to torture him for eight months, it would be worth it for enough money to really start farming. Once he was making money on his land, it wouldn't matter that no one spoke to him. He could come back here and live alone in peace.

He'd never been a gambler, but this time he might just roll the dice.

After cleaning out the refrigerator, he packed the one old suitcase he owned and set it by the door, then lay awake in bed until five thinking of all the reasons she might have asked him to marry her. None made any sense.

He called himself every kind of fool, but he'd always said he'd never had a chance. What if his crazy neighbor was offering him a chance? One slim chance to change his life. Did he really want to toss it away?

He got up, drank the last of the milk, and took a shower. It wouldn't hurt to go see if she was really waiting for him at the courthouse.

On his way out, he picked up his mother's thin gold ring and slipped it on his little finger, then locked up the house and headed for town in his pickup, with a rusty trailer pulling the one horse he owned.

While he drove toward town, he went over the contract one more time in his mind, looking for the deep well he was sure he'd fall into. All the details Nevada had talked about were there. From the day they married he'd have control of the Britain ranch as well as keep total control of his own property. If the marriage lasted eight months, he'd receive half the profits from both ranches. Since his would be lucky to make twenty thousand over the summer, he wasn't taking much of a risk compared to her. There was enough money in her accounts to buy several hundred more head, and the grass was already up high enough to feed them. They'd have a good season with cattle alone, not counting the crops he planned to get in the ground.

The deed to the three hundred acres had been

folded in the envelope. It already had his name on it. All it needed was her signature. She'd even included a title company's notarized statement saying she was the sole owner of Britain land.

He headed to the town square deciding he must be dreaming. Tomorrow he'd wake up and find himself back in the grease pit working. *But today,* he thought, *I might as well ride this dream out.* Maybe her insanity was spreading.

On impulse, he stopped in at Bailey Brothers and bought a suit. When Cord walked out in his new clothes, he couldn't seem to get comfortable. He felt like he was wearing a costume, trying to pretend to be someone he wasn't, but there was no turning back now.

He walked across the street to the post office. If he was really going to be getting married in a few minutes, he might as well change his address.

"Morning," the bashful woman behind the counter greeted him.

"Morning, Ronny," he answered, remembering the time he'd dropped in and asked her who'd paid for the postage on all the newspapers he got in prison after his folks died. She'd looked so shy and embarrassed; he'd left without waiting for the answer.

Since then he'd learned her name was Ronny Logan and he had a faint memory of her from school, only she was very timid and he'd been wild, running with a group of boys who called themselves "The Outlaws." She was still shy and he'd learned to avoid people, so that kind of made them alike. Not that it would be likely that their types would ever get together and form a club, but they had something in common, it seemed.

He picked up the change-of-address packet and headed out.

"Cord." Her soft voice stopped him.

"Yeah," he said, surprised she'd called his name.

"You look real nice today."

"Thanks, Ronny."

Stepping back out into the morning air, Cord straightened. Compliments were so rare he could almost feel them raw on his face, but he stood taller as he walked back toward the courthouse square.

# Chapter 4

## Courthouse

Nevada Britain watched from the third-floor window of the courthouse as Cord McDowell walked into the building. Her heart pounded faster and faster. She had hoped he'd come, but she hadn't believed he would.

He was bigger than any of her former husbands and solid as a rock, and handsome in a keep-your-distance kind of way. But his looks and his manner had nothing to do with why she'd asked him to marry her.

She knew she was taking a gamble that might get her killed, but she'd let others stop her from doing what she knew was right before and lived to regret it. If Cord was a cold man able to kill in rage, she'd know it soon enough. In a few minutes she'd be betting her life on one trait McDowell did show. He was a survivor.

Cord might turn out to be as mean as a snake like folks said, but he was easy on the eyes and she'd developed an instinct about when to run. She liked the power in his movements, like he was a giant trying to walk among fairies. When he wasn't in public, his shoulders were straight and he seemed taller, but now, while people were watching, he kept his head low and his shoulders rounded to pull his six-foot-five frame down a few inches.

When he stepped off the elevator and moved to where she stood by the windows, Nevada noticed his old boots had been polished and the suit was so new it still had wrinkles from hanging on the rack. His tan skin warmed against the white of his open-collared shirt.

"You came," she said, more to herself than him.

"I forgot to buy a tie. I'm sorry." He looked as

uncomfortable as she felt. When she didn't say anything, he added, "I brought the contract."

"My lawyer had another copy. We'll stop in his office first." She forced a smile she didn't feel. "Don't worry about the tie. You look fine." *A knight in not-so-shining armor,* she thought, *or a killer who'd honed his skills in prison.* Either way, her troubles would be over.

He just stood there looking at her. Finally, he said, "I know you said you don't want to tell me why you're doing this, but before we take another step I have to know what I'm getting into. Not all, maybe, but some."

She managed a nod. He was right. He should know. "I've got problems with the drilling business. I need to be at the office. The ranch is losing money. If I don't turn it around I might lose it too."

He met her eyes, and she knew that fighting for her land was something he understood.

She rushed on before she lost her nerve. "And I've got an ex who wants to make life miserable for me. If he knows I'm married again, he might move on." Nevada closed her eyes, knowing that she was leaving out boulders and talking about pebbles but she wasn't used to sharing her troubles.

"Fair enough." Cord seemed satisfied. "Let's do this."

They walked down the hallway, and he cleared

his throat twice before he said, "I've got a thousand questions about the ranch, but we can talk about them later." He seemed to be fighting to keep his voice conversational, to just talk to her like they were two normal people going to get married. "I jotted down some ideas I want to go over with you."

"I hope I know the answers. I gave everyone on the Boxed B the weekend off so we'd have time to look at the books and ride the land. You're not taking on an easy job, I got to warn you. I've tried to keep everything going, but half the ranch hands quit and the other half seem to be waiting around doing nothing until I fire them. I can't handle both the oil business and the ranch, so you'll be in charge there."

She wanted to add more about trouble sure to come, but it would be best to bring him in a little at a time. Letting him believe her biggest problem was the ranch would be the safest plan. If he knew more, he'd bolt on her.

They reached the office door. "Work doesn't scare me," he said before he turned the knob. "I didn't figure it would be easy. Nothing in my life ever has been."

She nodded, thinking they had more in common than he knew. "From this point on, I'll trust you, Cord, if you'll trust me. It's the only promise I can make, but you have my word." The lie only stung a little on her tongue as she told herself omitting a problem isn't lying. "I need you far more than you need me in this deal, and the strip of land between our places is a small price to pay. With you by my side I may still lose it all, but at least with you I have a fighting chance."

"I'll try trusting." He touched her arm. "But I'm not long on practice in that area."

The white-headed lawyer in a thousand-dollar suit rushed to greet them. "Welcome." He grinned. "We're ready for you, Miss Britain."

Nevada straightened, moving into her planned speech. "Call me Mrs. McDowell, and this is my husband-to-be, Cord. I've never given up Britain to take a husband's name, but I think I'll take this one. I'd like people in this town to know I'm married to Cord McDowell."

The lawyer grinned as if he thought she was joking. When she didn't say anything, he rushed on. "I'm happy to meet you, Mr. McDowell. If you'll just step this way, we'll get the papers signed and witnessed. Your bride tells me you both are in a hurry. The judge who'll marry you is already waiting in the conference room."

Nevada tried to keep her breathing slow, but it wasn't easy. She knew the routine. Said all the right words. Signed all the papers. Only she hadn't expected Cord to slip a thin gold ring on her finger when he said, "I, Cordell Harrison McDowell, take you, Nevada Britain, to be my wife."

The judge didn't say *You may kiss the bride*

when he finished. She guessed he figured she'd already been kissed enough.

Cord didn't move toward her, and she couldn't even bring herself to look at him. She'd rushed him into this only half believing he'd agree.

Now he shook the hands of the lawyer and the judge. He seemed in a hurry to be out of the office, but once they were in the hallway, he stood silent, looking at the rug beneath his boots while she tried to think of something to say. They'd been neighbors all their lives, but she knew little about him outside the young boy she'd once seen in school and the time he'd spent in prison since then. She'd heard that his parents had been quiet people already into their forties when he was born. Someone said his mother died of cancer and his father followed her in death a year later of a heart attack.

"You hungry?" Cord finally spoke as they waited for the elevator. "I didn't bother to eat supper or breakfast, so I could eat half a beef."

"All right." She wasn't sure she could keep anything down, but at least he had a suggestion. If he planned to wait for her to come up with something, they'd be growing along with the grass on the courthouse lawn.

"Where do you like to eat?" He waited for her to step into the elevator. When the door closed she became very much aware of him in the small space.

"I don't usually eat out in town. I have a great cook at the ranch."

"I like the diner across the street and down a few doors. I eat there now and then. Whatever's on the daily special is usually good."

She nodded, making note that he wasn't particular about his food, or apparently his clothes. The pant legs of the suit were an inch shorter than they should be, and with his light brown hair, the gray suit washed him out like a camera shot out of focus.

"I need to check in at the office, then I'll meet you there," she said as she moved outside.

"Fine," he answered. "There's something I need to take care of too. Thirty minutes?"

"Thirty minutes," she said, and almost ran to her car. As she drove the few blocks to her offices, she noticed him walking toward Parker Trucking and guessed he was going to quit.

Thirty minutes later, it was almost noon and the Blue Moon Diner was packed when they met at the door and walked in. Several people looked up, but no one spoke. She recognized a few of the town's folks but couldn't call them by name. The Britains didn't mix with the locals, never had.

"Friendly group," Cord mumbled as he slid into the booth across from her. "Must be you. I can't think of a thing I've done wrong lately."

She smiled. "If you weren't married to me, you probably wouldn't speak to me either."

"You got that right." He surprised her when he winked at her.

Nevada laughed. He was being honest, just like she'd asked. Suddenly it didn't matter that folks thought the Britains were uppity or that Cord was an ex-con. "If I weren't married to you I wouldn't talk to you either, Mr. McDowell."

"Sounds like a great way to start a marriage, Mrs. McDowell."

She caught the corner of his mouth lifting slightly before he raised his menu and said, "It's going to be a conversation-packed marriage. I can already tell."

Staring at her menu, she fought down a giggle. Maybe, just maybe, this marriage might be tolerable. At least until he got to know her. Then, like all the other husbands, he'd begin to pick her apart. Thanks to her father, her brothers, and three ex-husbands, she'd learned the hard way that something—no, maybe everything as far as they were concerned—was wrong with her. Only this time, after the eight months was up, she wouldn't stay around for the insults. This time she'd planned her escape ahead of time. She'd walk away with a working ranch, and he'd have money for a fresh start at his old place. If trouble didn't come, they might just both survive until winter.

They ordered, then sat in silence for a while. Absently, she played with the wedding band. "Thanks for thinking of the ring," she finally said.

"It was my mother's," he answered. "When you pull it off, Nevada, I'll pack. No discussion. No argument. Fair enough?"

"Fair enough." He'd just answered one of her worries as if he'd read her mind. Now all that she could hope for was that he might truly be a man of his word. "I'll give it back when we're over, but it was a nice gesture."

"I won't need it again."

She felt sad somehow for him. "You never know. You might marry again one day and want your wife to have the ring."

"I don't think so. You're the only woman who's come down the road asking in three years. What are the odds of it happening again?"

She laughed. "After being married to me for a while, you'll probably swear off women forever."

"You that much of a tornado, Nevada?"

She stared straight into his brown eyes. "And if I am?"

He didn't turn away. "I've always liked the wind."

She relaxed slightly. For the first time since she'd walked up to his porch last night, she felt like they just might have a chance of making this contract work for both of them.

They ate their meal in silence. The waitress brought the bill and he pulled cash from his pocket and paid. From the way he looked at his money, she guessed there was no reserve in his pocket.

When he stood to leave, he offered her his hand. She felt his strong grip around her fingers, and a bit of the nervousness that had kept her awake all night returned. For the hundredth time she wondered if she'd made the right decision. In a lifetime of turning the wrong way at every corner, fate had to let her make a right turn sometime, and maybe this was it.

He didn't let go of her hand until they were past all the people and out in the street.

"We need to stop at the bank," she said. "I called them this morning. They'll have everything ready."

He nodded, as if he knew what she was talking about.

When she walked in, she was halfway to the president's office before she realized Cord had turned off at the first teller.

She waited, trying to look patient until he joined her. "Have to stop and visit, did you?" The young teller was still smiling at Cord and acting like she didn't even notice Nevada.

"No." He didn't explain what he'd been doing. "You jealous already?"

The question was so ridiculous she almost laughed. "No, but I hate to be kept waiting. You might want to remember that. Let's get this done."

She marched into the president's office and they

began to sign papers again. Nevada couldn't keep from watching him shift slightly when the banker told Cord that he'd have sole control of the Boxed B Ranch accounts.

Somehow they'd managed to get him a leather folder of business checks with his name engraved along the bottom and the Boxed B brand just below.

"Nevada can still sign on the accounts, but she tells me you'll be handling them. If you have any questions, Mr. McDowell, just let me know. The general account has bonds in reserve, but if you need money for a short run, we'll be happy to extend you a line of credit."

The banker passed him a money bag. "This is the cash Nevada said you'd need to keep on hand at the ranch." He handed Cord a debit card. "This draws off the checking account for any little expenses. I'm afraid if you need more than a thousand in one day you'll need to write a check." He grinned. "I'm guessing you're going to pay off what's left of that loan on your farm today."

Cord raised his head slowly from the debit card. "You're guessing wrong. I'll be in next month with another payment if you've no objection. That's my land, my responsibility. I'll pay it off with my money."

"But . . ."

Cord put on his hat. "Thank you for the help, but we need to be getting home."

To her surprise, Cord offered his arm to her. When she took it, he walked out of the bank as if he didn't notice everyone staring. Half the people in the bank must have figured out that they were married, and they couldn't have looked more shocked if she'd hitched up with one of her daddy's prize longhorns.

As before, when they were outside, he let go of her hand. "Is that all we have to do?"

"Yes."

"Good. I've had enough of town."

"Me too." They agreed on something.

"I'll follow you back to your place," he said, pulling off his suit jacket as they walked toward the parking lot.

"Is that your trailer with a horse inside?" The old blue pickup she'd seen on their road was now hooked to the oldest horse trailer she'd ever seen.

"Yeah. I had to bring him along. I couldn't leave him behind, not knowing when I'd get back to feed him, and the pasture fences wouldn't hold him."

She ran to the trailer and looked inside. A powerful gray stallion stomped and pushed against the trailer wall. "Cord, he's beautiful." She hadn't expected that he'd bring more than a suitcase to her land and certainly not a fine horse.

Cord stood beside her and smiled. "His mother was my horse when I was a kid. Only horse we ever had on the farm. My dad wasn't fond of them, but my mother thought I should have a horse, so my dad found a gentle mare. When I went to prison, my dad just turned her to pasture. He wrote me a year later and said she'd had a colt. By the time I got out he was grown and wild."

"But who was . . ."

"They say mustangs run deep in the canyon, but I've never seen them. More than likely, one of your stallions jumped the fence and found my mare."

"My horses would never have come over uninvited. They're all thoroughbreds." She laughed. "What do you call him?"

"Devil. My grandfather told me once that his father said the finest horse he'd ever seen was named Devil, so I thought I'd call him that."

"Well, he's welcome to come over to stay, but I'll not have him mixing with my mares. I'll bet he doesn't even have papers."

Cord shrugged. "Nope, neither do I. You sure you want to take us in?"

"I'm sure about the horse. The jury's still out on you." A man who loved his horse couldn't be all bad, she decided. "I only ask one favor: If you come home with me, you've got to let me buy the right clothes for your life as a rancher. That suit looks like Bailey Brothers pulled it off a rack they had in the basement from the 1980s."

"I don't care much about clothes, and picking

this suit out was pure torture. Knock yourself out. I'll wear whatever you want me to as long as it's not orange. I hate that color. Mr. Bailey, back in the store, insisted on taking my measurements, so he should know the sizes. I don't plan on going in for a fitting again in this lifetime. Most clothes I've ever bought, I just held them up to see if they'd fit."

She stepped away from the trailer and hurried to her car. They'd just settled their first agreement in marriage. Maybe things would go smoothly for a change. She had a world of problems lurking like spiders in the shadows, and Cord might just take one of them off her hands.

Her last husband, rich with his family's oil money, wanted her ranch and thought she came with it. With the ranch crumbling from neglect and poor management, he might have had a chance to buy it, but if Cord could turn the Boxed B around, it would remain hers. She'd bought her brother's share when their father died and she planned to keep it, only Bryce Galloway had fought the divorce and kept her in court long enough to drain her reserves. She knew she had only one summer's stake left to make the ranch pay.

Driving onto her land, Nevada smiled. This was her home, and she'd never give it up without a fight. This land was not something her ex-husband could have just because he wanted it. It wasn't for sale, and neither was she. Bryce Galloway would just have to get used to the fact that there were some things no amount of money would buy.

She remembered Cord gripping her hand when the banker went over the accounts. It must have looked like a great deal of money for running a ranch, but it would be needed to make a profit this year.

Five hours later, she was frustrated and Cord was furious. They'd gone over the books, and even she could see that a ranch with the best equipment and finest stock around was losing money. It didn't appear that any of the three bookkeepers she'd had in the past year had embezzled, but all the part-time foremen were obviously wasting money and showing little profit.

"I'll go put on some coffee." She headed toward the kitchen. To her surprise, he followed her.

Without asking, he began opening cabinets.

"Looking for something?"

"Food," he answered, without stopping his search. "I've developed this habit. I like to eat at least a couple times a day." He pulled out a dozen eggs and a skillet. "Hand me the butter and cheese."

Before she knew it she was chopping up a salad while he scrambled eggs. She asked if he wanted her to open a bottle of wine, but he shook his head and poured two glasses of milk.

They ate in a comfortable silence, both calming down from the stress of the day. All afternoon Cord had asked her questions about the ranch, and her answer was always the same: *I don't know.* She had all she could handle taking care of her prize horses and running the trust as well as the oil corporation. At the end of the day there was never any time to study ranch business. The place had been running itself for two years, and it hadn't been running well. Since her longtime foreman had been fired by her last husband, the men who stepped into the job seemed to be progressing steadily into incompetence.

"Tell me how the house runs." He finally broke the silence. "I don't want to be in the way."

She thought about saying that it was the staff's job to stay out of his way, but she just stated the facts. "My cook usually comes about nine. I don't eat breakfast. She does the light cleaning, the laundry, and the cooking. She leaves about five unless I have guests and need her to stay. When I entertain, the bunkhouse cook, who is also her husband, usually helps her. A couple comes in once a week for the heavy cleaning and the yard work in the courtyard, but Ora Mae, my cook, has an herb garden off the back porch."

Cord listened as he ate.

"Ten years ago, before she ran off, my dad's last wife insisted on a courtyard, and somehow we've managed to keep it up."

"What time is breakfast at the bunkhouse?"

"Seven, I think."

"Monday morning we'll have breakfast in the bunkhouse with the men. After the hands settle into the fact that I'm running the ranch, you can sleep in if you like, but I'll eat with them every morning. After Monday, breakfast will always be served at dawn in the bunkhouse until fall."

He finished off her last bite of egg and added, "Ready to get back to the books? I thought when we're finished I'd like to see maps. As you know, I've flown over your land a few times, but I need to know every inch of it."

She groaned but followed him back to the massive old study she'd always thought of as her father's even though he'd been dead for two years.

After answering a dozen more questions, she tugged off her shoes and curled into her father's old leather chair. It still smelled of his pipe tobacco and the right arm had worn from years of balancing a whiskey glass. She didn't miss her father or mother, but now and then she missed the parents they might have been. She missed having just one memory of her father reading to her in this chair. Just one simple memory would have been something to hold on to.

An hour later she fell asleep wondering if this strange man she'd just married would ever stop working.

# Chapter 5

Duplex near the town square

Ronny Logan stood in the dark shadows of the front yard of the duplex she'd rented for two years. As the lights of the old town square blinked a shadowy yellow, memories flowed around her in the cool breeze. She felt like she'd been asleep the first twenty-seven years of her life, a shy child dominated by an overbearing mother. Through childhood she'd believed she was loved and her mother was trying to mold her into the perfect little girl, but during her teens she realized she'd never pass Dallas Logan's scrutiny. Her mother saw her as not just flawed, but damaged. By Ronny's twentieth birthday, her mother had convinced her that she was worthless.

Her father had simply been Dallas's first victim, and he hadn't done much better than his daughter. When he died, however, he left his half of the house to his only child. Since she finished school, Ronny had worked at the post office, as silent and invisible as a midnight mouse. She'd believed nothing would ever change, and then one day while making a delivery, she met a handsome man in a wheelchair, and her world moved from gray to bright colors.

Within a few months she bloomed, and when Marty Winslow left Harmony one night without saying good-bye, she ran away from home and moved into his old apartment. Dallas disowned her ungrateful daughter of twenty-seven years, and Ronny decided she'd survive better on her own. Marty Winslow might not have stayed around, but he'd believed in her, and one person believing is a long way from none. He gave her hope.

Only now, standing with the moonlight breeze blowing her long brown hair as the gentle sounds of Harmony surrounded her, Ronny Logan knew her life was about to change again, and this time was far more frightening than leaving home.

"You all right out here?" Beau Yates, her neighbor, startled her as he rounded the corner. Like her, he always dressed in a black jacket and dark jeans to move through the streets after dark.

"I'm fine," she answered as he seemed to materialize from the shadows. He was younger than her and always kind, even though with his black hair and late hours she often thought him more vampire than human. "I thought you were playing at the bar tonight."

"I am. I just ran home to pick up my new guitar. It seemed easier than driving the few blocks. My lungs could use the fresh air." He opened the unlocked side of the duplex and grabbed a case that must have been waiting at the door for him. "I have to get back before the break is over. The thought of Border playing on his own scares me." Beau laughed. "There's only a dozen drunks still in there tonight, but they'd give their best try at murdering him if he played."

Ronny didn't laugh at his joke, so he slowed, trying to see her in the poor light. "You sure you're all right, Ronny?"

"I'm all right, Beau." She couldn't think of a lie, and he didn't seem to need one. When you're twenty, nothing about life makes sense so you don't bother questioning.

He leaned against the wall as if sensing she needed to not be alone for a moment. "I like the stillness of this time of night. One of these days I'm going to write a song. I think I'm going to call it 'Between Heartbeats' because that's kind of what it feels like."

When she didn't say anything, he pushed away from the side of the house and headed toward the road with a wave and a flash of a smile.

As she listened to him jogging back toward the bar, she grinned at him even though he'd gone. Beau and his roommate, Border Biggs, made her life easier. Her neighbors reminded her of two pups, always getting into trouble, always hungry. They never went to bed before two and burned everything they cooked, but Beau could play and sing good enough to make you believe heaven was piped with country music, and Border was always there backing him up on stage and off.

Ronny closed her eyes and thought about what the kid had said about the night. She could almost feel the stillness, like daytime was for the heartbeats and the night seemed the silence in between.

A long black Lincoln turned onto her street and pulled up in front of her house, drawing Ronny's attention back to the present.

She looked toward town, making sure no one else was on the street. Her mother had been known to drive by, but never this late.

No one moved in the night. Beau and Border would be at least another two hours practicing their music at the bar. When they came in, they'd see her dark quarters and assume she'd gone to bed. No one would miss her if she disappeared for a while.

She walked toward the car as the driver stepped out and opened the back door for her. He nodded politely but didn't look up at her. Once she was inside, he climbed back into the driver's seat, put on music she knew someone had selected for her to listen to, and silently drove away.

As they left the lights of Harmony, she pulled the blanket from the seat beside her and leaned her head back. She had a long drive with little hope of finding happiness at the end. She'd made it before only to be turned away, but maybe tonight would be different. Closing her eyes, she wished for what might have been.

Ronny had no idea how long she'd slept, but the bright parking lot lights of a huge hospital woke her. As she straightened, the car pulled to a side entrance where a tall man in black waited. He was rail thin and his hair looked silver in the harsh light. When she'd seen him once before, he hadn't stepped closer; he'd only shaken his head as if to say *I'm sorry* and slipped back inside the hospital, closing the door so she couldn't have followed.

This time the driver remained in place as the tall man moved forward and opened her door. "Good evening, Miss Logan. I'm glad you agreed to come."

"I'll always come. Mr. Carleon, right?" she said, wondering if anyone else visited at this time of night.

"Yes. I'm the one who sent you the note. I feel as if I know you, miss."

They reached the hospital door and this time it stood open, waiting for her.

"If you'll follow me." Mr. Carleon moved swiftly. "He's expecting you this time and we have no roadblocks."

Ronny straightened and fought back tears. Two years without a word from Marty Winslow, and then a registered letter asking her to be ready an hour before midnight and to trust Carleon to make the plans. *I'll be waiting. Marty* was all the personal note she'd gotten from a man who'd stolen her heart just by being kind to her. He'd never pretended to be more than a friend, but for a woman starved of all love, it had been enough for her to build a world of dreams on.

"I'm sorry about last time, miss." Mr. Carleon kept his voice low as they walked the darkened back hallway. "There had been a shift change I hadn't been aware of."

She didn't care about the wasted journey she'd made a month ago. All that mattered was that Marty Winslow had contacted her. "How is he?"

"Weak, miss. Very weak."

Mr. Carleon moved from one hallway to another until they came to a freight elevator. When the man finally faced her, she saw kindness in his pale eyes and gray-salted hair that had once been black. He could have been anywhere between forty and seventy, but there was strength about him, a stillness that must have come with age.

"I've been with Mr. Winslow since he was ten. I was waiting at the base when the skiing accident paralyzed him almost four years ago." The older man's face wilted with sadness. "He's very near death, miss. This last surgery took all he had, and now infection has set in. The doctors are doing all they can, pumping him with drugs, monitoring him constantly. His parents are dead, but his older brother has taken charge. Daniel insists Marty suffer no pain, but if he takes all the pills, he'll sleep his last hours away."

A vision of how Marty had looked the day she'd met him flashed into her mind. He was alone and angry but very much a man in his chair. With his dark hair and fiery eyes, she'd thought he was a devil, and he'd been angry enough at the world to almost make her believe it.

"How long?"

Mr. Carleon shook his head. "I can only allow you an hour. Maybe a few minutes more."

"No." She didn't care how long the visit would be. "How long does he have left to live?"

"A few days. A week at the most, the doctors say. Even if the infection clears, his body is beginning to shut down. One of his doctors suggested flying him somewhere else for a therapy, but his brother was told he might not even survive the journey. So Daniel finally said no. Two years, five operations, and a dozen hospitals is enough. With Marty here, he'll be home when the end comes. The brother and doctors decided that's all they can do for him. He's out of time, miss."

Ronny fought back her scream. Marty had been there for her when she came alive, and if he asked her to, she'd be there for him when he died.

She had a hundred other questions, but Mr.

Carleon opened a door and she stepped into a private room lined with machines.

For a moment she didn't recognize him. Marty was thin and pale, as though he were fading away. She remembered how his strong arms had held her and how his laughter could fill a room.

It took all her strength to move to his bed and take his hand. Leaning close to his ear, she whispered, "One heartbeat past forever. That's how long I'll love you."

Marty didn't open his eyes.

Mr. Carleon pulled up a chair and offered it to her, but Ronny couldn't sit down. She stood like a soldier as one by one her memories of Marty faced the firing squad until the only reality left was the man in front of her barely breathing. His hand that had once set fire to her with a touch was now cold and limp. His lips that had taught her to kiss were almost white and thinned in pain. His laughter, his teasing, his loving words were all drowned out by the rattle of machines that played an out-of-tune death march through the night.

Minutes ticked by, but she refused to move. She stared, hungry for a sign from him. She took the pain of how little of him remained. A hundred things passed through her mind that she needed to tell him. She'd almost finished her degree in finance. She'd learned to cook. She'd bought a new car. She'd made friends in town. Like he told her to, she'd grown.

But she'd missed him every day that he'd been gone. It took her a while, but she finally figured it out. There was no forgetting Marty, no getting over him. She'd love him forever.

"Miss?" Mr. Carleon whispered beside her. "Miss, you have to go. The hour is up."

"But he didn't wake." She tightened her grip on Marty's hand, hoping he'd at least squeeze her fingers back.

"I was afraid he wouldn't," Carleon said, too calmly to betray any emotion. "I think he knows you're here, though. His breathing has calmed since you took his hand. I've been watching. His heartbeat is steady."

"Can I stay longer, please?"

"Miss, it would mean my job if Daniel knew I brought you here."

"Then why did you?" Never seeing Marty again would have been less painful. "He won't even know I'm here."

"Every time he wakes, he waits until only the two of us are in the room, then motions me near. I lean close and he whispers your name." Mr. Carleon stared at Marty. "I know you're always in his thoughts. I know his brother thinks I work for him, but I work for Marty Winslow and I will until the day he dies."

"Can I come back?" She kissed Marty's hand as she pulled her fingers away.

"I'll send the car every night I can an hour

before midnight. It will wait ten minutes. If you can't make the trip, I'll understand. If I don't meet you at the back door of the hospital, you'll understand. There are very few people I can trust."

"I'll come if the car is there." She walked to the door, not daring to look back. The only man who'd ever thought she was beautiful was dying, and she was allowed only an hour a night to see him, with nothing but a promise of a next time.

As she rode back toward Harmony, tears ran unchecked down her cheeks, and she knew that when Marty Winslow died, so would she.

# Chapter 6

Almost dawn
Duplex

Beau Yates leaned against the windowsill, his body so slim and still he almost looked like a part of the frame. He watched his neighbor step out of a late-model Lincoln and walk slowly toward the porch they shared.

He couldn't help but wonder where she'd been.

If Ronny Logan had been another kind of woman, wild or even normal, he would have guessed she'd had a wild night out, but she wasn't the type. Ronny was warm hot chocolate on a cold night. She was kittens and apple pie and all the kind of things he thought of as pure good. He'd never heard her say a bad word or claim she hated anyone. She didn't even complain about her witch of a mother, who flew by now and then on her broom just to remind her only child that she still hated her.

Beau picked up his guitar as his neighbor went into her side of the duplex without raising her head. Somehow, she had a secret. He didn't know what it was, but he knew it was good. Maybe she prayed at church all night?

As his fingers began to play across the strings, he smiled, thinking of his secret life. He also climbed into a car now and then with a girl he called Trouble, and they raced the moonlight. It seemed the only time in his twenty years of life that he didn't feel like he was waiting for something to happen. With the girl in the ponytail, he just relaxed and breathed in life.

Slowly, he picked out the melody to a song about how most folks while their life away waiting for lightning to strike and set the dullness of their days afire, when all they'd have to do is pull the box of matches from their pocket and strike one.

Maybe Ronny was doing just that.

Beau smiled, thinking that he was one of the waiting ones. His father, a preacher to the bone, was convinced Beau lived in sin. He'd left home. He played in a bar. He shared an apartment with a guy who had tattoos and drove a motorcycle. He stayed up all night writing songs.

Setting the guitar down, Beau watched the first pale light of dawn. With luck, he could be sound asleep before full sunup reached Harmony. At least he'd break the bad habit of staying up all night his father thought he had.

Pulling off his shirt as he walked toward his bed, he thought of Trouble in her car as she let the night wind blow her hair. If she ever came around again, he could get used to her as a keeper in the bad-habit column of his life.

# Chapter 7

Boxed B Ranch

Cord worked until after midnight, then turned off the study lights and carried his sleeping bride to what he hoped was their room in the rambling old ranch house. She'd set his suitcase by an empty closet door, but she hadn't bothered with a tour of the place.

He pulled back the cover on one side of the king-size bed and laid her down. Slowly, he tugged the tie from her hair and let the long white-blond strands spread out across the pillow in streams of gold. With a hunger for something he'd never known, he watched her breathe. She was so lovely, this wife of his, and fragile despite all her tough-girl attitude. For a few minutes he just studied her, learning the curve of her face and the beauty of her hands as he wondered if he'd ever know her better than he did right now.

Neither of them had said a kind word all evening. He'd asked questions and she'd answered, pouting when she didn't know the answer, sharp when he pushed, but always honest. He didn't have to tell her what a mess the ranch was in; she saw it same as he had. If the spending continued without any profit coming in, the Boxed B wouldn't last another year, and she obviously had no one to turn to if she'd come to him.

He doubted she even liked him, but she needed him, and he planned to be there for her—though they both knew they'd be counting this marriage in months.

In one evening with her he'd figured out two things. He already knew more about the ranch than she did, and no other man besides her father had left his fingerprints on the maps in the study.

No brother of hers. No husband had cared about the ranch. He'd be the first since her father to take charge, and that was one question he hadn't had the nerve to ask why.

He told himself that the ranch was why she'd brought him here, but deep down he knew there was more she wasn't talking about. He felt it. A shadow hung over the ranch like an aging dragon waiting to fight one final battle.

When he'd asked about the oil business, she'd said she almost bankrupted it buying her brother's half of the ranch. He'd walked away with millions and left her with two lame businesses about to fail.

*She's a fighter,* Cord thought as he covered her and went to the other side of the bed. The night was warm enough that he spread out on top of the covers and fell asleep to the soft sound of her breathing.

When he woke it was after nine. The glare of full daylight shocked him awake. Cord had gotten up early for so long, he felt disoriented at first.

He didn't see the note on the pillow between them until he stood.

*Gone shopping. Be back at noon.* She'd signed her initials, like he might not know who'd left the note.

He walked around the room, unsure what to do. When he realized he was alone in the house, he went through each room. Five bedrooms, each with a bath. All but the master looked to have been closed off years ago. Two living areas, two dining rooms, one small, one huge. A breakfast nook off the ranch kitchen and a big bathroom next to the back door. The wide office they'd worked in had windows facing west.

Two facts about it tumbled in his mind. One, he could almost see his farm if he stared hard enough, and two, a loaded Colt rested in the bottom drawer of the massive desk. Maybe Nevada kept her father's Colt there to remember him, or maybe she felt there was a need to be armed.

When they knew each other better, he'd act like he'd just noticed it and ask. Maybe. His headstrong wife was afraid of something . . . something more than him. She was skittish as a pony who'd heard a rattler.

Cord found another office upstairs next to an exercise room and a game room. The pool table looked as if it had never been used, but animal heads covered the walls and full gun racks braced each corner. Most of the weapons were classic Remingtons that looked like they'd never been fired.

Cord felt a little like a robber casing the place, but he needed to know the house and he wasn't sure she cared enough to show him around.

The upstairs study was cluttered with papers and books. This was Nevada's world. He could almost feel her here. It looked newly painted in pale blues and greens with sketches of horses covering the wall. When he moved closer he saw dates on each frame along with *N.B.* scribbled in the corner of each. She'd been painting pictures of horses since she was seven, each year getting better and better. Her office was the only room he felt reluctant to leave. The only room that wasn't cold and aged.

He knew without asking that this place might be her house, but she had never made it her home. There were no pictures of family, no trophies, nothing that looked like it might have belonged to any one person.

By the time he got to know the house and showered, Nevada was back. She walked into the bedroom as he buttoned his Levi's. When he looked up she was standing in the door, her arms loaded down with bags and her blue eyes watching him.

He'd never thought of himself as shy, but darn if he didn't feel himself blush. "Any chance you bought me a shirt? The only dress shirt I own is pretty wrinkled after I slept in it." On this full day together he didn't want to wear one of his old work shirts.

She popped out of her trance. "I did. Most of what I bought is being altered or ordered, but I did pick up a few things. You're about the same size as my brother, but I tossed all his clothes when he left." Like a rabid squirrel, she dropped the bags and began rummaging, then proudly showed her prize to him.

"Thanks," he managed to say as she stared at his chest. "You finished looking?"

She ducked her head. "Yes," she mumbled as she went back to digging in the bags.

While he pulled the pins and cardboard out of an eighty-dollar pale blue shirt with pearl snaps, she lined up socks atop a boot box. "I just told the Bailey brothers to load me up with a week's worth of work clothes. They said that after forty years in the business they can guess a man's sizes down to his underwear when he walks in the door."

Cord pulled on the finest shirt he'd ever owned, thinking that she thought it was a work shirt. The cotton had to be blended with silk or something. He thought of telling her a twenty-dollar shirt would do fine, but he'd already agreed she could dress him, so he might as well play along. Shopping was something she probably had made pro in before she was out of high school.

Five minutes later he realized the boots fit perfectly as well. They had an inch heel and the leather was soft. When he faced her, he held up his hands, feeling a little like the world's largest paper doll. "Do I pass?"

"You passed, Cord, when you were just wearing your jeans, but now you look like a man who runs a ranch. Ready to see the place?"

"No," he said. "First we eat. I've already missed breakfast and it's almost noon."

"This feeding you might be a problem. When Ora Mae shows up Monday, I may have to give her a raise."

"Come on, Princess. I'll show you how to make sandwiches. We can eat once we're in the saddle. I plan to see every square mile of this place before dark."

"Let me change first. You can put your things in that closet while you wait." She pointed to the closet where she'd left his suitcase as she crossed the room to the other walk-in closet and bathroom. "And," she yelled over her shoulder, "don't call me Princess."

"Fine," he answered as he stepped into what was now his closet. "This place is bigger than my bedroom at home and there's a dresser built in here."

She didn't answer, and he hoped she hadn't heard. He was sounding like a hick. The walls began closing in on him and he fought to keep them at bay. Years of living in a cell so small he could almost touch the walls played on his mind and made him crave open spaces. Even a closet this big wasn't a place he wanted to spend any time in.

Dropping the bags, he moved back to the door and took a deep breath. Air. He needed fresh air.

In three long strides he was at the wall of

windows and noticed that none were built to open. What kind of idiot builds windows that don't open?

Looking toward her closet door, he saw her standing among her colorful clothes. She'd stripped off her dress and was tugging on her jeans. The bra and panties were little more than lace.

Cord gave up breathing altogether. He'd seen pictures of women nude, movies with beautiful bodies, but nothing had ever affected him like the sight of Nevada. He couldn't have turned away if she'd threatened death.

He watched her button her pants and then pull on a white T-shirt that fit like a second skin. Over the tee, she wiggled into an oversized sweater that hung off one shoulder. Turning, she looked up and smiled. "Finished looking?"

He'd lost the power of speech, so he just stood as still as a tree.

What few brain cells he had left knew he should probably apologize, or something, but all he could get out was, "I . . . I . . ."

She walked past him and picked up her hat. "Look, Cord, we're going to be living together for a while. We might as well get used to each other. I've never been shy and it's nothing I'm sure you haven't seen before."

When he didn't move, she added, "I'll pack up some water and fruit while you collect your thoughts."

With that she was gone. He felt like he was one of those backward people on *Star Trek* who got beamed up on the teleporter of the starship *Enterprise*. He couldn't understand what was going on. Had she just told him it was all right for him to watch her dress? Hell, he felt a habit coming on.

When he finally found the new hat she'd bought him and made it to the front door, she was waiting for him. They were saddled up and riding full out before he could clear the vision of her standing in her underwear from his mind.

Nevada had obviously gotten over the view of him much faster, because she was rattling off facts about the ranch. She might not know anything about the day-to-day running of the place, but she knew its history.

She also knew how to ride across the open land and where all the watering holes and roads were. She could recite facts about the oil production that had been going on since long before she was born.

Again and again he climbed down to feel the earth. The land was good, but very little of it was being used. Except for the pasture where her twenty prize horses roamed, most of the pastureland was empty, if you didn't count jackrabbits. The land that had been plowed under for crops had been abandoned years ago to weeds, and he'd seen records of where hay had been hauled in for winter feed even though there were more than enough barns to hold a homegrown supply.

"There's a great deal to be done." He saw potential.

"Hire who you need," she said. "The money you put in the safe last night should pay any day labor, but the regulars draw ranch checks. I've been advertising for a new bookkeeper for the ranch. You might as well do the hiring. Ora Mae will call those who applied for interviews when you have time. You'll meet all the staff on Monday."

"Who pays the hands?"

"I have been for the last four months since the last bookkeeper quit. Cattle started disappearing about that time, and lately I've noticed the men hanging around the bunkhouse kitchen waiting for orders. Some are good men, I think, but they need a leader. They're not comfortable handling things."

"How many foremen you been through since your dad got ill and stopped running the place?"

"Four. The last one was just a hand, but he tried. Mostly he made mistakes and I wasn't much help to him."

"How many bookkeepers?"

"Three." She didn't need him to say more. "I know. I've got a problem. I have to take off work at the office to show them around, and then about the time they learn everything, they leave. I think someone is buying them away, offering more money. No matter what I do, I can't keep more than the cleaning staff and a handful of cowhands."

Cord swore he saw a tear slide over her cheek, and he had no doubt that she had tried. "I'll make mistakes too. Lots of them." He stared at the sky, giving her time to relax. She'd acted as if he might criticize her for not making a go of two businesses at once. "Can I count on you standing with me, right or wrong? I don't want men going around me and you changing things I'm setting up. If you don't like something I'm doing, I expect you to tell me first."

"You have my word." She climbed down and pulled a water bottle from her pack. "I love this place, but Dad never thought I needed to know ranch business. He didn't even like me showing up at the roundups. To him the ranch was my brothers', and the oil business was a place he'd let me work. It didn't matter that they all three hated it. When my two oldest brothers died, Dad just doubled his efforts to force Barrett to take over. I think Barrett left a week after the funeral, fearing that somehow the land might trap him even with Dad gone. He signed it over to me, and I gave him all cash on hand along with stock in the oil. Sometimes I think I paid too dearly for land I don't even know how to run. I sometimes think maybe the only reason I wanted it was because of my horses, and maybe because Dad didn't want me having any part of it."

"It's beautiful country," Cord said as he swung out of the saddle and took the drink she offered. "You could show a good profit, and you're right —one good season is all you need to turn this place around."

"No. I can't. I've tried." She looked up at him. "But you can." She looked straight at him. "You should know there are those who do not wish you well."

He walked his horse closer to her and whispered, "What else is new?"

The wind blew a few strands of her hair from the clamp she'd twisted back as they mounted up.

"Bring it on," he smiled.

She smiled back at him. "Bring it on," she repeated as they kicked their mounts into action and rode straight into the wind.

# Chapter 8

An hour before midnight
Duplex

Without a single word, Ronny Logan climbed into the black Lincoln and closed her eyes. This was her third ride on the interstates to Marty's hospital room. Each night she thought the car might not come for her, or Mr. Carleon might not meet her at the door. Marty might not still be alive.

She felt like a zombie, walking the waking world but not part of it. Each morning she'd manage to do her job and study. She could sleep in the back of the post office at noon instead of eating, but no matter how tired, she would be waiting in the dark. Each night she dressed in her best clothes and waited for the black car.

The second night she'd been awake enough to realize they were heading toward Oklahoma City, but mostly she slept in the car with its smooth music and warm blanket. Last night after she'd left without Marty waking yet again, she'd felt herself crying in her sleep, but it didn't matter.

All that mattered was Marty and the tiny hope that she'd be there when he opened his eyes.

Tonight Mr. Carleon was there, his hand offering to help her from the car, his face blank of emotions. There was no time for greetings as he rushed her through the hallways and up the elevator.

"How is he?" she asked, not expecting Carleon to say anything.

"He's awake," Mr. Carleon whispered as he opened the hospital room door, "but I don't know for how long."

She moved to Marty's side, afraid to even breathe.

"Hello, beautiful," he said, in a low voice that wrapped her in love as it had once before.

"Hello." All the things she'd thought she would say to him vanished when she realized it was enough just to hear him.

"You wouldn't want to crawl up here and sleep with me, would you?" His voice was barely more than a whisper, but his hand gripped hers. "God, how I've missed you."

She glanced at Mr. Carleon standing in the shadows. He'd told her Marty was dying, not from the illness but from the cures they'd tried. Even the family composed of one brother and a handful of cousins had given up hope weeks ago. Now, his brother checked with the doctors a few times a day but didn't bother to visit a man sleeping away his last hours. Daniel had left orders to be notified if there was a change, and a few of the cousins still brought flowers but didn't stay.

Having her near had been his last wish, and Mr. Carleon was there to help. If nothing else, he'd block the door tonight.

The older man nodded slightly, and she carefully leaned down beside Marty and laid her hand gently over his heart. "I'll love you one heartbeat past forever," she whispered, and thought she saw him smile just before he drifted back into a drug-induced sleep.

After three nights of midnight rides, Ronny felt her body relax. She knew she was probably breaking every rule the hospital had, but she closed her eyes and took the ounce of happiness in her world without love. Her friends had told her to move on after Marty left, find someone else, but how could she settle? She'd rather hold on to a memory.

As machines ticked the minutes away, she let tears flow, wondering if every person just has so many they have to cry in a lifetime. If so, she must be near her quota. Once, Marty's hand touched her hair, moving through it slowly as if remembering every minute he'd touched her in those few months they'd known one another.

Mr. Carleon nudged her gently an hour later and woke her. "It's time to go, miss."

She nodded and moved slowly away as Marty

remained sleeping. For the first time, on the way home, she didn't cry.

She slept and worked and ate . . . and waited for the night.

At eleven the next night the car ride seemed endless, but when she walked into the room, Marty was waiting. His dark eyes slowly moved over her, and then he raised his hand. "You finally got here, honey. I've been waiting."

She sat on the edge of his bed, not knowing what to say and very much aware of Mr. Carleon listening.

Marty wove his fingers between hers. "Tell me about Harmony, beautiful. Tell me about your life. Tell me about your day and every day you've had since I walked out on you."

She could see pain in his dark eyes and wondered if he'd declined the pain meds so that he could be awake with her. If so, she needed to make their time count.

"I moved into your duplex after you left. It's still like what you described once, a cuddly dump." She had so many questions she wanted to ask, but she didn't know if he was up to answering. Did where he'd been really matter? He was here now. "I found the money you left with the cookbook and used it to enroll in online courses. I love the computer you sent. Every time I turn it on, I think of you."

Marty smiled. "I knew you'd need it."

"It's become my life. I carry a full load of classes online, and with each class I make friends going to school in their pajamas. Now I have friends all over the world."

"How's the post office?"

"The same. My route that started with your house and the fire department is the whole downtown square now. It takes me an hour to walk it after I've sorted all the incoming mail. I love walking it, watching the seasons change."

"Do you talk to the people now?" He studied her hand in his as he spoke.

"Some." She remembered how shy she'd been, thinking every stranger might be the one who would harm her. "There are a few that I'm just on nodding terms with."

One by one, Marty asked about all the people who had been in his world when he'd lived in Harmony. Summer, the friend of Ronny's who'd let her room with her when Ronny first left home. Tyler Wright, the funeral director who had always been kind to her. The Biggs brothers, who lived in the other half of the duplex, and Beau Yates, who'd moved in with them.

They were people from a sliver of his past, but she had the feeling he cared about each one. Until the accident he'd lived an exciting life: the best schools, the most thrilling vacations. Money had never been a problem. She knew he'd come to Harmony to hide out in his wheelchair, but somehow he'd found a peace there, and he'd found her.

When she paused, he gripped her hand tighter. "I always meant to come back to you, honey. I swear."

Ronny couldn't answer. She didn't know if he meant it or not. It didn't matter. She believed it, she always had.

"Tell me more," he whispered. "Hearing you makes me forget about the pain."

He fell asleep as she talked about learning to cook.

Mr. Carleon moved to her side. "It's time to go, miss."

She nodded. "I wish I could do something."

"You did, miss. You helped a great deal. You gave Mr. Winslow peace for an hour. You let him go back to Harmony to visit, something neither his brother nor the doctors thought would be wise."

Ronny looked up at the thin man. "Why'd you let me come here?"

"Because he never stops asking about you or for you. He's been all over the world seeing doctors. His brother persuaded him to concentrate on getting better. At first when he asked to see you and his few close friends, the caretakers put up roadblocks by promising only delays. It wasn't hard. He wanted to walk, and the thought of walking back to see you kept him going.

"By the time he realized Daniel wasn't going

to allow him any visitors, his cell phone and computer were gone and a nurse guarded him all hours. He had no way to get to you. Two months ago, after yet another surgery, he was confined to bed, unable to manage even the wheelchair. I watched him turn inward, not wanting the world to see him, but still he'd ask for me to check on you.

"Once we settled in here, Daniel didn't stay around much and the few cousins he never really talked to lost interest in doing their family duty. They had lives to get back to. Hour visits became five-minute drop-bys, and daily trips stretched into weekly stops."

"But you stayed?"

"I stayed. When he ran to Harmony two years ago, I thought his family was right—if I didn't go to help, he'd come back. But now I know I was wrong. If I had gone with him then, he might have made a life even in the chair and not had to go through all the cures that didn't work."

She looked around the room. "You live here, don't you?"

Mr. Carleon nodded. "I leave to sleep a few hours in the morning and shower, then I'm back. I won't leave him again. Even when the private nurses were hired, I remained."

Ronny raised an eyebrow. "The invisible private nurse?"

Carleon smiled. "With all the machines and

nurses just down the hall, the private nurse saw no need to sleep in a chair. I played along with her conspiracy to slip away about midnight and sleep across the street in a hotel where I provided her a room. She's always back by five, and I've promised I'll be here with him and notify her of any change. On weekends I hired her friend under the same arrangements. Both know I'm near if there is any problem, but he sleeps through the night and most days away."

"Thank you," she said as he opened the back door of the hospital. "For being his friend."

Mr. Carleon nodded once. "I wish I'd known you, miss. I would have made the arrangements earlier, but I believed what the doctors and Daniel kept saying about distractions impeding his progress."

She had to ask. "Will you let me know if something happens? I don't think I could bear it if the car just didn't come one night and I never knew."

"I promise." His smile was sad as he closed the door and she stepped into the waiting Lincoln.

# Chapter 9

Monday
Boxed B Ranch

By the third night of his marriage to Nevada, Cord decided they'd developed a habit. He worked until he was dead tired. She fell asleep watching him. He carried her to bed. Then he lay three feet away from her and tried not to think about her or the way she smelled, or how she moved, or how the shadowy outline of her body curved beneath the covers. From the looks of things he would have to learn not to think at all if she was within fifty feet of him. He had a feeling if he complimented her she'd fly into that tornado he'd been expecting since they'd left the courthouse.

Nevada Britain wasn't like what he thought. She didn't seem as wild or crazy as people said. She just seemed lonely and, of course, spoiled. She was a hard worker, not much for talking unless he mentioned her horses, and cold in a way he never thought a woman who'd had lovers would ever be.

Near as he could tell Nevada didn't trust anyone, but for some reason she'd been forced into trusting him with her land. Other than that, she didn't even seem to like him most of the time or want him involved in her life. They talked about the ranch and nothing more. If he mentioned her family, she'd fire up and say she didn't want to talk about them, or her ex-husbands for that matter.

Like they had the first night, Sunday night they'd cooked a simple meal together, and then he'd eaten and she'd picked at her food. When she'd pulled on her riding boots, he'd followed. They'd saddled up and ridden under the evening sky, not getting back until full dark and not having said more than a dozen words to one another.

He helped her with her horse in the new barn for just her herd, and then they rode double over to the main barn, where she watched him take care of Devil. Without a word, he took her hand and they crossed the last forty feet to the back gate of the main house. He guessed they were both tired and maybe a little nervous, but he couldn't think of anything to say as he followed her into the house and back to their bedroom.

They'd settled into a few habits that he didn't mind at all. Neither made any pretense of not watching when the other dressed or undressed. She even rushed into his closet wearing only her underthings to lecture him about maybe burning the clothes he'd brought with him to the ranch. They finally agreed on his packing them in the old suitcase he'd brought and promising to try wearing only the clothes that she bought him. In truth, he'd gotten used to the luxury of well-fitting clothes.

Cord thought of telling her she should never argue with him wearing only a bra and panties, but then she might take his advice and he'd hate that. He fell asleep each night planning what he'd do tomorrow and wishing that he could touch her.

When he woke Monday, she was already in the shower in her bathroom. It seemed strange for a room to have two complete bathrooms, but he'd figured out two days ago that the whole place had been designed by idiots. Half the windows didn't open. Most of the rooms had no use, and if the huge fireplace in the living room was ever lit it would warm all the ranch and half of western Oklahoma.

She came out of the bathroom with a thin robe plastered around her damp body. "I'll be ready in ten for the breakfast with the boys, but I can predict they won't be happy to see us. As far as I know, a Britain has never eaten with them."

"I'm not a Britain."

She frowned as if she wished she'd thought to add that into the contract. "They just won't like it." She lifted her arms to pull off the towel covering her hair. Her short robe moved up a few inches.

"Not my problem," he managed to mumble before stepping into his bathroom, all of his body now fully awake.

After a quick shower, Cord pulled another one of his new shirts from the rack and decided to try a pair of jeans that she'd picked out for him. He wanted to look like he knew what he was doing this morning when he faced the men for the first time. The jeans fit snugger than he usually wore, with a boot cut on the cuffs that was just right.

When he walked past the mirror to grab his hat, Cord noticed his reflection. A rancher, not a farmer, looked back. In this case, he hoped clothes made the man if he was to have any chance at pulling this charade off.

Nevada was waiting for him at the door. To his surprise, she wore a business suit. Her beautiful blond hair, which he'd gotten used to watching sway over the weekend, was now tied atop her head in a little knot that he hated. Everything about her was all business.

"I'll drive you over and introduce you to the men, then I have to get to the office." Nevada straightened her jacket. "I have a board meeting at nine and I need to go over a few things at the office first with my staff."

"You work all day?" Somehow he thought she mostly shopped and had lunch.

"Eight to five, sometimes later." She shrugged. "Between husbands I managed to get a business degree with a minor in law. Never finished in law, but it comes in handy in dealing with contracts and leases."

He didn't miss the sadness in her blue eyes when she added, "I love being here with my horses, but I understand oil." She handed him a small cell phone. "If you need me, just hold down two and I'll answer. I'm the only one who has your number, so unless you give it to someone else, it'll be me calling if the phone rings."

"Fair enough."

The smile on her now-painted lips didn't reach her eyes. "You ready to go face the world as husband and wife? When we step out of this door we've got to make them believe it, and with my record with men it won't be easy. Remember, no one is to know of our agreement. As far as anyone knows, including the staff and ranch hands, we married for love and you're here to stay."

He thought about yelling, *No way can we pull this off,* but something in her stare stopped him. She was silently pleading, begging him to go along with her plan, and he couldn't let her down. He had no idea why it was so important to her, but he'd keep his word. A bargain was a bargain. Until now he'd thought running the ranch was the most important part of the bargain, but now he realized that to her, their playing the happily married couple might be.

Taking her hand, he walked her to her car and they drove to a long bunkhouse a few hundred yards away from the main house. The ranch headquarters was built like a small town with the big house in the center. Trails, two tracks wide, joined most of the buildings like wagon spokes, and he noticed a few four-wheelers around that were probably used to haul goods from one building to another.

Beyond the bunkhouse was a small gravel lot that had been empty when they'd ridden by yesterday but now held several cars and trucks. Nevada had already explained that all but a few cowhands drove into work every morning. The rest went home on weekends but stayed over during the week. Her housekeeper and the bunkhouse cook had a small cabin on the property but spent their weekends at a lake cabin over near Twisted Creek.

Three men stood on the porch watching as Cord and Nevada walked up to the bunkhouse that looked big enough to be a small hotel. One tipped his hat slightly; the other two just stared. None spoke.

Cord tensed, realizing they might not know him, but they had no respect for Nevada. He knew without hearing that these men had talked about her, probably even joked about her behind her back. One of the silent men looked at her with hunger in his eyes as if she were not the boss but a streetwalker passing by.

Cord opened the door for her and waited until she stepped in. When he followed he took in the room slowly.

A dozen more ranch hands were in a great room with a long table that could easily seat thirty on one side of the room and comfortable leather chairs on the other. A middle-aged man with an apron stepped from the kitchen and smiled at Nevada. His was the only smile in the room.

"Morning, Little Miss," the cook said.

"Morning, Galem. I'd like you to meet my new husband." She brushed Cord's arm, showing the first affection she'd ever shown. Her sudden caress made him jerk slightly. "Honey." She leaned into him slightly. "This is the bunkhouse cook and a friend. He's been with the ranch for twenty-three years."

Galem wiped his hand on his apron and offered it to Cord. "Nice to meet you, Mr. McDowell. I heard you were coming. My youngest daughter works at the courthouse and said Nevada married Friday."

Galem might be thin and balding, but his smile was warm and a kind of friendly Cord had rarely seen. Open. Trusting. Accepting.

Cord managed a nod as he sized up all that Galem hadn't said. He hadn't mentioned that she'd married for the fourth time, even though he must have known. He also hadn't told the others, for several in the room coughed. And last, he hadn't lied about hearing about the wedding.

"Galem, if you'll call the others, I'd like to hold a meeting over coffee this morning." Cord moved into his planned speech. "It will only take a few minutes and then the men can ask any questions while we eat. I'll be here for breakfast every morning at dawn, and any man who is tired of working for the Boxed B won't need to join us. Any man coming in after breakfast has missed a day's work."

Galem smiled. He didn't need to call anyone; the men scattered in every direction. Some ran to get the others; some took their seats at the table. Change was on the wind and they all knew it.

"You like it black, Mr. McDowell?" Galem guessed.

"I do, and call me Cord. We've got a long day and no time for extra words."

Galem nodded once at Cord, but Cord didn't miss the wink he gave Nevada. To his surprise he felt a bit jealous, especially when she winked back.

She'd just flirted with the cook more than she'd flirted with him all weekend.

Putting his arm around his wife, Cord turned her toward the door. "I can handle it from here, Nevada. You probably need to get on to the office."

She agreed, and by the speed of her walk, he guessed she wasn't comfortable among the men filling the room. Not one man said a word to her, and she called none by name.

As soon as they were out of anyone's hearing, she whispered, "Galem likes you. Can you believe it? He likes you. I can tell."

"Stop winking at the cook," Cord ordered, but she wasn't listening.

"He never liked any of the others. Wouldn't even speak to my first husband. Spilled boiling coffee on the second, and the third was afraid to go out to the bunkhouse when my brother told him that number two had his privates so scalded he was in constant pain for a week. You'd think Bryce would have known better than to believe my brother; they'd roomed together in college."

"You care about what the cook thinks, Nevada?" Cord's brain was still focusing on the wink.

"Of course. When I was little and he started working here, he was my guardian angel. More than once he stopped my brothers from picking on me. A few years ago he married Ora Mae, and she took over managing the house. He adopted her three daughters, but you'd never know they weren't his blood from the way he brags about them. I've always thought Galem and Ora Mae made a cute couple. You'd think they were in their twenties and not their forties."

Cord relaxed as he opened her car door.

She stood next to him. "I think we fooled even Galem. He seemed to really believe we were a couple. He won't inform on any ranch hand, but he won't lie for them either. If he thinks we're real, so will the others."

"Then this should help seal the deal," Cord said as he put his hands on Nevada's waist and pulled her to him.

Before he could change his mind, he kissed her full on the mouth. She hesitated, trying to pull away for only a few seconds before she seemed to understand. To his surprise, she wrapped her arms around his neck and kissed him back.

He lifted her off the ground as he straightened, letting her body mold along his. The taste of her, the feel of her, the hint of apricots from her shampoo almost buckled his knees.

When she pulled away, she touched his jaw. "That should do it. Thank you for thinking of it."

"You're welcome," he whispered against her cheek.

He lowered her back to the ground and she added, as cold and formal as if the kiss hadn't just happened, "Don't wait up for me. I may not be home until late."

Cord watched her drive away, thinking about how kissing her for real had felt so much better than he'd thought it would. He figured he'd shock her if she knew that when he dreamed of loving, he dreamed of her. He'd even hung the clipping of her riding in a parade on his cell wall once. She'd fascinated him with what his life might have been like if they'd gone on that date ten years ago.

The clipping had lasted only a few months before his cellmate tore it down and told him to stay in the real world for a change. The picture and the dreams had lasted about as long as this marriage probably would, but while it lasted he could feel like, for once, he didn't need to dream.

He walked back to the bunkhouse knowing everyone inside was staring at him.

When he took the seat at the head of the table, Galem came from the kitchen with a steaming cup of coffee. Cord watched as the cook set the cup down carefully in front of him.

"Thanks," Cord said to the cook as the last of the cowhands took their places.

While Galem served coffee, Cord started, "I've studied the books. No one here has had a raise in two years. That ends today. Next, we work with the sun, not on the clock, and every man stops at six unless I've asked for overtime. We'll run a five-man crew on weekends from now on, and any who want to work then will draw time and a half. When it's cold we'll start later, and we'll end earlier when the weather turns bad, but you'll still draw the same pay. Fair enough?"

No one said a word. A few looked shocked, but

most looked like they were calculating next month's paycheck. Cord knew that raising wages on a failing ranch was risky, but these men would bring the place back to life.

"I want to talk to each one of you and see what you like doing best, but understand, until we get this ranch in working order, we all do what needs to be done. If you can't do a job, let me know when it's assigned, not when you fail.

"I count twenty men. We'll need forty, so if you know someone who's honest and wants work, bring him to breakfast tomorrow. If I hire him, he needs to be ready to work. If not, he'll have had a meal for his trouble."

As he talked, Galem put food on the table. By the time they began eating, four men had walked out and the others were asking questions and making suggestions. Most, he figured, were hands who had been around for at least a few years and were happy to have someone finally ask for their opinion on the running of the ranch. By nine, Cord was in the saddle and working. Everything had to be ready to get crops in the ground and cattle in the pastures as fast as possible.

About two the phone in his pocket sounded. Cord walked away from the corral so he could hear Nevada. It seemed like days since he'd seen her, not hours.

"How are things going?" she asked. "This is the first break I've had."

"Fine," he answered, surprised at how fast the morning had gone. "Four men quit. I fired three others." The man who'd glared at her had been one Cord let go. "We're trying to get ready to move what cattle you have left to the north pasture. I'm planning to buy at least a hundred new head tomorrow. The auction is in the morning, and Tannon Parker says he can have any cattle I buy delivered before dark. I've got a crew mending fences now."

"Not the ranch, Cord, how are you doing?"

"I'm good." He thought about saying that he was great. Inside he felt like he was walking in boots that didn't quite fit, but he was giving being boss his best try. One of the men he'd fired had cussed him out, calling him nothing but a con. Normally he would have gotten mad, but Cord knew it was coming. He'd planned what he'd say and how he'd walk away. He had a ranch to run and didn't have time to talk about the past.

"I hired three brothers who rodeo on weekends. They may cut out on me early on Fridays, but they know cattle. Galem calls them the presidents since they're named Johnson, Jefferson, and Jackson."

"Oh," she said, sounding as if she were only half interested. He could hear papers shuffling in the background.

All he could think to say to her now was, "Did you eat lunch?"

"I rarely eat lunch at work. I live on coffee."

He growled like a bear, and she laughed.

"Everyone cooperating?" She changed the subject.

"Everyone except Ora Mae. I went in about an hour ago to grab something for lunch and she ran me out with the broom. Said if I wanted a noon meal she'd serve me on the porch. I told her I didn't have time to sit down, so she threw a couple of apples at me and told me she'd have supper ready at six after I cleaned up. Now I know why you got that room off the back of the kitchen. Your housekeeper won't let anyone in who smells like a cow or is dripping dirt."

"She likes you too." Nevada laughed through the phone. "If she didn't, she wouldn't have tossed apples."

"I don't think so. I'm thinking lunch around this place may be hazardous to my health."

"Of course she does. She threw skillets at my last husband. When he told her he only wanted green for lunch, she mowed the yard and served it up."

"I like her better now." In truth, he liked that Nevada was talking to him about her past. "I'll give Ora Mae another chance, but it'll be from a distance." He hung up and walked back to the corral. As soon as he got more men hired, he'd move a few to his land and get a crop in the ground. The cowhands had been cold at first, but as the day aged and they saw that he had a plan, they chipped in to help. Some of them even took up a challenge to keep up with him and work as hard as he did.

When he walked past the bunkhouse a little before six, a lanky stranger stepped off the porch. His legs were slightly bowed and he wore his hat low. Cord decided he could have stepped out of the past, a cowboy from a hundred years ago just getting in from a trail drive. The sound of his spurs clinking reached Cord, and he stopped and waited to see if the man was flesh and blood.

"I'm Zeb Darnell." The stranger offered his hand, rough with calluses and scars. "Galem called me and said I might want to work for the new boss on the Boxed B. Said you had plans and might could use a cowhand."

Cord nodded and shook hands. "I told men applying to come to breakfast."

"I know, but I've worked here before. I'm a good hand, but I was no foreman. Nevada's last husband fired me 'cause I couldn't read the notes he kept leaving me when I took over the job."

Cord waited, giving the man rope.

"I understand you're buying cattle tomorrow. That's why I came tonight. I've been working at the stockyard, but I'd like to hire on here. I think I could be some help at the auction tomorrow. If you're interested in me working, I'd need to quit there and be started here before the show opens. I know cattle, Mr. McDowell, and I can help you with the buy."

Cord realized he'd learned a great deal about reading men in prison. If Zeb was lying, he was far better at it than any man Cord had come across. Also, he wasn't the type to brag. If he said he knew cattle, he probably did. "I'll see you at the stockyards tomorrow. You're hired."

"I'll go there early to quit." Zeb smiled. "I'll have the stock checked before you get there."

"Fair enough. You're working for the Boxed B now, and I'd like to pick up a hundred head tomorrow. You think we can manage that?"

Zeb tipped his hat. "Yes, sir. Thanks, Mr. McDowell, you won't be sorry."

"Call me Cord, and I'm the one who needs to thank you for coming out tonight. Once we're finished with the buy, we'll eat lunch and wait for the trucks. I'd like you riding back in the trucks with the cattle. You'll know where to tell the drivers to unload if you worked here before."

"I was planning on riding back. I brought my horse here tonight just in case I got the job." He touched his hat. "See you tomorrow."

The man walked toward the parking area at the side of the bunkhouse as Galem stepped onto the porch.

Cord waited until Zeb's old pickup pulled away before he said, "You being my guardian angel, Galem?"

The cook smiled. "Maybe. That cowhand knows cattle better than any man I've ever seen. He's honest too, but he won't work for a fool like Bryce Galloway, who only wanted to play at ranching. When Nevada married Bryce, I knew Zeb wouldn't hang around long, and he didn't."

"He can't read." Cord's words were a statement, not a question.

"No," Galem answered, "but the cows don't notice."

Cord laughed. "Thanks. He'll be a big help walking me through the sale tomorrow. I'm pretty green."

"He needs a job on land, not in feedlots, and he'll help you build the herd. I think he was nervous coming out, being fired once from this place."

"Tell the men that they all start fresh with me when they hire on. No past hanging on."

Galem nodded. "No past," he echoed.

Cord turned toward the house, knowing Nevada had been right about Galem. The cook had just filled a weak spot Cord had been worried about. He knew farming and land, but he didn't know enough about cattle. Zeb wouldn't need to read, just point at what to buy to build the best herd that had ever roamed the ranch.

After a few steps, he stopped and looked back at Galem. "Any chance you know a bookkeeper?"

"Nope, but you might ask around."

Cord almost laughed out loud. He didn't have anyone he knew to ask. If he asked anyone in town they'd probably have him arrested for speaking to them.

After a shower and a shave, he walked into the dining room in clean clothes. The table was set for one. Ora Mae had left a note. *Little Miss's food is in warmer. She said to tell you to go ahead and eat, she won't be in until late.*

He read the note twice, noticing Ora Mae had used the same nickname as Galem had for Nevada. He figured he'd have to hang around a lot longer than eight months before she'd let him use one, if ever.

Cord took his plate to the study and looked over past cattle buys. Every bone in his body hurt from work. He'd pushed the men, but he'd pushed himself twice as hard. At ten he could keep his eyes open no longer. He stripped down to his underwear and crawled into his side of the bed. He was asleep before his head hit the pillow.

Deep into the night he felt the bed shift and knew Nevada had climbed in on her side. She might run around half the night, but she'd kept her word. She'd come home to sleep in his bed.

# Chapter 10

March 14
Winter's Inn Bed-and-Breakfast

Martha Q Patterson was exhausted. When the funeral director's little talk with Joni Rosen didn't seem to work, Martha Q knew she had to think of another plan for emptying her house of widows. She liked the idea of being an innkeeper. It somehow sounded romantic when she started, but since then she'd heard that the two happiest days of an innkeeper's life are the day he opens his doors to the public and the day he closes them.

She needed rest, not more work, but the three widows showed no sign of leaving.

Even worse than having to get dressed and put on her face each day was the problem of writer's block. They were slowing down her great career as the next top writer of sexy, intriguing, apocalyptic murder mysteries. She'd decided from the first to write a book with everything in it. Masochistic shape shifters who time-traveled into Rome as it fell. They ran around producing zombies in togas while they became wine experts.

Her book would hit the best seller lists, she was sure of it.

Martha Q thumped her own forehead. She was getting off track again. She needed to plan.

Maybe ants or termites. The widows would hate that.

Red ants would send the ladies running. Or bedbugs. People hated bedbugs, thanks to the idiot who'd blown them up to puppy size and put them on the Internet. If the bugs had just been butterfly cute, no one would have minded. They'd just toss back the covers and smile as feathery bedbugs flew by.

Off track again.

Martha Q considered hiring a prowler, or a Peeping Tom. She grinned. That would make an interesting story if a Peeping Tom fell in love with an exhibitionist. They'd be neighbors. He'd wear out the grass between their houses and she'd save enough money on window blinds to replant. Every night, no matter the weather, he'd pull on his coat and stand in the flower beds until she turned out the lights after blinking three times, their secret code for *I love you*.

"Off track again," she mumbled as she reached for her bowl of chocolate-covered peanuts.

Half a bowl later she realized every single plan she came up with to send the widows away would also hurt her business. She liked people, with their secrets and stories, coming into her home, making her feel as if she had a big family and wasn't alone.

But she also admitted she was a fair-weather liker of people. It was grand when they came on weekends or even odd days of the week. It was the every-day thing that bothered her. She needed a vacation. Maybe she'd drive up to Kansas and stay at someone else's bed-and-breakfast.

The doorbell pulled her out of her worrying and away from the now-empty candy bowl.

"Darlene," she yelled up the stairs where she thought the newest housekeeper might be. "Stop eating my candy."

"Yes, ma'am. I'll be down in a minute to fill it back up."

"Thank you," Martha Q said over her shoulder as she rushed to the door. One of the widows probably forgot her key, or maybe a few of the half dozen things she'd ordered from the shopping channel had arrived. Every time she couldn't sleep it cost her twenty-nine ninety-five plus shipping. The cleaning products, Christmas lights, and one-size-fits-all cuddle pillows never looked the same in daylight as they had at two in the morning, but the anticipation kept her hoping.

She pulled open the heavily carved door as she plastered on her best smile.

The nice-looking man on her porch didn't appear as if he came as part of any midnight deal. Tall, well built, thirty-five maybe.

"Yes?" Martha Q straightened to her proprietor pose. "May I help you?"

He ducked his head slightly as he faced her; a smile sparkled in bedroom eyes. "I'm sorry I didn't call ahead, Mrs. Patterson, but I hoped you might have a room for a weary traveler. I'm here on business for a few days. I was told this was the best place in town, though I never had a chance to visit during the short time I lived here a few years ago."

After seven husbands, Martha Q had learned to mistrust flattery, but the sound of his whiskey-smooth voice made her wish she hadn't given up drinking. "We do have a room, but I'm afraid it's on the third floor."

"I could use the exercise." He smiled again, and she thought he might be an actor playing a part. She knew she could read people, even if she sometimes read them wrong. That didn't change the fact that she could usually read them, and this one seemed to be printed in smaller type than normal. Like the last crossword puzzle in the book, he wouldn't be easy to figure out.

Maybe he was a famous actor; after all, if he hadn't appeared on *Gunsmoke*, she probably wouldn't have seen him. Maybe he was here scoping out sites for a new series or a reality show based on innkeepers.

Martha Q rattled her head, hoping to shake a few brain cells awake. This guy had *never worked a day in his life* written all over him. "I'll show you the room. Mr.—"

"No need to look it over. I'll take it," he answered, a bit too fast.

She noticed his leather hand-tooled bag already at his feet. Cocky, she decided, like her first boyfriend, who'd always carried three condoms in his pocket. But this one was much better-looking than any guy she'd ever dated, and he was dressed like he had his clothes made just for him. "Come on in, Mr. . . ." She tried again for the name.

"Bryce." He smiled with his too-perfect teeth. "Bryce Galloway."

"Any chance you play loud music and stay up all night smoking and swearing?"

"No. I'm pretty quiet."

Martha Q sighed. "I was afraid of that. I take two nights in advance. Every third night is free and breakfast is at eight thirty." She opened the door wider and invited him in, having no faith that he'd have any effect on the widows. He was too young and too smooth for them to give him a second look. Widows like a man who's lived long enough to have a few bad habits and rough corners they can work on. The first husband might be married for love or even lust, but the second one was usually a fixer-upper.

The good news was that now the inn had only one room left vacant. The bad news, she'd be the first woman in history to scrub her nose off trying to get her makeup removed every night.

Bryce Galloway might be easy on the eyes, but having another guest would simply mean more work.

When she walked into the kitchen to tell her cook that there would be another mouth to feed for breakfast, Martha Q was surprised to see Mrs. Biggs's grandson Border sitting at the kitchen table.

"Is it Sunday night already?" Martha Q said, as if she were really asking a question.

Border, unlike his friend Beau Yates, never knew how to take her. "No, Mrs. Patterson, it's only Wednesday. I just came over to say hello to my grandmother."

Martha Q frowned. The idiot thought she was senile. *This day was going downhill. A change of subject was needed.*

She sat down and cut herself a slice of the pie Border had already had half of. "Border, did you know that I was thinking about becoming a great writer?"

"No, Mrs. Patterson. That's really something. I've never known a writer before. What are you working on?"

Martha Q hated questions about her work. "Well, I haven't worked much yet. First comes the thinking."

"Of course." Border actually looked interested. "That's the part I would have trouble with."

"I have no doubt, but you know Beau and he writes songs. How does he get his inspiration?"

Border shrugged. "He says sometimes he feels like they're already in his head and he's just fighting to get them out. Like the other day I asked him about this girl who sometimes picks him up after work, and he said she'd been on the back roads of his mind. I found out later that them words were in an old song. I swear, he don't just write songs, he talks them too."

Martha Q knew she would get little help from Border. She finished off her slice of pie. "Mrs. Biggs," she said to the cook. "Have you got an extra pie to send the boys? Maybe it'd help Beau write."

"I'll do that." Mrs. Biggs smiled at her tattooed, two-hundred-pound, shaved-headed grandson like he was adorable.

Martha Q decided the pair were proof that love is blind, and with that thought came an idea for a story about a beauty who fell in love with an ugly beast of a man.

She made the mistake of telling Border her idea, and he said he loved that movie even if it was a cartoon.

Martha Q marched off, frustrated that a storyteller had stolen her great idea before she could even get it down on paper.

# Chapter 11

March 15

The Lincoln hadn't shown up in front of the duplex on Monday night, but Ronny trusted Mr. Carleon. On Tuesday when it came, she saw that Marty was still alive but too weak to wake. On Wednesday, he talked a few moments then drifted off. By Thursday, she wasn't sure she'd find him alive. The week had been a roller coaster with little sleep. Even Cord McDowell told her she looked pale when he came in to mail Boxed B letters.

She sometimes wondered if Cord had guessed she was the one who made sure he got a newspaper mailed to him in prison after his folks died. She couldn't think of another reason for him to make a point of speaking to her when he came in while he ignored everyone else. They were two usually invisible people who saw each other.

With the days at work and the nights at the hospital, Ronny realized she was wearing down, but she couldn't stop. When someone is in the hospital, everyone around them dies a little. Each night she saw Marty, she felt his pain as she watched his life slipping away.

The newest rumor Ronny's mother had started was that Ronny's living alone, when everyone knows a girl should live with her mother until marriage no matter how late in life, had led to an unwanted pregnancy. Dallas Logan had a hard time pulling off the rumor because Ronny looked like she was losing weight, not gaining. Plus folks talked to Dallas Logan only long enough to plot their escape.

Ronny no longer worried what her mother told people. She'd said she never wanted to speak to Ronny again, and Ronny planned to do her best to honor that request. Dallas Logan didn't miss having a daughter; she simply missed having someone to control and lecture. Marty had given Ronny the strength to walk away from her mother two years ago, and she'd silently thanked him every day. He'd pulled her out of hell, and even if she hadn't fallen in love with him, she still owed him.

When the black Lincoln arrived an hour before midnight on Thursday, Ronny let out a long breath she hadn't realized she'd been holding and walked to the open door, letting all her worries and problems slip away. Seeing Marty was all that mattered.

Mr. Carleon met her at the back door of the hospital, his face as stony as always.

"How is he?" She braced herself for bad news.

"He's awake but in pain," Mr. Carleon whispered as he moved down the back hallways with her, almost running to keep up.

Ronny felt both happy and sad. She knew Marty had skipped some of his medicine so he could see her. Being awake meant pain.

She almost ran into his room but took a moment to calm, preparing herself for whatever might happen. Reason told her that one night he'd be gone, but reason didn't reach her heart.

When she entered, three men blocked her path to Marty's bed. They were all three tall and lean like runners. One, the oldest at about forty, wore khakis and a bomber jacket. Another, maybe five years younger, was dressed like a hunter, and the third seemed just as comfortable as the others in his suit.

All three stood shoulder to shoulder in front of Marty's bed. They'd been waiting for her, for they showed no surprise. The urge to run washed over her, but she stood her ground. If they wanted her out of the room, they'd have to use force.

"You Ronny Logan?" the one in the suit asked, as if he were quizzing a witness.

"Yes," she answered.

The man who looked like a bush pilot took a step toward her. His eyes were steel and his face weathered past his years. "You sure she can handle this, Marty? The little lady looks like a frightened mouse."

The suit raised an eyebrow. "I don't know about this one, Marty. She looks like she'd break under pressure. You need a bulldog, partner."

Ronny had had enough. She might not be brave enough to talk to them, but she could try pushing through the line.

Bumping the suit's shoulder and the hunter's arm, she darted between them and rushed to the bed. Marty's smile was all she needed to calm.

His fingers closed over her hand as he said, "She can handle whatever comes along. She made it through you three clowns, didn't she?"

Ronny could see the pain in his eyes, but Marty smiled at her. "Honey, these are my three best friends. They were with me when I tumbled off the mountain. The one in the jacket is Ross. He thinks he's the best pilot ever born. Ivan may look dumb in that suit, but he's the best lawyer Austin has to offer. And last is Glen. He's half mountain man, but he did manage to make it through med school even after I dropped out and stopped helping him, so we call him Doc. They said they'd come if I ever needed them, so I called."

"We're here to try and talk Marty out of his craziest idea yet." Doc's voice was low and flavored from the deep South.

"What's that?" Ronny squeezed Marty's hand,

letting him know she was on his side no matter what the idea.

Ivan, the lawyer, took over. "He says he wants to go home with you, if you'll have him. Wants to set up housekeeping in Nowhere, Texas."

Ronny couldn't speak. She just stared at the three men.

Doc took over again. "He's rallied the past few days since I've seen him. I'll give you credit for that. And, considering his condition, if the move doesn't kill him, then his chances aren't that much different here or in Harmony. If he dies, he'll die where he wants to be. While he's living, he'll be with you."

"Right. You might want to think about this and join our side of the debate." Ivan tugged off his suit jacket and stared at Ronny as if he thought she might not be stable. "If he lives longer than expected, you'll be stuck with him, Miss Logan. Our Marty's not an easy man to live with when he's healthy, and when he's in pain, he's the devil. We should know. We carried him off the mountain after he broke his back. More than once we considered knocking him out with a right cross. If he wasn't cussing, he was giving directions and pushing all of us."

They all three agreed. The doctor picked up the debate. "He'll need home nursing, round the clock, and machines. More as time goes on and his body begins to shut down. Near as I can tell, all the hospital is doing right now is trying to make his last days as painless as possible. It looks like the doctors and his brother are just waiting."

"Have you given up on him?" she whispered, knowing that Marty was hearing every word even though he'd closed his eyes.

"No, Miss Logan, we didn't give up on him on the mountain. It took us three days to get down to him and dig him out, then we lashed our skis together and carried him out. We know Marty like no one else knows him. He's a fighter. This move may shorten his life, but he's willing to take that chance. At the worst, it'll make his last few days happier being with you. At the best, it might add some time, but you got to understand from the first, we're counting time in days, not weeks."

"Don't listen to him, honey," Marty whispered. "He's an OB and pediatrician in a little town that makes Harmony look like the big city. Bottom of his class. I'm betting he's wrong."

Doc laughed. "I just might be wrong and I wouldn't have been at the bottom, Marty, if you'd stayed in school. But I'm a realist and don't believe in lying to a patient or a friend."

Marty squeezed her hand. "I'm down, Ronny, but not for the count. Not yet. If Doc's right and I only have a few days, I want to spend it in Harmony with you. But I want to be straight with you from the first. I knew these guys would make sure you understood before you said yes."

Everyone was silent for a moment as Ronny leaned over Marty. Her kiss on his cheek was all the answer they seemed to be waiting for.

Ivan pulled a paper from his briefcase. "When he stopped e-mailing us last year, the three of us stayed in touch with Marty through Mr. Carleon. I believe we've figured out how to make this all happen if it's what he, and you, Miss Logan, really want. The discussion stops here if you're not willing to sign these papers." He straightened. "And as your lawyer, almost, I'd suggest you do not sign. If Marty's brother gets mad and finds a way to cut him off, you could end up going bankrupt trying to care for him. You wouldn't be able to work."

"I've got enough money of my own to ride this out," Marty whispered between clenched teeth.

Ronny thought about it. The only thing she had of value was half of the house her mother lived in. She'd gladly sell it to stay home and care for Marty. "Where do I sign?" She grinned.

"You'll want to take a few days to think about it," Doc added in his slow southern tone. "You'd be taking over legal and medical power of attorney for him. We'll help all we can, but I know his brother. Daniel Winslow won't make it easy on you."

She looked at the three men. They were Marty's true friends. At one time he would have stood equal in strength to them. All three looked like they had doubts about Marty's plan.

"What do you think, Ross?" she asked the man in the leather jacket. His arms were crossed and he'd been frowning the whole time the other two had talked.

"I think I'd rather live a day near someone I love than a lifetime without them. You're going to be taking on hard times, girl, but you got to ask yourself how hard it'll be to walk away."

Ronny could have kissed the pilot right there in front of everyone. He'd turned the problem around. It wasn't Marty's choice or even just what Marty wanted. It was her decision. Her choice. Her life.

Marty didn't seem to be listening. He'd drifted into the twilight between pain and reality, but his hand still held hers.

"I'll sign the papers." There was no pull to walk away. One day, one week, one month, she'd take it. "When can I take him home?"

Ross smiled. "Saturday morning. Doc and I will start for Harmony before dawn by plane. We'll have a day to make arrangements to get all the right equipment installed and a nurse on call at all hours. He'll also meet with a local doctor and fill him in on Marty's condition. If you'll hand us your keys tomorrow, we'll have everything set up by the time the ambulance brings him to your place. Marty told us once that the place is not big.

We'll knock out walls if we have to, but we'll have it ready."

Ronny tightened her grip on Marty's hand. "Is this what you really want, to go back to Harmony?"

His answer came in a slight nod and a whisper: "In a perfect world, I'd come home to you."

"Where do I sign?" she said again. She was no child. She knew what she'd be getting into. A battle to keep him alive. A possible battle with his brother. It wouldn't be easy, but she had friends who'd help her.

As she moved through the papers, she planned. "I'll go to work tomorrow and ask for a vacation. I've got enough days not to have to worry about working for a while. I'll move all the furniture into the bedroom and kitchen. You can put his bed and the machines in the living area."

The three men nodded as if they'd already talked everything out with Marty.

When Mr. Carleon walked her to the waiting Lincoln, he said simply, "If you want to come back tomorrow night, miss, you can ride down with Marty in the private ambulance. Ivan and a medic will be with you and I'll follow in a van with his personal items. We'll have you both back in Harmony by one. I'll stay with you until you feel comfortable and the nurse is satisfactory, but I'd like to get a room nearby. Then I can sit with him some and run errands for you both to make this time easier. Do you have a suggestion where I can stay?"

Ronny couldn't stop smiling. After all he'd done, he was talking as if they were simply planning to visit. "There's a bed-and-breakfast close. In fact, Martha Q Patterson owns the duplex I rent. I'm sure she'll have a room."

He nodded as he opened the back door for her. "I'll be in touch with her about the lodging. Try to get some sleep. I'll send the car tomorrow night."

"I'll be waiting. I'd like to ride down with him."

Ronny turned toward Carleon as she stepped out into the night air. "So, you come with this bargain?"

"I'm afraid so." He bowed slightly like the butler he probably had been. "I promise no inconvenience on your part. I hope to be of service."

She leaned over and kissed his cheek. "Thanks. I'm sure you will be a great help."

He took the kiss with a slight nod and opened her car door. "Until tomorrow," he said as she slid into the Lincoln.

This time she sat in the dark backseat and cried with joy and fear and hope as the Lincoln pulled away from the hospital.

Marty Winslow was coming back to Harmony.

# Chapter 12

Friday

For the fourth day in a row Nevada woke with her husband already gone. They were passing in the night, and that deep pit of loneliness she sometimes felt seemed to be settling in again.

She told herself he had the ranch and she had her work. That was the way she'd wanted it from the beginning. He was only following the rules of the bargain. Each called the other a few times a day, but the conversations were short and usually formal, since others were in her office or he had men working nearby. No unnecessary words, never any endearments.

Unbelievably, Nevada could already see changes in the ranch. He'd hired a dozen more men and an independent contractor to repair roads crossing the Boxed B land. Trucks and tractors were on the farm roads now, and more horses were in the main barn. Cattle roamed land she hadn't seen grazed in years. She'd told him every day to remind the new guys to stay away from her horses. Her mares had their own stable and pastures. She'd handpicked the trainer who drove out from town to work with them every morning. Her one rule was that no one else was ever to go near her horses. Her very sanity depended on it, she sometimes thought.

She wished she could be home to watch over things, but she was needed in the office. Lawsuits were still coming in claiming her father had promised something he hadn't delivered, or he'd forgotten to pay a bill near the end of his days, but that was not Cord's problem. It was all hers.

Bryce Galloway had also contacted her, reminding her that he'd be happy to take the ranch off her hands at a rock-bottom price. He could afford to pay more, but he wanted to humiliate her. He thought of her as weak. When he'd left her before her father died and her brother ran, he'd thought she would crumble and come begging to him for help, but instead she'd served him with divorce papers. The divorce was final before she'd inherited the land.

Bryce knew she loved the ranch, and he wanted to hurt her by taking it from her. Almost from the first she'd known that Bryce wanted her, not to love, but to control. Even after two years he still thought she was his to play with and taunt for fun.

None of this was Cord's problem. She wanted to keep it from him mainly because if he knew she'd married a man like Bryce, he'd think her a spoiled fool who only saw the Galloway money.

The reason was far darker. She'd married Bryce and put up with him for months, not out of a need for money, or even love, but simply because she thought she didn't deserve anything better. He'd reminded her every day he'd lived on the ranch that a tramp like her was lucky he married her. He was good-looking, rich, from a powerful family, and she was simply his.

Nevada had worked hard to prove him wrong. She was worth more, she told herself. She deserved better.

The first Monday after she'd married Cord, she'd made up an explanation as to why she was often late getting home, but Cord had never asked. When she left in the morning she sometimes saw him from a distance, but he was never close enough to speak to. He never kissed her again. She didn't know whether to be happy or sad about it. She only knew that to protect herself she needed to stay away, not just from Cord, but from all men.

As the days passed, one fact became more and more evident. He hadn't let her down. Cord was holding up his half of the bargain. She only prayed he would continue to do so if trouble stormed. She could feel problems mounting at the office; she just couldn't gauge where they might spill over next and who among her staff of thirty might be feeding the fire. Bryce's lawyers seemed to know where her business was weakest and kept striking with offers to buy or rumors of poor management of her business.

Right now her ex-husband was playing with her like she was no more than a mouse and he was a cat that hadn't gotten hungry enough to eat her yet. She guessed he hadn't heard about her marriage to Cord, and to say he wouldn't be happy was an understatement. Even the day he'd left her, Bryce had sworn he'd be back to take over the ranch. Now, with Cord there, the take-over wouldn't be as easy as he might have planned.

Cuddling into the warm covers, she forced aside Bryce Galloway and the memory of his fist slamming into her face the last time they'd met and concentrated on Cord. In many ways she thought of him as a simple man, not dumb or backward, but simple in his needs. He worked, he slept, and he ate. That seemed enough. He talked of plans for the ranch and his little farm, but he never mentioned dreams or goals for himself. He didn't seem to care about how he dressed, but he worried about her eating, like she was a child who might starve if he didn't pay attention.

She'd never be attracted to a man who didn't have grand dreams, but she liked the way Cord looked and the polite, almost hesitant way he sometimes acted around her. And, of course, she loved the way he wore the clothes she bought. The way he moved and, most of all, the times when he was perfectly still, as if he'd paused just to treasure something like the morning air, or his first bite of a sandwich, or her as she dressed. A simple man in a complicated world. Life could never be so easy. Not for her.

If it hadn't been for the kiss and the looks he gave her when he watched her change clothes, she'd think he wasn't attracted to her. But he had to be. She knew men, and no man looked at a woman like that who didn't want her. No man kissed like he had without wanting more.

If he was only pretending, he should win an Oscar.

Kicking her way out of the covers, Nevada stretched and leaned her head back to shake her tangled mass of hair behind her. They'd been married a week today. Her plan was working. Galem had kept her up on what was happening. Cord was a hard boss, but the men respected him. He never talked about anything but the ranch and he listened to all suggestions. Zeb Darnell, a loyal hand who'd been fired a few years ago, had now become Cord's right-hand man. Zeb's knowledge seemed to fill in the gaps in Cord's knowledge of ranching.

She had to give Cord credit. He'd shown good sense to hire Zeb.

As she dressed, Nevada wondered if there was any kindness or loving left in Cord. Prison must have been hard. She'd asked Tannon Parker a year ago how Cord was doing at work, and Tannon had said simply that he was a shell of a man. All he did was work, and it didn't seem to matter if he was on his land or hers; Cord was determined to work himself to death.

Maybe Tannon was right. She'd hoped for a man but got only a shell. She could live with that for eight months. She'd learned she could live with almost anything. Only this time, living with Cord might gain her the one thing she'd never had . . . security. By the first hard freeze she'd be so solid no one would ever take anything from her. No one would hurt her.

When she stepped from her bathroom, she almost collided with the object of her thoughts.

"Cord," she managed to say as she pulled her blouse around her.

Mud covered one side of his body and his hat was missing. "Didn't mean to startle you. I took a fall and decided it would be easier to change clothes than to beat myself to death trying to brush off."

She laughed. "You do look like a mud man." For the first time in a week she thought he looked adorable, like a big kid who'd rolled in the corral. "How'd you get past Ora Mae?"

"Came in the courtyard door. It's never locked. Keep your voice down so I can get cleaned up before she sees me."

"Of course," she whispered. "I'd hate for my

housekeeper to murder you for tracking in mud after I left for work."

He raised an eyebrow and glanced down at her open blouse. "You don't look ready to leave."

She didn't bother to button the blouse together. "I took the day off. I wanted to work with my horses and I've got shopping in town. I thought we could have dinner together tonight if you've no other plans."

"That would be a change." He began stripping off his clothes and tossing them into the sink.

She leaned against his bathroom door and watched. "Ora Mae says you go through two sets of clothes a day, sometimes three."

"If I were home I'd just hose off in the yard and drip dry, but I figure you'd be upset. If I stripped outside, Ora Mae would have a heart attack. She thinks I'm not housebroke because I drink out of the cartons of milk and juice, but when I lived alone there wasn't much need for glasses."

"I'll pick up more clothes today. I wouldn't want everyone seeing you strip."

"There's no need. I can make do."

"I don't mind. I'll be in town anyway, and you're right, I do like the way you look in the clothes I buy." She hesitated and added, "As well as without them. You've got a fine body, Cord."

He unbuttoned his trousers. "If you don't turn around, Nevada, you're about to see the without view right now."

127

She didn't move.

He took the challenge and finished stripping. Once he was in the shower, he yelled, "I expect the same views."

She laughed. "Dream on." Even through the glass door she watched the frosted shadow of his frame. He wasn't all tanned and perfect like a male model. He had muscles hard from work and parts of his body that had never seen sunlight. He had hair on his chest and scars. A scrape ran the length of his arm from elbow to wrist and she guessed he hadn't simply rolled in the mud when he'd taken the fall.

"You fall off your horse?" she asked as she reached for the first-aid kit.

"No, he actually tumbled out from under me. Zeb talked me into trying his cutting horse, and the mare shifted faster than I could move. I tried to tell Zeb that until a week ago I was a farmer, but those new clothes must have convinced him otherwise."

"What did he do when you fell off?"

"Laughed over my cussing."

She heard the shower go off. When he stepped out, he'd pulled a towel around his waist as he kept talking. "I'm thinking of having a long talk with that horse."

"Put your arm on the counter."

"It's nothing." Cord looked at the scrape, now bubbling fresh blood. "It'll scab over."

She blocked his bathroom door and repeated, "Put your arm on the counter."

For a few seconds they stared at each other, and she wasn't sure which one would win this argument. She wasn't even sure why she was fighting. If the man wanted to bleed, let him bleed.

Without breaking his stare, he lowered his arm, scab side up, and she watched the muscles of his arm tighten as she neared.

Nevada dabbed the blood, sprayed antiseptic, and wrapped the scrape from elbow to wrist with first gauze and then tape. "There, that wasn't so bad. Now at least it will stay clean. You can unwrap it when you get home and let it air."

She looked up and found him still staring at her.

Feeling very mothering, she shooed him with her hands. "Now go back out and play."

A slow smile finally tugged his lip up. "I'd better dress first." He moved to his closet and pulled out the first shirt and jeans he saw.

"I hadn't noticed," she lied as she ran across the room. By the time she'd pulled on trousers and her boots, he was gone without another word.

That night at dinner she was still thinking about how good he'd looked nude. They were little more than polite strangers, but they were getting to know one another. He never complained or asked too many questions. He didn't try to keep up with her or boss her around. This might be the best marriage she'd had so far. Of course, if it lasted eight months it would break a record.

She pushed her food around on the plate as she thought of the morning and how they'd almost been a normal couple for a few minutes.

"I can't get the windows around this place open," he said from across the table.

"What?" She realized she hadn't been listening. "Oh, yes, the windows. You told me."

"I like to sleep in fresh air, and whoever built this place forgot to buy working windows."

She thought of telling him that windows were the dumbest dinner conversation subject she'd ever heard. She'd known the man a week and he'd never bothered to ask her what books she liked, or what was her favorite movie, or even who she voted for. At this rate they'd never learn each other. "Well," she said, trying not to sound bored, "just knock one open."

"Or we could just move the bed out in the courtyard. There's plenty of fresh air out there among all those strange flowers."

"My stepmother, who lasted one summer around here, had the flowers brought in from all over the South. My father wouldn't let her redecorate the house. I like the courtyard, but I'm not sleeping outside."

"You are if I do." His words were a challenge.

"Right. Our bargain. For eight months I sleep with you, right?"

"Right."

Ora Mae walked in to say she was leaving, and the discussion dropped. He talked about what he'd done on the ranch, and she talked about a problem at the office. Neither understood much of what the other one was saying.

When they went to bed, he sat in a chair by the sealed windows and pulled off his boots as he watched her. She always turned her back to him when she slipped off her bra and tugged on her nightshirt. If he'd asked her to turn around, she told herself she would, but he'd have to ask. Otherwise, she had no intention of putting on a show.

When she crawled into bed he walked over to her side and flipped off her light, then pulled the cover to her shoulder, and she had the feeling he'd done the same thing every night they'd been married. One week.

Nevada lay awake waiting for him to say something. She guessed he wasn't a man who asked for things, and she wasn't a woman who waited for what she wanted.

After ten minutes she was still wide awake and waiting. "I've had it," she broke the silence. "I'm tired of lying over here every night waiting for you to reach over and touch me. If you're gay, that's fine, but if you're not, I'd like to know why you're not attracted to me like every boy I've known since I was old enough to car-date."

Practically every man she'd spoken to since she'd been fifteen had hit on her. Before she became the CEO of Britain Oil and Drilling, almost every male in the office had brushed against her, or acted drunk and made a pass. But Cord had been sleeping three feet away and hadn't even tried. She'd never played hard to get. He must know that.

"When I suggested marriage I meant it as a business arrangement." She tried to calm. "I knew you'd be good at running the ranch, but then you added the bit about my sleeping in your bed and I thought, great, he's just like all men, he wants a piece of me. I've given away so many pieces in the last ten years I didn't figure one more would matter. Then you marry me and I do my part of the bargain and crawl into bed with you, and you don't even bother to touch me. I'm lying here wondering night after night when you're going to pounce on me. I swear, it's downright exhausting."

"You coming up for air anytime soon, Nevada?" Cord sounded more concerned than interested in her crisis.

She sat up and tried to glare at him, but the room was too dark to pull it off. "I see you looking at me, taking off my clothes with your eyes. But when I'm right here all night long, you don't cross the three feet of bed between us. We might as well be sleeping in cots, or better yet have a

132

bundling pillow between us like the Victorians did. I don't know why you asked me to be here anyway. We'd probably both be more comfortable in separate rooms; after all, you've got four others to pick from. Which reminds me, you don't make a sound all night or move. You just fall into bed like you were shot and sleep without even pulling covers. Corpses don't lie as still as you do at night, Cord McDowell, and I can tell you for a fact it's unnerving. Twice last night I woke up and couldn't even hear you breathing. I lay there thinking, great, I'm in bed with a dead man."

He got out of bed and circled round to her side. "You finished?"

She shrugged, thinking she'd made a fool of herself, but she'd always had a problem slowing down once she got rolling. He was about to be husband number four to tell her to shut up. She'd really outdone herself in finding something wrong with this one. Why couldn't she just have been happy with his plain conversation and simple ways? It wasn't like he had habits hard to put up with. The man didn't even leave his socks on the floor.

Cord sat down beside her and turned her shoulders until they were facing each other. "I'm an only child. I've always slept alone. When I went to prison I slept alone. Since I came home three years ago, I've never shared a bed with anyone."

Her vision adjusted to the light enough to see his face. "You asked me to be in your bed because you didn't want to be alone? That's it! I don't know if I'm more insulted or confused."

"It seemed like a good idea." He sounded tired, not at all like a man who planned to take his turn listing her faults. "I didn't know your sleeping in my bed came with touching." His big hand moved down her arm. "But I could get used to the idea if it bothers you so much."

"Oh, it's all right now that I understand; forget about it. I was just feeling rejected. Now that I know you wanted to sleep, I'm fine, really." She pushed his hand away and turned her back to him.

He sat on the bed awhile, but she wasn't about to start rattling on again.

She felt him stand and heard him walk to the windows. The drapes swished as he opened them, and she guessed he was looking out into the night. Another one of his simple habits, she thought. Something scraped across the floor.

Glass shattered with a crash vibrating like a gunshot through the room.

Preparing for flight, Nevada jumped to her knees on the bed. His broad-shouldered body shadowed across a seven-foot window, now without glass. The heavy iron luggage rack she'd always hated now rested upside down atop one of the rosebushes.

Cool night air flowed gently around her as the

room settled back into silence. "What do you think you're doing?" she whispered, afraid to confront him too strongly.

"Opening a window," he answered as he walked back to her side of the bed.

"Have you lost your mind? You've probably broken half the branches on that rosebush, and it will be a mess cleaning up all the glass."

"Stop talking, Nevada, and lie back." He lifted her covers and she leaned back against the pillows. Without another word, he moved in beside her, pushing her over to allow himself room. With one arm around her shoulders, he pressed his body along hers. "I don't want you to feel rejected. I'm not going to pounce and attack you, but I think I might like to be close enough to touch you for a while."

They were both nervous, but neither one moved away. She told herself she wasn't afraid of him, but the man had just knocked open a floor-to-ceiling window. She corrected her evaluation of him from simple to unpredictable.

He placed his hand on her waist and pressed his cheek against her hair.

"I like the way your hair smells." He pulled the covers over them both.

She wiggled to a more comfortable spot beside him, deciding that she might need his warmth now that they had cool air coming in. "You going to touch me while I'm asleep?"

"I might. You got any objections?"

"No. I guess not."

It took a while, but slowly both calmed and she fell asleep.

Their night together set a pattern. Whoever went to bed first picked the side, and the other cuddled in. If he explored her body during the night, she wasn't aware of it. As the days passed, she realized that if they'd had sex she would have felt wanted, but by gently holding her Cord had made her feel cherished, and she'd never felt cherished. Somehow it was more intimate than sex. She'd never had a lover who'd held her all night.

In the mornings he moved away from her. With a light kiss on the cheek, he vanished. If she saw him before she went to work, she made a point to walk over to wherever he was and kiss him good-bye. He'd always cup the back of her head and stare down at her as if he wanted one last look before she left. Days passed, drifting into spring, and one by one all the windows were fitted with windows that opened.

On cool evenings they always rode, Cord on his gray horse named Devil and Nevada on one of the mares from her own private stable. Slowly, they grew used to the other's touch. The way he put his hand on her leg when he checked the stirrup. The light touch of his fingers against her back when they walked. Her pats on his forearm when she wanted his full attention.

There were no words of endearment between them except when they knew others were listening, but there were few words of anger. He was stubborn about running the ranch and seemed to trust his judgment more and more. She rarely came home in time to eat dinner with him, and he was often gone before she woke up.

At night, she'd bring her dinner into the study and watch him work at her father's old desk. Once in a while he'd tell her about something that happened at the ranch. She'd usually fall asleep watching the news and he'd carry her to bed. The next morning she'd wake up with her clothes still on and raccoon eyes from sleeping in her makeup. And . . . she'd smile, remembering that she'd slept soundly in his arms.

The only time he slowed his routine was when he watched her dress, and she made sure that was as often as possible. She liked the idea that she affected this cold man. Sometimes, if they went to bed at the same time, he'd just sit in the chair with a clear view of her closet and watch. Sometimes he'd stand at the door and study her as she changed into riding clothes after work.

They were like two people occupying the same space, but in different dimensions. If she hadn't felt his warmth against her at night, she would have wondered if maybe he was simply a machine and not a man.

As she cuddled next to Cord, Nevada told

herself that a machine was exactly what she needed to marry. She was no good with people . . . with relationships, and neither was he. If there was no passion, she could live with it. He apparently didn't have any for her, and she'd learned from others that what she'd thought was passion had been simply lust. Once lust cools, it shrivels into indifference to the point of cruelty. Her last husband's bruises had taken weeks to heal.

Bryce liked to play rough with her, half teasing, half cruel, to prove he was stronger and in control. At first he'd said he was sorry when he hurt her in his play before he took her to bed, but after a few months he stopped caring. He only wanted control, and if she didn't respond fast enough, he made her pay.

When she'd shown her bruises to her father, he'd told her to stop lying; Bryce had already told him she'd been drinking again and that he'd had to restrain her when she'd gone wild. By the time her father grew ill, she knew Bryce thought he'd broken her. She'd followed his every rule and she'd learned to curl into a ball if he raised his hand. Most of the time, he'd laugh and forget about hitting her.

He thought he'd take charge of everything but couldn't stand the depression of watching her father wither away, so he'd left, thinking to make her suffer without him. But while he partied in

Vegas, she'd served him with divorce papers. He hadn't thought she would go through with it, so he'd ignored the court date. The divorce was final before he could contest it.

The last words Bryce said to her when he'd collected his things had been that she'd never belong to anyone else. Even knowing that he was miles away didn't keep the shiver of fear away. Bryce wasn't finished toying with her. He'd been wealthy and worthless all his life. Like a big-game hunter who kills for the thrill, Bryce wanted her. He told her once that she was beautiful and he wanted everyone to know that she was his. At the time, she'd been flattered, not realizing he saw her only as a toy.

His words would have been funny later in the marriage, if she hadn't felt his anger so many times. In truth, she'd never belonged to Bryce, or anyone else.

At first, when Bryce had been courting, she'd noticed pats that were a bit too hard, always followed by apologies. She told herself he was showing off in front of her brother, proving he was the boss. Then after they married, even his grip often left bruises. She'd been a fool not to see the signs early, but he'd always talked his way around her hurt and anger, until finally he no longer cared and hurting her became pure entertainment when no one was around to see. He'd always been attentive in public, explaining her bruises as drunken accidents as he served her another drink.

Bryce didn't want her, not then and not now. He'd made it plain within days after they married, but he did like playing the rancher.

She'd married Cord McDowell for more than his help on the ranch. She married him to be a barrier between her and the man who swore he'd finish the job of killing her one day. It wasn't fair to Cord. Much as she hated herself for it, Cord was just one more wall she'd built to feel safe.

She'd realized when the bargain first occurred to her that she might be putting him in danger, but there had been no family, no friends to turn to. She'd told herself the risk was worth taking. After all, if she hadn't picked Cord, he might have lost his farm. Only now, she felt guilty for not telling him more about Bryce. He had a right to know. She'd only been thinking of herself.

As worry swirled in her mind, she pulled her hand from the covers and moved her fingers slowly over Cord's bare shoulder. "I'll protect you," she whispered, hoping that she could find a way to make it true.

A memory surfaced in her tired mind.

She'd been more drunk than sober years ago when a group of her friends gathered for a party at the lake one July Fourth. In the shadows she watched a man coming toward the camp, flashing his light like a weapon and shouting orders.

Then he grabbed a kid's arm and jerked him up.

The kid came up swinging and the invader crumpled after one blow. The reflection of a badge on his shirt blinked in the flashlight's beam. Then Nevada remembered running into the shadows, leaving the kid and the deputy behind.

She rested her head on Cord's arm, knowing the kid she'd seen that night had been him. Not one of the dozen teenagers drinking around the campfire came forward the next day to testify to what happened. She'd tried to talk to a cop that night, but he didn't seem interested in listening to a drunk sixteen-year-old. When she'd wanted to go in the next morning, her father had demanded she remain silent.

The deputy claimed he'd been attacked, and there was no one to say otherwise.

# *Chapter 13*

Martha Q Patterson thought she might have a stroke before she got up all the steps at the front of Wright Funeral Home. If she did, Tyler better do her funeral for half price, since he insisted she come over to his place to talk.

She knew she'd called him three times in less than two weeks, but she needed someone to talk to. Since he'd be getting her business someday, he might as well earn it now. Only this time he'd said he couldn't leave his pregnant wife even for ten minutes, so here she was climbing Heart Attack Hill. It occurred to her that some of Tyler's business might walk in and go out boxed.

Martha Q knew she wouldn't complain. She cared about Kate Wright, so she came to Tyler's office this time. In a strange way they were in the same business, innkeepers and funeral directors. They both laid people to rest.

Martha Q was laughing at her own joke when Tyler opened the door.

"Good morning." He made a slight bow of his head, as if she were the queen come to call. Martha Q would have been flattered, but Tyler pretty much treated everyone like royalty.

"How is Kate?" Martha Q wasn't in the mood to waste words and any more energy. She needed answers and a chair.

"My Kate is resting. She won't admit it, but I think this pregnancy has been hard on her these last few months. She said something about how going into a war zone was nothing compared to carrying a baby." He motioned for her to follow him into his office.

"Well, see that you two don't get in this situation again," Martha Q huffed. "There are ways to prevent this disease from happening again."

Tyler laughed. "You sound like you're talking to two kids. Once Tyler Two is born, I think we'll be happy with one child. Kate and a son are far more than I'd hoped for in this lifetime."

Martha Q squealed. "Please, Lord, don't tell me that's what you're naming the poor child?"

"No," he grinned. "That's just what Kate calls him."

As always, Tyler's love for his wife showed in his face. For years the man hadn't been able to get a date in town, what with his occupation and his build, and then he found Kate. Martha Q had heard several women wishing they'd given him a chance before he went off the market. Nothing makes a man more handsome than when he cherishes his wife.

Martha Q moved into Tyler's messy office, mumbling that she hoped the kid had his father's sense of humor and his mother's looks.

Tyler acted like he didn't hear her as he offered her a seat beside the windows. "When you called, I asked Autumn to make a fresh pot of coffee for us. With the cool morning I thought you might like a cup. Kate always tells me how nice Winter's Inn was when she stayed there before we married. She said you'd have tea every afternoon in the style of a grand lady. I'm afraid all we can manage here is coffee and scones from the bakery. Autumn's been too busy to bake lately."

She straightened. In one lifetime she'd gone

from being called the town slut to being called a great lady. Of course she was smart enough to know that a fine tea set doesn't make a lady any more than fishnet hose make a slut.

As Tyler always did, he lowered his voice and asked, "How may I be of help to you?"

Martha Q finished off a corner of her scone before she stated her first fact. "I think we got one of those serial killers living right here in Harmony. Nobody knows it, and by the time they do, there'll be a line of bodies waiting at your back door."

Tyler frowned. "Who?" He said the word so slowly it sounded like a hum.

"A good-looker named Bryce Galloway. About thirty-five, all fancy, real nice. Too nice. You know, the kind whose neighbors are all interviewed after he's arrested and they all comment on how 'polite' he was."

"Bryce Galloway? Wasn't he married to Nevada Britain a season or two? Seems like she got divorced right before her father died. If I remember correctly, he was from old oil money down near Houston or Dallas. Folks said he was crazy about her the minute he saw her."

"You know him?"

Tyler shook his head. "He didn't help Nevada with the funeral arrangements. Far as I know he didn't even attend. Her only brother refused to come too, said he hated the old man. She looked so alone there in the family pew, her back straight, her eyes staring ahead like she saw nothing but trouble coming to blow her over."

"I'm not surprised he didn't help. Probably wouldn't have even if they'd still been married. He has that none-of-my-family-has-worked-in-three-generations look about him, but I'd bet his Italian loafers he's never worn out a pair of boots."

Tyler nodded as if he knew what she was talking about.

"And besides"—Martha Q pointed her finger at some invisible point floating between her and Tyler—"who *wasn't* married to Nevada Britain? Just split the population of Harmony and you'll hit the number she's planning on stopping at. Somehow I heard she talked Cord McDowell into marrying her the other day. Not that anyone else would want him, but—"

Tyler raised his eyebrow. He was not a man to gossip . . . at least not for long. "What makes you think Bryce is up to something illegal?"

She thought of mentioning how the man sometimes, when he thought no one was looking, would huff and puff as if fighting to control rage. He ate strange too. Eggs with no yolks, bread with no flour, milk that didn't come from a cow. Everything else had to be fat, sugar, and caffeine free. The last time he gave the cook, Mrs. Biggs, his order for breakfast, she told him to just gnaw on the table until she got back. Martha Q didn't usually pay much attention to the breakfast part of her business, but since Mr. Galloway arrived she'd been running to the store to pick up food that wasn't even real.

There was no way out; she had to be honest with Tyler Wright. He'd know what to do. "It's just a feeling," she began. "It's not any one thing he does or says. It's more like the pieces of him just don't fit together. I get the feeling I'll be that person interviewed about how well I knew him." She leaned forward. "I know men, Tyler, and I'm telling you this one is not right."

"You want me to have the sheriff evict him from your place? I'm not sure how she'd do it, but you might be able to say you had folks coming in who needed the room."

"No. I don't want to make him mad. I just want you to tell Alex and a few of her deputies to keep an eye on him. He only lived here when he was married to Nevada, so he's not one of us. I keep wondering what kind of business brought him back. Now think about it, Tyler; if you were rich and could live anywhere, would you move back to a little town and stay on the third floor of a bed-and-breakfast just to be next to an ex-wife who probably wishes you were dead?"

"How do you know that?"

Martha Q raised an eyebrow as if questioning his IQ. "Most ex-wives do; it's a fact."

Tyler shook his head. "If you don't like having him under your roof, something needs to be done."

"I'll call Rick Matheson and take the lawyer to lunch. He'll tell me how I can get him out of my inn with the least trouble." They both nodded as if something had been settled.

Martha Q figured Tyler just thought he'd listened to the latest in a long line of problems she'd made up, and maybe he had. Since she didn't have a quiet house to write in, she might as well make up drama in real life.

She finished off her coffee, tucked the rest of her scone into her purse for later, and made Tyler promise to talk to the sheriff. It shouldn't be much of an inconvenience; he had breakfast with Hank and Alex once a week at the diner. Hank was the fire department chief, and his wife was the sheriff. Between the three of them they knew everything happening in Harmony.

When she drove back to the B&B, a man dressed in black was sitting on her porch steps. He was tall and thin, and for a moment, before he noticed Martha Q, he seemed to have the weight of the world on his shoulders.

Martha Q swore. She was starting to feel like her place was the pound for lost singles.

To the man's credit, he stood when she headed toward him. A formal kind of stance, like a military man or butler. She'd guess him near sixty with beautiful silver-gray hair.

"Mrs. Patterson, I presume?"

"Correct." He didn't look like he was selling anything, but if she'd been a few years younger she might have been interested in buying. "I'm Martha Q Patterson."

"I'm Anthony Carleon. I work for Marty Winslow, who I believe rented half of a duplex you own a few years back."

"It's rented right now, if he's thinking of coming back." Martha Q frowned. If Marty could afford to hire a man like this to work for him, surely he could get a better place than her duplex to live. It had been a dump when she and her first husband bought it almost forty years ago.

Anthony Carleon smiled. "Mrs. Patterson, if you'll allow me a bit of time, I'll try to explain the situation, but first I must ask if you have a room available here." He motioned toward the house behind him. "I'm in need of lodging."

"I have one left, but it's on the third floor. Marty would never be able to get his wheelchair up there."

"No, the room is for me. Marty will be staying at the duplex with your current tenant, Ronny Logan. Of course, we'll expect you to increase the rent and we'll check with you about upgrading or painting."

Martha Q unlocked her door and turned back to Carleon. "This sounds like a sit-down story. Won't you step into the parlor, Mr. Carleon?"

Half an hour later she handed Carleon the key to the third-floor bedroom next to Bryce Galloway. As her latest boarder moved up the stairs with his one suitcase, she thought of calling Dallas Logan and giving her a heart attack. The old bag had been making up stories about her poor homely daughter ever since she moved out. When Dallas heard that her only child had a man living with her, Dallas would take it like a full-power Taser jolt.

## Chapter 14

Ronny Logan wasn't sure she'd slept at all after signing the papers and leaving the hospital. Her world was about to change. She'd always dreamed Marty Winslow would come back to her, but she'd never thought it would be to die.

As she stepped out of the Lincoln one last time, she wondered if the long black car would be coming with them. Somehow she doubted it.

Ross and Ivan called and said all was ready at her place by the time Ronny walked into the front of the huge hospital. They told her Doc had already sent a nurse with all the equipment needed. Mr. Carleon, of course, had driven over yesterday to make arrangements, then driven back to the hospital to see that Marty's things were loaded properly. A little after dawn he'd be following the ambulance toward Harmony.

As she walked down the front hallway for the first time, Ronny answered Ross's questions on her cell and added, "I think it would be nice if Marty could see out the front windows from his bed."

"We already got it, Ronny. Mr. Carleon found a few extra chairs and a cot for the nurse on the night shift. We'll have everything ready by the time you arrive."

Ronny clicked the phone off as she reached Marty's hospital room door.

"Ready?" Mr. Carleon interrupted as he stepped into the hall. "If we leave soon, his brother isn't likely to confront us."

Ronny nodded. The sooner she got him away, the better.

Marty was either asleep or drugged so heavily he didn't make a sound when the EMTs moved him. Even with Doc running the show, moving a man from this hospital was like prodding a near-frozen snake along. One minute everyone at the hospital thought they were in charge and needed to be checked with, and the next no one was responsible for anything.

Once they were on the road, Doc insisted she sit in the chair next to the driver, and within minutes Ronny drifted to sleep to the low sounds of the machines just behind her and the rhythm of the road beating out the miles until she was home.

She sometimes dreamed that Marty had never been hurt and they'd fallen in love and married just like all happy couples. Only even in her dreams she knew she would have never met him if he hadn't been crippled and hiding away in Harmony.

A small part of her wondered if she wasn't more needed than loved. If he'd been walking, running a business, wheeling and dealing, she never would fit into his world. Only now with him hurt and dying, she'd made room for him in her world.

She remembered he'd said something that always echoed in her memories of their days together. "In a perfect world," he'd said, "I know we would find each other. Some people are just meant to cross paths."

# Chapter 15

## Boxed B Ranch

Cord pulled the powerful pickup behind the house and parked next to his twenty-year-old truck. He'd driven his pickup only once since the day they married. Galem had handed him the keys to the special-edition Ford F-450 Platinum and said, "You'll need the power, Boss."

Cord smiled, remembering how he'd driven out to a dirt road and spent an hour reading the owner's manual. The learning curve around this place was huge. Surprisingly, a few of the courses he'd taken in prison helped. The auto mechanics and computer classes along with the two he'd taken on bookkeeping were wonderful, but he still hadn't figured out how to work the cell phone. Not that it mattered. The only person he wanted to call was Nevada.

She'd been home all day and he'd been working. So many little things were going wrong on the land, like fences cut and gates left open, that he was starting to wonder if a few of the men he'd fired weren't coming back to pester him. Today, even though it was Sunday, he'd been out driving the roads, checking. At noon he hadn't made it in for lunch because a farmer wanted to meet him to buy off the last of Cord's equipment on his parents' place.

The money was enough to pay off the loan on his land, but Cord knew if the marriage didn't make the eight-month mark he'd be hurting. Owning the land, even the three hundred acres Nevada had signed over, wouldn't help if he had no money to buy what he needed to farm.

When he walked into the house, he grabbed an apple and ate it as he ambled around looking for Nevada. His mind was on an idea he'd had of using the new land to raise horses. A stream ran through the land most months, and two windmills would serve the dry times. He didn't want to have fancy horses like she raised, but good strong ranch horses. He might even use Devil for stud.

Cord found her in her little upstairs study. She was so engrossed in painting she didn't even notice him watching her until he crunched down on the apple.

"Want to tell me what you're doing?" he asked.

"Nope," she answered. "Want to tell me where you've been?"

"Nope," he echoed. If he told her of some of the problems, she'd just worry, and he was doing enough of that for them both.

He watched her a minute, wondering how this angry woman could possibly be the same person he cuddled with at night. Something was bothering her, but he had no idea what. She went back to painting and he stood at the door. He hadn't been invited in.

She signed the painting and smiled. "Finished," she said as she turned the canvas to face him.

Cord grinned. "Very good." A horse standing in a pasture. It was nice, real nice, but what kept him smiling was that she'd signed her initials *NM,* not *NB.* She'd meant it when she'd said she wanted his name.

"Want to go into town and have supper? We could walk the town square."

She made a face. "Sounds charming."

Cord frowned. "Does that mean yes or no?"

She was out of her chair so fast he didn't have time to get out of the doorway before she bumped her way around him and headed downstairs. "Yes. I'll go. Why not?"

Cord figured he'd pushed conversation to the limit, so he just waited downstairs. He didn't have long to review their confusing conversation before she stormed out of the bedroom with her jacket and purse. When she bumped past him on her way outside, he decided he was no more than a turnstile.

He followed and was surprised to see her climb into his truck instead of her little car she usually drove back and forth to town, but he didn't ask questions. He just headed to town.

They were halfway there before she spoke. "There's something I should tell you. I've heard that my ex-husband is in town. Has been for a few days, I think."

"I'm not giving you back," Cord said simply, and winked at her.

To his surprise, she laughed. "Don't worry, I wouldn't go back."

Cord decided now was as good a time to ask as any. "How do you think we're doing?"

"Good. I'm happy with the agreement. You?"

He thought about it for a while before answering. "It's different than I thought it would be. The days are long and the work is hard, but you and me, we seem to be getting by." From the way she'd cuddled close last night, he could have no complaints. "We mostly just stay out of each other's way."

He stopped at a Mexican food place she claimed she'd never noticed. She ordered a salad and he ordered a platter. It was so noisy they barely talked, but he felt a little of the tension leave her. While they waited for the check, he rested his hand over hers, and she didn't pull away. He had no idea if she liked it, but touching her hand made him feel more normal, like they were just another couple out for dinner.

When they walked out, all four tires on his truck had been slashed.

Cord walked around the truck twice, swearing to himself. When he passed her the second time, he asked, "Got any idea who might do this?"

"Several," she said. "One of the men you fired. Any one of my three ex-husbands. Wild kids causing damage just for the hell of it. Some guy who thought you got his parking place."

Cord rolled his shoulders to relax. "In other words, anyone."

"Pretty much."

Nevada wanted to call the sheriff's office, but Cord didn't want them involved. The chances were slim they'd catch whoever did it, but he'd bet the cop coming out would know him and give him a hard time. He didn't care about the cop, or the hard time, but he didn't want Nevada to see him as all the cops around saw him. An ex-con. A wild kid who'd sent a sheriff's deputy to the hospital with one punch. Cord would have to keep his gaze to the ground and be extra polite, but they'd still talk to him like they knew he must be doing something illegal.

"I could call Galem," Nevada suggested. "If you insist on not calling the sheriff."

"Galem and Ora Mae are at their cabin at the lake. He said they didn't plan to drive in until early tomorrow."

"We could walk home." She began to pace.

"Not in those heels, you can't. I'd end up carrying you the last few miles."

"I could call a cab," she smiled.

"Or we could catch the subway." He bought into her joke. The closest thing Harmony had to mass transit was the little Joy bus that picked up folks at the nursing homes on Sunday for church.

A tall man dressed in a black suit walked past them. He paused, and in the twilight Cord saw intelligent eyes take in the crime and understand.

Cord expected him to walk on. No one in town ever spoke to him, and Nevada didn't speak to anyone she didn't have to. But the man turned toward them as formal as a royal guard.

"Pardon me for interrupting, but do you two need a lift? I have to drop off a takeout order to my employer a few blocks away, but if you don't mind waiting, I'd be glad to take you somewhere."

Cord could already see Nevada shaking her head, but he answered, "We'd be much obliged, but we live a few miles out of town."

"No problem." The man smiled as if happy to be of service.

They crammed into the front of a U-Haul van with takeout orders in their laps. Nevada looked like she thought she was being kidnapped, but Cord relaxed.

When the tall man started the van, Cord listened as he shifted and said, "Sounds like the transmission is going out."

"I fear you may be right. As soon as I get time

to unload it, I plan to turn it in. This was a sudden move, and I had to take whatever they had. My employer is very ill, so his needs have to come first before the unpacking or my frustration."

They drove a few blocks toward downtown before he pulled up at an old duplex. Nevada held on to Cord's leg as if she feared death coming. He spread his hand over hers, but she didn't relax. He wished he could tell her that he'd seen enough bad guys in his life to know the gentleman in black wasn't one of them.

"I'll be a few minutes dropping these off." The man added, "I hope you don't mind waiting."

The thin fellow was so polite, Cord felt bad for adding to what was obviously a long day for him. "If you don't mind me taking a look under the hood, maybe I can make sure this engine lasts until you get it turned in."

Carleon straightened, then smiled. "I would be much obliged." He said the words with the same Texas drawl that Cord had used. "I'll just deliver these to the people inside and make sure the night nurse has arrived."

Nevada pouted while Cord looked at the engine. Finally, she got tired of waiting and climbed out to stand next to him. "We should have just called someone," she whispered. "Who knows how long we'll be stuck here? One of the guys at the bunkhouse could have come into town and picked us up."

"Sorry, Princess."

"Don't call me that, and why do I have to be nice to this stranger? I've never seen him before and I'll probably never see him again."

"You don't know how to be nice, do you, Princess?" Cord didn't bother to look at her. He knew she was pouting.

She caught him on the shoulder with a jab that surprised him so much he jerked up, banging his head on the open hood.

When he stepped back, rubbing his scalp, the tall man stood three feet away.

"Everything all right?"

"Yeah, I was just having a discussion with my wife. She tends to storm." Cord winked at her as if they'd been playing.

Nevada looked at him like she might swing again.

Lowering the hood, he said, "I think this thing will make a few more miles."

Carleon nodded. "I need to get one box out of the back, and then we can be on our way. There will be plenty of time to unload the rest when I return."

To Cord's shock, Nevada smiled at the very proper gentleman raising the back door of the van. "Please, allow us to help. We'll be happy to move the boxes onto the porch for you. It'll save you time."

Carleon started to protest, but Nevada picked

up a box and headed for the porch. Cord had no choice but to follow. She matched him trip after trip, taking her share of the load. He knew she couldn't be comfortable in high heels, but she never complained. She was too busy proving that she wasn't a princess.

On one of the last trips Cord thought he saw Ronny Logan standing just inside the window of the duplex. She didn't seem to notice him, but Cord couldn't help but wonder if the boss Carleon had said was so ill had something to do with why the lady from the post office looked so sad.

By the time Mr. Carleon took them home, it was long past dark and they were exhausted. Without a word they moved to their separate bathrooms and showered. Cord could hear her drying her hair as he tumbled into bed. He was almost asleep when she cuddled next to him.

With her warm and in his arms, he whispered, "That was a good thing you did tonight." When she didn't say anything, he added, "I'm proud of you."

He knew she wasn't asleep, but she didn't move. After a few long breaths he felt a tear roll off her cheek and onto his arm.

The next morning, Cord got the men started working and headed into town in his old truck to get his tires fixed on the Ford. He stopped by the garage and paid for four new tires with the cash in his wallet, something he'd never imagined being able to do. The salesman said they'd put them on at the restaurant parking lot and then drive his truck over to the shop to have them balanced. No one argued when Cord said he'd be back in an hour to pick up his truck. They simply answered, "Yes, sir."

His next stop was the post office. He didn't have to ask about Ronny Logan; one of the postmen was complaining about her taking a few days off and now everyone had to help get the mail sorted.

Cord left the post office and drove to the duplex. The U-Haul was gone, and so were the boxes that they'd left on the porch.

He felt like a fool, sticking his nose in someone else's business, but Ronny Logan was as close to a friend as he had in this town. He needed to know she was all right.

He tapped on the duplex door and was surprised when Ronny opened it so fast she must have seen him walk up.

She didn't say a word, just stared at him with big brown eyes red-rimmed from crying.

"I'm sorry to bother you," he stuttered. "I just came to see if you're all right or if I can help." It didn't come naturally to him to offer help, but he had a feeling she'd never ask, no matter how dearly she needed it.

Ronny nodded and opened the screen door. He backed up as she moved outside.

For a minute, they just stood there. Two people

who hardly ever talked to anyone were about to have a conversation.

Finally, she blew her nose on a ball of a tissue and said, "You know how to build a ramp for a wheelchair?"

A hundred questions came to mind, but Cord simply said, "Yes. Where do you want it?"

She took a deep breath and walked around to the back of the house. He saw the remains of a ramp that didn't look like it had been built solid enough to stand one winter.

"The doctors think my friend, Marty, came here to die. None of them, not even Mr. Carleon, believes he'll ever sit in a chair again, but I believe and, if I had the ramp, Marty might believe."

Cord looked at the rotting lumber that would no longer hold a wheelchair. "I'll have you one built by tomorrow."

"I can pay," she whispered.

He shook his head. "I'm happy to help. I'll worry about this. You worry about getting that friend of yours well enough to use it."

He put on his hat and headed for his pickup. When he backed out, Ronny was standing on the porch staring at him. She didn't wave or say a word, but he thought he saw a hint of a smile.

Within thirty minutes he'd collected supplies and called Galem to tell him to round up Jefferson and Jackson. Johnson, the youngest of the president brothers, could help Zeb with the cattle, but he needed the other two and Galem. "Meet me at the hardware store. Tell them to wear carpenter belts fully loaded for work."

Galem didn't ask questions; he just said, "We're on our way."

Cord closed the phone and smiled. They were seasoned ranch hands. The two could handle pretty much any job, and he had no doubt Galem would keep advice flowing until they were finished.

When they arrived, pickups were loaded with supplies and they headed back to the duplex. Cord saw no sign of anyone inside either side of the place, so he set to work.

Halfway through the job, Martha Q Patterson pulled up in her old car, which rattled to a stop. Everyone in town knew the owner of the bed-and-breakfast. She'd been so wild in her youth that folks still told stories about her.

"Cord McDowell?" she yelled as she rushed toward him.

He straightened and reached for the shirt he'd pulled off half an hour ago. "Yes, Mrs. Patterson."

She was out of breath by the time she reached him. "What in the hell do you think you're doing?" Her eyes never left his chest.

"I'm building a ramp for Ronny."

Martha Q folded her arms and finally looked up at him. "You want to tell me why?"

"She asked me to." He didn't see any need to tell her more. Cord didn't like questions and never gave more than a short answer. He stared down at the lady, wishing she'd go away.

To his surprise, the tall, thin man who'd offered them a lift yesterday stepped out the back door of the duplex and rushed to Martha Q like she was an old friend. "I'm so glad you came by," he said to Martha Q before offering his hand to Cord. "Mr. McDowell, I don't think I properly introduced myself to you last night. I'm sorry; exhaustion is my only excuse. I'm Anthony Carleon, and, if you've no objection, I'd love to explain to Mrs. Patterson exactly what is happening here."

Cord nodded once and went back to work, happy to be out of the conversation. Hell, he didn't really know what he was doing here. This had nothing to do with his farm or Nevada's ranch. He had plenty of work to do on both, but, strange as it would sound to most folks in town, he and Ronny were friends. Ever since he'd gotten out of prison he could count on her saying "Good morning" to him or talking about the weather when he came in to get his mail. When no one talks to you for days, such a small kindness meant something. It meant even more when he watched and saw that she was so shy she barely looked at others.

As he worked, he listened to the man who'd

called himself Mr. Carleon explain that some guy named Marty Winslow might one day be able to sit in a wheelchair, and Ronny promised him when he did that she'd wheel him out of the house and they'd take a walk.

When Martha Q finally drove off, Cord thanked the man, and Mr. Carleon laughed. "She only wanted to be part of what was going on," he said. "Despite her bluster, she thinks very highly of you."

"She does?" He didn't think someone like Martha Q would even remember him.

"Yes," Carleon smiled. "She was telling one of the other boarders at the inn just this morning that your wife had picked a fine man this time." Carleon looked around at the ramp. "From your work, I would have to agree. This looks like it will still be standing when the house falls down."

"Thanks." Cord wasn't sure for what—for passing on the compliment, or for his work. "If you're staying here, you'll let me know if Ronny needs anything?"

Carleon straightened but didn't answer.

Cord knew he'd have to say more. "She's a friend. I'd like to help if I can."

The older man must have believed him, for he said, "I will. But I work for Mr. Winslow. I board at the inn. Marty, my employer, has round-the-clock nurses to help him, and I'm here to run errands, but I'm guessing Ronny could always

165

use a friend. I hope you'll stop by often. I'm here whenever I'm needed."

He pointed at the dried-up creek that ran behind the duplex. "If I cross the creek, I'm actually very close. Thanks to Mr. Galloway for pointing out the shortcut."

Cord stopped breathing. "Bryce Galloway?"

Carleon answered casually, "Why, yes, do you know him? He's one of the boarders at the inn."

"No, but I've heard of him. My wife thought he might be in town, but I thought he was just passing through." Bryce Galloway had just moved to the top of his list of who might have slashed his tires.

# *Chapter 16*

March 21

As the days rolled into spring, Martha Q and Mr. Carleon developed a habit of sitting on the porch after supper. They found that both enjoyed watching the day age into evening. She decided he was a pleasant man. At her age, pleasant men could fill the lonely hours sometimes far more than women friends.

She'd learned that he'd lost his wife to cancer twenty years ago and had no children. Which, to her way of thinking, was a blessing for her. Everyone she knew had not only children, but grandchildren, and they were simply boring when Martha Q knew she had no chance of one-upping them with a better story.

As they took their places among the wicker furniture, Martha Q began. "It's a really nice night tonight, Mr. Carleon, don't you think?"

"I do." He waited until she was settled in her chair before he sat down. "Here among all your huge old elms, it reminds me of New England."

"Me too," she answered, even though she'd never been to New England. In fact, she wasn't even sure where it was. Up north somewhere, but all the states got fuzzy past the Mississippi.

"How was Marty today?" Martha Q figured she'd better change the subject before he asked where in New England she'd visited.

"He's weak. Very weak. I can't say I was much for moving him, but like his friends, I couldn't just stand around and watch him die. Now at least when he wakes up, he smiles through the pain. His first word is always *Ronny*." Carleon stared out at the trees' shadows crawling toward the house. "I don't know if he loves her so much as the dream of what might have been between them, but she is very dear to him."

"She's a good girl, I can tell you. I've known

her all her life. Some say a man like him wouldn't be loving her if he were healthy, but I say it doesn't matter why he loves her. The important thing is, he does. Having a special man like that care about her will make all the difference in her life. In her later years, she'll have him to remember and know that, even for a moment, she was special to someone."

Mr. Carleon nodded. "I see their love more every day. Each time he stays awake an hour longer or manages to move his arms to do a few simple exercises, her face lights up like Christmas morning. I don't think she believes he's going to die. That'll make it harder on her when it happens."

"There is no easy where death's involved."

"How right you are."

They grew silent as Bryce Galloway walked up the walkway. Unlike the other boarders, Galloway never bought the simple supper at the inn. He usually went into town or to the bar for his dinner, unless of course it rained; then he drove the black Rover he'd rented to a drive-through and bought a bag of junk food. The smell of fast food often drifted down all the way to the first floor from his room. For a man who insisted his food be cooked with no dairy, fat, or sugar, Bryce sure brought a great many greasy bags in.

Martha Q had no idea where Bryce went, but he seemed a busy man for someone who never mentioned a job or friends in town. His rental car looked like it was built for off-road travel. But he seemed more the type who thought he was roughing it if he stayed anywhere without a golf course connected to the property.

"Evening," Galloway said with a wide smile that flashed for only a moment when he looked up.

Mr. Carleon leaned forward and welcomed him without a smile. "Evening."

Bryce didn't bother with small talk. At some point he'd quit trying to make an impression on them. Maybe because he knew they'd already figured him out. He simply tipped an imaginary hat and went into the bed-and-breakfast.

Martha Q waited until she heard him tromping up the stairs before she said, "If I were writing a mystery right now, that man would be the character who did it."

Mr. Carleon laughed. "I believe you're right; though I don't have a single fact to back up my opinion of him, I'd bet a month's pay that he's up to something."

Joni Rosen, dressed in her usual black, joined them on the porch. Martha Q didn't mind, except that Widow Joni was petite, and little women always made her feel bigger. She solved the problem by moving to the swing and covering up with a blanket, which she really didn't need.

Joni had that sadness that hangs around after a

funeral. At a certain age Martha Q decided it makes people over fifty feel comfortable around each other. They've all spent time in that well and know it.

Martha Q knew the only way to cheer Joni up was to gossip. The little woman never started gossip, but she didn't mind spreading it along. She and Joni filled Mr. Carleon in on what they knew of Bryce Galloway. He'd shown up in town two or three years ago like he'd just bought the place at a half-price sale. He was friendly and outgoing, becoming buddies with everyone right away—or at least with all the people he thought counted.

Barrett Britain, Nevada's brother, introduced him to everyone as the man who would someday take over the Boxed B. They'd been roommates in college, but Bryce had never visited Harmony before. He came one summer to ride dirt bikes, but he stayed fascinated with Nevada.

Strange thing was, no one in town ever saw him with Nevada until they saw the wedding announcement in the paper. By the time he married her a few months later, you would have thought she was the outsider, judging from all the hugs he got. Of course, the wedding was at the country club with all the important people attending. Martha Q heard all about it because some guests stayed at the inn and felt the need to fill her in on what she'd missed.

Joni explained how Nevada went right on being her wild self even after the wedding, and folks started feeling sorry for the city boy who'd moved in and tried to handle her. She was always wrecking a car or making a scene. Word was she was once so drunk, she fell down a flight of stairs and bruised up one whole side of her body. The poor man had to nurse her back because nobody in town wanted to go out to the Boxed B with her there drinking and the old man dying.

The marriage was over after a few months. Bryce left saying they'd get back together, but it never happened.

When Joni went in for cocoa, Mr. Carleon told Martha Q about the look he'd seen on Cord McDowell's face when he'd mentioned Bryce.

Martha Q returned the honesty by saying there was something about the polished Bryce Galloway that bothered her. "I've taken to locking my bedroom door at night and hinted that the widows do the same. He hasn't done one thing wrong, but something about him doesn't add up."

"Maybe we should keep an eye on Galloway," Mr. Carleon suggested. "I have a friend on the Houston police force. I might just give him a call tomorrow. He might be rich, but probably not rich enough to make police records disappear. If he had problems, they'd be filed somewhere."

"Would you?" Martha Q squealed with excitement. She was living a real-life mystery.

Joni Rosen picked that moment to step back outside and insisted on knowing what was going on.

Martha Q had to include her; after all, it would have been rude not to.

With their heads together over cocoa, the three planned to set up their own neighborhood watch on Bryce Galloway.

The next morning at breakfast they enlisted the other two widows. While the ladies went out to buy trench coats and black hats, Mr. Carleon crossed the creek and went to work for Marty Winslow. He'd already decided that their little spy game was harmless and would be something interesting to tell Marty when he woke. He might even go with Martha Q to her writers' meeting at the library. Maybe he'd hear a few bits Marty would find interesting. Carleon had always thought him a brilliant young man.

When he stepped on the porch of the duplex, Carleon almost collided with the big kid next door named Border Biggs. His head was freshly shaved so even more tattoos were visible than usual.

"Morning," Border said in almost a growl. "Mr. Carleon, ain't it? I heard you came with Marty when he arrived."

"Yes," Carleon smiled, remembering that the tattooed biker was, hard as it might be to believe, sweet Mrs. Biggs's grandson. "And you must be Border. Your grandmother makes the best pancakes I've ever tasted."

The big thug raised an eyebrow and nodded. "She's something, ain't she?"

"Yes. I'm enjoying the breakfasts she makes immensely." Carleon knew he hadn't won the kid over by simply one compliment.

In an offer of friendship, or at least peace, Carleon pulled up his sleeve. "What do you think of that?"

On the older man's arm was an eagle in full flight with an American flag between his claws. "I got it in 'Nam. I don't remember why, but it seemed a good idea at the time."

Border didn't look less frightening when he smiled. "That's so cool, man. Really cool."

Somehow they were no longer strangers. The kid stepped off the porch and headed toward his Harley. "See you later, man."

Mr. Carleon buttoned his cuff. "See you later, Border."

As he walked into Ronny's little apartment, he thought about how this was the strangest town. He was part of the widows' detective agency, hunting a man they thought looked like he might do something wrong, and he was also friends with the local Hells Angel. No wonder his boss, Marty Winslow, loved this place.

# Chapter 17

March 23

Frustrated and exhausted, Nevada came home later than usual. She'd spent an hour longer at the office than she'd planned. Bryce had dropped by the office as if he thought he'd be welcomed back after two years. Though he'd been polite to all, it set her nerves on edge and she couldn't get back to work for an hour after he'd left.

When no one was near enough to overhear, he'd whispered, "You about ready for me to come back, Nevada? You know you can't handle the ranch and this business without me. I've grown up in the oil business and I like the idea of playing rancher."

"I'm married," she said, holding out her hand with Cord's mother's ring.

"Yeah, how long will that last? Even an ex-con is too good for you. He wouldn't put up with you for long. You're the kind of woman who needs a strong hand." He stared at her. "He'll be gone soon and you'll need me back."

Despite his family's deep pockets, she'd heard

that he'd failed at several ventures since he'd left her. Maybe he figured running a ranch was easy. She really didn't know or care what he thought. "We'll never be together again, Bryce. Never."

He smiled that playboy smile that she'd loved when she'd first seen it. "Don't be too sure about that, Nevada. I haven't been able to get you out of my mind, and I'm a man used to getting exactly what he wants."

"Not me. I'm married."

He smiled. "What's he going to do to stop me? If McDowell lays a hand on me, he'll be in prison the rest of his life. All I'd probably have to do was say he threatened me and there are cops in this county who'd lock him up."

Nevada felt a chill. She told herself Bryce was lying, but she wasn't so sure. The thought of how gently Cord held her at night crossed her mind, and she decided she'd keep this problem with Bryce between them. She didn't want Cord involved or hurt.

Bryce made a polite bow and left her office, probably knowing just how badly he'd frightened her. Before their honeymoon was over, he'd begun playing a game with her. He liked to plant the seed of trouble or place a threat as if casually making a bet that he knew he'd collect on later.

The *later* always came after he'd had a few drinks and they were alone.

When Nevada left the office after sunset, she

asked security to walk her to her car. Bryce wouldn't try anything in public, that wasn't his style, but she wasn't sure what she'd do if she had to face him alone.

*Storm.* She thought of the word Cord had used when she got angry. He'd said it so simply. *"My wife tends to storm."* Like it was something she just did from time to time. Cord had said it as if storming were a part of her character that he didn't mind at all.

Nevada could never remember knowing that kind of acceptance in her life. It seemed every day of her life someone had been trying to change her, mold her, control her.

She'd always worked hard, even when her father didn't notice, but all he'd ever done was criticize her. When he died, she walked into the company her grandfather had built and took over without missing a step. There had been no one to pat her on the back and say *Good job,* but for every mistake she made there were whispers.

Only now, Bryce was back in town and the constant feeling that she was being watched fed a bad mood she'd had all week. Bryce thought he'd keep pushing, keep pestering, until she caved.

He didn't know her as well as he thought he did, she decided. All she needed was the weekend off and she'd come back fighting. She wanted to relax at home and ride her horses, and sleep without an alarm. Maybe she'd even say she was sorry for barely speaking to Cord, if he ever stopped working long enough to listen.

Her short-term husband deserved better.

Bryce Galloway would eventually go away. She didn't like the idea that he'd come to Harmony. Maybe he thought his downhill slide started when he walked out on her to teach her a lesson. She knew he hadn't expected her to go through with the divorce. Even now, he hadn't fully accepted that they were over, forever and ever over.

She wasn't afraid of him anymore. He might hit her, if he got the chance, but he'd never own her again. No man ever would. Two years ago her father was dying, her brother was planning his escape from the ranch he hated, and Bryce had left her to deal with it all. It was the lowest point in her life. Strange thing about dropping to the bottom of a deep well—you've got nowhere to go but up. She had begun to climb.

The only thing that did frighten her was how he might try to hurt Cord.

As she walked into her cool home, Nevada set her packed briefcase on the nearest chair. *Home,* she thought, *I'm finally home.*

Her day had started out a disaster. The designer briefcase she always carried back and forth to the office had toppled over that morning when she was leaving, and she hadn't had time to get all the papers back in order. Then she had to deal with a lightning fire at one of the rig work sites. Her secretary had called in sick, something Bridget never did, and from there the day dropped even lower when Bryce came in. Now, she just wanted to forget about everything and relax.

When she walked by the kitchen, she almost didn't notice Cord sitting at the breakfast nook table, his meal half finished.

"About time you got in, Babe." He sounded cold, almost angry.

She stopped. He'd never questioned her hours and he'd never called her Babe.

"I told you several times, I don't like nicknames. Maybe it's time to test your hearing." She moved closer to the table. "And . . ." She drew a breath, knowing that she had to nip his questions about her time in the bud. "It's none of your concern where I've been. I told you from the start I often work late."

"I waited dinner for you."

"Why, so we could have another meal not talking?" She was being bitchy, but she didn't care. Her head hurt. Her feet hurt. Her emotions had been shredded like cheap confetti.

"Don't pick another fight when we're in the middle of this one." Cord's cold eyes drilled into her. "You weren't late working. I called your office. You weren't there. No one was. Even the answering machine must have taken off early."

"You could have called my cell. We've been

getting some odd calls at the office. I have the systems turned off at five so no one can get through." She didn't add that it was her ex-husband she feared would call late.

He didn't look away. He only asked, "So you could lie to me and tell me you were working late. I don't care what you do or where you go, Nevada, I just hate being lied to."

*This is it,* she thought. *This is where the marriage starts to turn. From now on it will start to rot and nothing can be done to save it.* She held her ground. "I don't want to lie to you, Cord, but it's none of your concern. I thought we had that understanding from the first. I don't want you worrying about me; that's just one step from controlling me."

She expected him to accuse her of having an affair or of drinking or even shopping too much, but he said simply, "Want to tell me about the odd phone calls?"

She shook her head. "No. It's just business." She felt terrible for lying. He didn't deserve it. He'd been straight with her, but she saw no point in telling him about Bryce. There was nothing he could do.

He stood and walked to her. For a second she flinched, a tiny part of her bracing for a hit. Cord was bigger than Bryce. If he hit her, it would break bones.

But he only walked around her and pulled her

plate from the microwave. When he'd set her food on the table, he pulled out her chair and waited for her to join him.

She took the offered seat, unsure where she stood with this husband she rarely talked to.

While she picked at her food, he pulled a note from his pocket and slowly unfolded it. Before he placed it between them, she knew what it was. A note from Bryce. Three had come to the office, always addressed personally to her. Always the same.

She didn't pick up the paper.

"You know what it says?" Cord asked. "I wasn't prying. I found it on the floor next to where you always leave your briefcase. It must have fallen out."

"I know what it says. It says the same thing as the odd phone messages I've been receiving at work." She couldn't lie anymore. Not to him.

Just to have something to do, she picked up the note and saw four words written in bold print. *Missing you. Coming soon.*

She expected Cord to accuse her of having a lover, but he just waited. "It's not a love note. It's a threat, and I've taken measures at the office. It's not something you have to worry about, Cord."

To her shock he seemed to believe her. He took the note, folded it back into his pocket, and said simply, "You'll tell me when it is?"

She thought about hugging him for not asking more. This was her problem, and she'd made up her mind after talking to Bryce that she'd do her best to keep Cord out of it. "I promise." She'd dealt with Bryce two years ago, and she could deal with him now.

"Then let's eat, Babe." He smiled. "And I thought we'd talk at meals from now on. Maybe not rattle on, but it doesn't have to be so silent."

She realized he was dropping the subject. No drilling of questions. No yelling. All he asked for was that she didn't lie. "Back to argument number two. Don't call me Babe."

Now, when the argument turned to nothing of importance, he frowned. "I like calling you Babe, but I could change to Honey. Honey sounds a little too sweet for you. Darling or Sweetie wouldn't be right. No, Babe has to be it."

*"No,"* she yelled. "Babe is the name of a pig."

Cord thought about it. "Yeah, I know, but it was a cute pig."

She took a bite of pot roast, chewed while she thought about him, and then said, "Are you trying to pick a fight?"

He smiled. "Maybe, Babe. I like to see you fired up. It's better than worried."

She considered hitting him with her baked potato, but she doubted it was hot enough to do any real damage.

He read her mind. "If you toss one bite of that food I swear I'll—"

"You'll what?" Even play-fighting with him could get her hurt.

He grinned. "I'll think of a worse name to call you than Babe."

She smiled, settling into the nearness of him like she always did. "If you call me Babe, I'll call you Pa because it fits you. I swear, Cord, you look young but you've got the ways of an old man." She guessed he'd had very little time in his life to have fun.

Then it hit her. He'd gone to prison about the time he turned eighteen. He'd never had time to flirt or act silly. The man was almost thirty and he'd never flirted with a woman. Even when he'd asked her out once when they were still both kids, he'd just asked, no smiling or *How are you doing,* just "You want to go out?" She'd said no more because of the way he asked than because she didn't want to date him.

"Cord," she said, before he thought of another topic to bug her with tonight. "How about we go sit on the couch and watch a movie?"

"Why?" He looked like he smelled a trap.

"I could pop some popcorn and we could hold hands and pretend we're at the movies on a date. You're right. I need to leave my worries for a while and relax. You're the only one around, so I guess that makes you my date."

He stood and collected the plates. "You pick the movie, I'll pop the corn. It sounds like a dumb idea, but I'll go along with it."

When they were settled on the couch and had munched on half a bowl of popcorn, she took his hand in hers. For a few minutes he didn't seem to know what to do, and then hesitantly he began to move his thumb over her palm. When she shifted and pushed her shoulder against him, he lifted his arm and pulled her to him.

Halfway through the movie he lowered the volume and whispered, "I wasn't checking up on you today. One of the men said he found you one night a few years ago between here and town. You'd totaled your car. He claimed you must have taken the curve at sixty instead of thirty. I called because I thought you might have had car trouble or wrecked another car. I tried your cell first but you didn't answer."

"I remember that night. I don't know how fast I was going, I only remember crying so hard I couldn't see the road." She leaned her head back against his arm. "Funny, I don't remember why I was crying."

"I was worried about you tonight."

"I know," she answered, "but don't expect me to report in. Just know I'll always be coming home as soon as I can. I'll keep my promise to sleep in your bed every night."

"Fair enough." He kissed her cheek.

"And, anytime you call, always leave a message. Sometimes I step out of my office and forget to take the phone." When he didn't look like he understood, she added, "You know, to the ladies' room."

"Oh."

She swore he blushed.

She placed her hand on his jaw and turned his head toward her. The kiss was soft, gentle, like a first kiss. Neither seemed to want it to end, but neither pushed for more. For now, it was enough. This wasn't a peck on the cheek or a kiss for show. This kiss was real and they both knew it.

When she finally pulled away, he smiled and turned the movie back up. A settling had passed between them and an acceptance that neither one had ever felt. It took her a long while to realize what had happened, to recognize the feeling blanketing over them both.

It was simply a trust unlike anything she'd ever felt. He trusted her without questioning when she'd given no answer. All he'd asked for was not to be lied to, and she swore she never would. She'd keep her secrets, but she would no longer wrap them in lies.

When the movie ended, he took her hand and they walked to the bedroom without a word. He stripped off his clothes, watching her do the same. Neither bothered to turn on a light. The open blinds and windows let in enough moon-light to see.

He pulled back the covers on his side of the bed and waited for her to climb in. When she did, he moved in beside her and kissed her lightly. "The movie wasn't such a bad idea after all," he whispered against her ear. "I wouldn't mind having a date with you again."

She stretched, letting her body settle against his. All the stress of the day moved away, and she finally felt safe. She wouldn't have cared if he kissed her again, but he only whispered, "Good night, Babe."

She poked him gently in the ribs and felt his laughter against her throat.

## Chapter 18

March 24
Duplex

Ronny slipped out the back door of her little apartment and into the cool night air. She had to force herself to think about what day it was. The twenty-fourth, she thought. One week since Marty had moved in with her. The days, even the hours flowed together. There was so much to be done, and time passed not from morning to night, but from the precious hours Marty was awake.

They'd almost lost him the second day. She didn't sleep for more than thirty hours as she stayed by his side. Something in her tired mind said she'd lose him if she didn't keep watch. Finally he calmed, and she slept for twelve hours only to find him smiling at her when she ran in to check on him.

Mr. Carleon tried to keep time in balance. He insisted she eat breakfast even when she didn't notice it was morning. Beau Yates, next door, played his guitar every evening he didn't work, and Marty would hold her hand as if they were at a great concert.

Dr. Addison Spencer came every day to check on him. She kept close records and tried to balance his pain medicine so that he could keep his wits about him. Ronny teased him that the doctor was fighting a lost cause because after falling off a mountain he didn't have many wits left.

Marty, in his usual superior way, claimed he'd been born double-witted and could stand to lose a few. The first time he laughed, everyone in the room stopped. Ronny fought back tears as she realized teasing him just might be the magic that helped him live one day longer.

As always, Marty complained. He didn't like the

food or it was too hot or cold in the room or the sun bothered him or the room was drab. He even complained about the color of the paint.

Ronny frowned at him. "Well, in a perfect world, what color would this room be?"

"Green," he said. "Deep forest green."

That afternoon, while he slept, everyone grabbed a paintbrush, and when he woke up the room was green. Of course, he reminded them all that it was the worst paint job he'd ever seen, but no one listened.

Tonight was the end of his eighth day and he was still alive. She walked to the ramp Cord and his men had built for a wheelchair. Marty was no closer to being able to sit in a chair than he'd been the day he came, but seeing the ramp brought her promise.

Someday, she hoped, she'd roll him down the ramp and they'd go the block to Main Street. They'd go past all the stores and look at the courthouse. Maybe they'd stop at the diner for lunch or go over to Buffalo's Bar and Grill and have a beer. She'd sit beside his chair and they'd hold hands as they listened to Beau and his partner in the band play. It would be like a real date, something they'd had very few of.

Marty would always say that Beau was a dreamer, his head full of songs, and she'd argue that it might not be a bad way to go through life.

Ronny wasn't a big dreamer. She'd never wanted a great passion or riches or to travel the world. All she'd ever wanted was for someone to love her. She wanted to hold someone's hand and smile. She wanted one person to care when she had a cold or lost weight or cut her hair.

"I don't want much, God," she whispered into the silent night around her. "If you could see your way to give us just a little more time."

Marty was asleep and the night called her out for a walk.

The sudden sound of a car moving slowly down the street made her move back into the shadows of the duplex. In the foggy glow of the streetlight half a block away, she watched her mother's car circle the block. Once. Twice.

On impulse, Ronny walked to the curb. If her mother wanted to say something to her, Ronny decided she'd listen. She no longer had any energy left to be angry at Dallas Logan for kicking her out. In truth, it had been the start of her awakening, and she knew, even if asked, she'd never go back.

When Dallas's old Buick circled one more time, she made it almost even with Ronny before she gunned the engine and sped away.

Ronny smiled at the taillights as she buttoned her coat and tied back her hair with a band she kept in her coat pocket. She was sure her mother thought the gesture of driving away fast would hurt Ronny. One more insult. One more time that Dallas could reject her child.

Only Ronny no longer felt it. She knew she was loved and needed by the man inside, and her mother's anger no longer mattered. She moved silently through the streets, no more than another layer of shadow between the streetlights. She liked the night when she could disappear and let the darkness hold her for a while.

When she went back inside, Marty was awake. He must have been watching her from the window. "Come here, honey." Not only did his eyes show the pain he felt inside, but he seemed sad for her as well.

She walked to the chair that always sat close to his bed. "You saw my mother's car?"

"I did. If I could I'd take away all the bad memories of your growing up with that woman, but I've come to believe that the bad only makes us appreciate the good, and you are the best thing that ever came into my life."

"Really?"

"You're the only person who ever needed me. I wish I could always be here for you. When I was away, every day I tried to remember details about you. The way your hair moved. The way you stood up to me that first day we met even though I was yelling at you. I even remember that funny hat you used to wear when you delivered the mail. I thought it was the ugliest hat I'd ever seen, but you were cute as a bug wearing it. Funny, no matter what was going on when I was away, the thought of that hat would always make me smile."

She laced her hand in his. They'd agreed days ago not to waste time saying things like "How do you feel?" or "You need to rest" to one another. They took the short periods of time they had. It was all that was left and somehow, it had to be enough.

"Tell me about your adventures," she said, curling against the bed so that she was as close as the machines would allow her. "Tell me about the world you've seen."

He began telling her of mountain climbing and hang gliding and skiing in the Alps. For a moment, as she listened, he wasn't a frail man in a hospital bed. He was the man she had met and fallen in love with. He was whole again, pulling her along with him on his adventures . . . pulling her into a perfect world.

# Chapter 19

April 4

They'd been married almost a month when Cord woke Nevada at dawn with a rough kiss. They'd kissed good night for over a week—soft, gentle kisses—but this was different. This tasted of passion.

"I can't hold out any longer, Babe." His hand spread wide along her side. "I got to get closer to you, so if you don't want this, you'd better stop me now."

She stared up into his warm eyes, still half asleep. He looked more like a man being tortured than someone about to make love to his wife. His jaw was set. His gaze never left hers as his hand moved down her, hungry for the feel of her. The silk nightgown bunched and tugged against his callused hands. He wasn't holding her, only brushing over her, as if learning her every curve.

"You're so soft," he whispered against her ear. "So soft."

She didn't budge as he pulled off her short gown and moved above her. The feel of his body pressing over her warmed her as he shifted her arms and spread her blond hair across the pillow. For a minute he waited, matching his breathing to balance hers, letting his warmth blanket hers.

He braced his elbows on either side of her face and kissed her with feather kisses along her cheek. With each breath his hard chest lowered and pressed against her as his lips trailed over her skin. When he returned to her mouth, she opened to his hunger and moaned as the kiss turned molten.

The kiss was deep, and neither thought to breathe. When he finally broke away, she gulped for air and waited for him to pull her into heaven.

His big hands moved into her hair and tugged her gently as he tasted the flesh of her throat like a man starving for her.

She could feel her whispered moans of pleasure pushing him beyond reason.

If she didn't tell him how she felt, he'd move away and she'd never know this man she'd married any better than she knew him now. Pressing her lips against his ear, she whispered, "Make love to me, Cord. Just love me."

He pulled away and looked into her eyes, then lowered his mouth to hers with one last gentle kiss before passion consumed them both.

Without a word he made love to her with great tenderness. The only sound was her soft cry when he entered her. He wasn't taking, but giving in loving touches and slow kisses that moved over her skin like warm water. What he lacked in polish, he made up for in gentleness. He hesitated at times, giving her moments to anticipate pure pleasure and rushed at others as if he couldn't wait to be closer to her. His body never smothered or dominated, but comforted and sheltered her from all the world except his touch.

As he moved over her, so close they became one, she had the sense of coming home, of being complete.

When they were finished and both too tired to do more than breathe, he pulled her against his chest and floated the covers over them both without saying a word.

Even in the shadows of passion, he held her as no man had ever held her. His hand moved slowly down her body, cherishing one last touch before he fell asleep.

Tears dripped down her cheeks. She'd wondered what making love to him would be like. Violent, savage, wild, but it was none of those. He'd made no promises. Whispered no endearments. Told no lies. But his every touch told of caring deeply, so deeply he'd lost himself in satisfying her.

An hour later, he was dressed by the time she woke and crawled from the bed. For a minute they just looked at each other. He wore his jeans and western-cut shirt with the snaps, all pressed and starched. His winter-wheat hair was still wet from a shower and she could smell the shaving cream he'd just used. Down to his handmade boots he looked every bit a successful, powerful rancher.

She stood before him with wild straw hair and a gown strap hanging to her elbow. The top of one breast showed, but after he'd handled her so completely at dawn she didn't think it would matter much.

"About this morning . . ." He finally broke the silence.

"Don't you dare apologize," she interrupted.

He raised an eyebrow but didn't move any closer.

She crossed half the distance between them. "No one's ever made love to me like that. Not ever. You made me feel like I was special. Like I was priceless, and I'll not have you ruin it by saying you're sorry or that we shouldn't have done it."

A slow smile spread across his face. "I was going to ask you if it really happened or if I was just dreaming. Either way I had no intention to apologize."

She felt like a fool for her outburst. "It happened," was all she could manage.

"So, I take it, you've no objection to it happening again sometime."

"I'm looking forward to it." Crossing her arms,

she tried to look proper. "In fact, I wouldn't mind at all if it became a habit between us."

She wanted to run to him and kiss him, but something in the way he stood told her he wanted to keep everything in a compartment, even her.

For a man who never touched anyone, he had certainly touched her before dawn. Even now she could still feel his big hands sliding down her body, moving her gently so that he could satisfy every part of her.

"I have to get over to the bunkhouse." He pulled her back from her thoughts.

"All right," she answered, not knowing how to talk about how perfectly they'd made love.

He nodded once and walked to the door. "You might want to go shopping for more of those little gowns that aren't long enough to cover anything or thick enough to hide anything. I like them."

Looking down at the silk slip of a gown, she smiled. It had cost her a hundred dollars, and until last night she hadn't thought he'd noticed. She'd order half a dozen online today and have them sent overnight.

# Chapter 20

At nine in the morning Martha Q found herself totally alone in the inn. All the widows went to the first-day sale at the Sears outlet store. Mr. Carleon left to stay with Marty in one of his usual pressed black suits. Bryce Galloway said he would be gone all day, and the housekeeper took Mrs. Biggs grocery shopping.

Martha Q wasn't sure what to do. She hadn't had the run of the house, completely alone, in months. She told herself she wasn't a nosy person, but it seemed like a good time to look in every room. After all, it was her house.

She collected the master keys and decided to start on the third floor. Mr. Carleon's room was perfect. Three black suits, an overcoat, and a half dozen white shirts were lined up in his closet. No color, she observed. All his personal things were lined up neatly in the three dressers. Underwear. Handkerchiefs. Socks. A black shaving kit. Several books were on the shelf by the bed, all in order of size. The man even made his own bed. He folded his underwear and left a thin bookmark in the paperback he was reading. No excitement, no surprises.

In Bryce Galloway's room, she found the opposite. Nothing was picked up or cleaned. Dirty clothes scattered on the floor, the suitcase left open atop the dresser as if he didn't realize he had drawers he could have used. The maid had already complained that his was the hardest room to clean. He'd left shaving cream and stubble in the sink, towels on the floor, water stains where his glass sat on the nightstand, and crumbs on the desk along with dirty dishes he'd carried up from the kitchen.

Leaving the door open so she could hear anyone coming up the stairs, she went through his belongings like a spy. Papers were piled on the desk, but they all looked like legal documents or geographic maps, except for one that had simple times written down. *6:10, 6:22, 7:03. All in by 7:15,* and so on. There was another list of times with initials beside them, but they made even less sense. Each time had an *A* or *B* before it, like he was keeping a log on two people or two houses at the same time. Galloway was watching people come and go, but who and from where had not been written down.

Martha Q fought the urge to call Tyler Wright again and fill him in on the details. Since the man had found out he was going to be a father, he didn't seem to give his full attention so easily, but the funeral director was the only man she could think of who might be able to solve the riddle.

Bryce Galloway didn't belong here. He wasn't one of them. From the look of him, he had enough money to stay at a grand hotel, not a little bed-and-breakfast in the old part of town.

Harmony had its share of nuts and odd characters, but Bryce was different. If there was a town somewhere where he'd fit in, Martha Q didn't want to go there. Tyler Wright would listen to her and probably pat her hand and tell her she didn't have anything to worry about. He'd be gone soon. After all, if he'd planned to stay, wouldn't he have bought a house and not stayed at the inn?

She grinned, remembering how she'd driven by the funeral home a few days ago and seen Tyler helping his Kate out of the car. For a moment in the quiet morning air when they thought no one else was around, he'd kissed her cheek as he'd spread his hand across her swollen belly. If Hallmark could get that emotion of pure love on a card, they'd sell a million.

As she walked down the stairs, Martha Q decided she'd have to depend on the widows' detective agency to find out more about Bryce. She'd put one of them on him from the time he left after breakfast until he returned. No, she'd better make them go in twos. One was bound to get distracted. Martha Q wanted to know where he went, who he talked to.

At the bottom of the stairs, the fat cat swore in cat talk when Martha Q tripped over him. Martha Q swung in an attempt to kick the cat, but Mr. Dolittle just walked away mumbling to himself. If cats really were reincarnated people, he must have been a bachelor. No woman would put up with him if he weighed more than twenty pounds.

"I might as well get dressed," she said to no one. "I may have to do some investigating of my own. I'll have to stop by the bookstore and buy a tablet first. He's not the only one who can keep records." If Bryce was keeping track of someone's comings and goings, she'd bet it was for no good.

# Chapter 21

April 4

Cord spent the morning trying to keep his mind on work. No matter how hard he pushed, there never seemed enough hours in the day, and now he had a feeling there wouldn't be enough hours at night either. If Nevada was ever agreeable to it again, and she seemed to be, he'd die of exhaustion before he'd give up making love to her. At one point he was so wrapped in passion that lightning could have set fire to the bed and he wouldn't have noticed.

But as the day aged, he told himself he didn't have time to think about her and what they'd done at dawn. The ranch had more than its share of problems. One of the fences was down in the north pasture and cattle were everywhere, even on the county road. Galem said men had to stop their trucks and shoo a dozen cows away before they could get to work. An hour later they discovered that the pump to one of the main water supplies had broken.

To make matters worse, the day turned cloudy about eleven and so did his mood. Try as he did, he couldn't keep his mind away from thoughts of Nevada. There were probably words he should have said to her before he left, but he had no idea what they would be. He found himself wishing for the night as thunder rolled in the distance. Wishing it could be just the two of them in the world again. She'd looked so adorable with her hair all wild and her little nightgown half falling off.

The thought of how Nevada felt in his arms returned again and again like a merry-go-round of pleasure circling in his mind. She'd lain back on the pillows and let him touch her, only moving slightly now and then when she showed her pleasure. He'd taken his time, learning every part of her. The softest spot just beneath her breasts and the way she laughed when he brushed his fingers down her spine. He loved the smell of her when she was warm and wrapped in the sheets. He loved the taste of her throat as he felt her pulse against his open mouth.

"You asleep, Cord?" Galem shouted above the thunder.

Cord jumped out of the way of a cow coming down the branding chute. A few men smothered laughter until Cord laughed at himself, and then full all-out teasing began.

"You'd think the boss was on his honeymoon," one said.

"He does look like he needs sleep."

"Got that calf-eyed look about him."

"We'd better watch out for him or he's liable to get trampled."

"Maybe you should consider taking a nap somewhere besides where five hundred pounds of beef can knock you down."

Cord grumbled, but he couldn't hide the smile or even fake anger at the time they were wasting. Let them laugh; in a few hours he'd be going home to Nevada and it wouldn't take long to get her back between the sheets.

"Let's get back to work," he ordered, and added to himself, "We've got loads to do before it rains."

The men went back to business, and Cord forced his mind to focus on what he was doing.

Around one o'clock he ordered everyone to take a break. Galem handed him one of the sandwiches he'd packed for the men. They were too far from headquarters to go in, so sandwiches and luke-warm water would hold hunger at bay. The men broke into groups, most talking about plans for the weekend, while Cord sat down beside Galem.

"Wouldn't do you no good to go back to headquarters for lunch anyway, Cord," Galem said. "Ora Mae went to Amarillo with Little Miss. Phoned an hour ago to tell me they were in the middle of a shopping spree and would be lucky to make it in by six."

Shaking his head, Cord admitted, "I don't see why she likes to shop. I always hated it."

"Ora Mae told me once that Nevada's mother only showed her any attention when they shopped. She liked to dress the little girl up. I guess that was her way of showing love."

Cord almost mentioned that Nevada was probably shopping for him, but he doubted she considered it a show of love in his case.

He took another sandwich. "Why do you call her Little Miss? She's five seven before she puts on her heels. She's not exactly a little miss." He smiled, thinking of how his chin touched the top of her head.

"I know, but I remember the skinny little girl who followed me around when I came to work at the Boxed B. I was still in my teens when I quit school, my folks kicked me out of the nest. Helping out in the bunkhouse wasn't just my first job, it was my only home. Back then Nevada's father was running the place and he wanted men at the bunkhouse day and night. We didn't just work hours, we signed on for the season. He was always pushing his three grown sons to cowboy up, but he ignored his half-grown daughter. Near as I could see, the boys followed his lead. I never saw them do anything but tease her or tell her how dumb she was 'cause she couldn't keep up with them."

Galem took a bite of his sandwich and continued, "I never heard the old man say a kind word to anyone. He mostly yelled at everyone, except Little Miss. To him, she wasn't even there. He told me once that she was something his wife wanted, like she was nothing but a pet around the place. I didn't know a lot, but I taught her to ride and tried to teach her to cook. Cooking lessons were a waste of time, but I never saw a kid love horses like she did and still does. She'd come home every summer and nag her mom until she got a new mare. She always said she'd raise horses to sell as show horses. Her mom gave in to her, kind of the anything-you-want-as-long-as-you-go-away brand of raising a kid. By the time she was fifteen she was showing horses and winning every trophy around."

"I've never seen a single trophy around the house," Cord commented. "You would have thought they'd let her put them up somewhere."

"That stepmother she had one summer tossed them all out, I bet. She even tried to get the old man to sell off Nevada's horses. Only her daddy had promised Nevada's mother before she died that he wouldn't mess with them, and the old man kept his word. Maybe he figured as long as Nevada had the horses she wouldn't spend much time at home. I swear that summer the step-witch was here, Nevada slept more in the barn than she did in the house."

"Thanks for telling me." Cord realized Galem must trust him to so openly talk about Nevada. "And thanks for yelling. That steer almost bloodied one of these shirts Nevada bought me. I was daydreaming on the job."

"No thanks needed," Galem answered. "I'm guessing you got a problem on your mind."

"Right," he managed to say as he looked up and saw the *problem* headed straight toward him in her grandfather's old Jeep.

Swearing, Cord swung over the fence thinking he should have stripped all the gears except first so she couldn't go over twenty. He headed toward the spot he hoped would be where she stopped before hitting the corral.

Her own little cloud of dust swirled around her as she hit the brakes and slid to within three feet of him.

Cord waited. He knew it wouldn't be long.

She climbed out of the Jeep talking. It took

his mind a few beats to catch up with her.

"Hold on now, Nevada. Take a long breath and start over."

"What is the matter with you? Didn't you hear what I said?" She folded her arms over her chest and stared at him as if he were brain dead. "I swear if I have to tell you everything twice, we'll never finish a conversation."

Cord moved closer and lowered his voice so none of the men could hear. "I just need time to get over the sight of you before I can think. You're beautiful even when you're upset."

He fought the urge to kiss her. "I thought you weren't on the ranch. I heard something about you going shopping." He grinned. "You do look great in that sundress." He closed his mouth and his eyes. He was starting to sound as scattered as she always did. Maybe being brain dead and chattering on about nothing was catching.

"The men are staring at us," she whispered. Thunder rattled the air and the first raindrops plopped in the dirt, but she didn't move.

"They're staring at you and that cotton dress." He'd thought she looked and felt great in silk, but now he couldn't imagine anything finer than cotton brushing her legs.

"We need to talk. Something happened in town that I should tell you about." She took his arm and pulled him toward the Jeep. "Go for a drive with me."

"I can't," he started, as huge drops splattered around him. The sky darkened as if someone had turned down the dimmer switch on the world. Big drops of rain hit the hood of the Jeep like tiny bombs spraying inch-wide circles across the hot metal. "We need to finish here."

Horses danced nervously as lightning flashed and the men scrambled for the rain slickers tied to their saddles. This wasn't just a light afternoon shower coming; something strong was blowing in.

Cord turned back to his men. "Close it down, boys, and call it a day." Even if the rain stopped soon, it would be too muddy to get much work done. He saw Zeb running for one of the horse trailers as the cowhands loaded up their mounts. Riding home in this storm might get horse and rider killed.

He put his arm over Nevada's shoulder. "All right, let's go talk, but I drive." In the drafty old Jeep they'd both be soaked in minutes if they didn't find cover fast.

As he circled the corral, he made sure all cowhands were loaded into trucks, horses were ready to move, and gates were closed. Cord didn't want to come back in the morning to find fifty head of cattle wandering the west side of the ranch. He'd had enough accidents happen lately. So many, in fact, he was starting to think someone had it in for him, making trouble run double time. In the back of his mind the name of Bryce Galloway kept echoing even though he didn't have an ounce of proof. He wouldn't put it past the ex-husband to try to make things hard for Cord just for the fun of it.

Since Cord was closer to his farm than the ranch house, he headed down the dirt road toward his home place. He'd sold his old tractor and his horse trailer, hoping to make enough money to pay off the last of his loan. The buyer was supposed to pick both up yesterday. He'd left them parked in the yard between the house and the barn and had planned to drive over to his place today anyway just to make sure they were gone.

As they drove he could feel them racing the edge of the storm, and he guessed if he slowed it would catch them. Rolling down the window, he let damp air fly past him as lightning danced along the horizon. In this country it paid to watch the weather.

Nevada chatted about her trip to Amarillo and all she'd bought as he drove. He knew she wasn't talking about what she needed to. She was nervous about something more than the lightning. Like him, she grew up with the sudden storms and knew to take cover.

When they turned onto his land, he slowed. The storm hadn't caught up to them yet, and the last thing he wanted to do was accidentally flip the old Jeep in a pothole. He knew his place needed repairs, but somehow the Boxed B always drew his attention.

"You need to get the crew out working on this road." She voiced his thoughts. "I don't want you neglecting your farm. I always thought this was a nice place, like one of those pictures of what folks in cities think farmhouses should look like."

He'd never thought of it that way. It had always been just a house. Even though he grew up there, it still seemed more his folks' place than his.

"That's not what you came out to talk to me about." Cord was ready to hear whatever she had to say. "What brought you back from town so early?"

"There was another note on my car when I stopped at the mall. We weren't there long and I saw no sign of him, but Bryce left it. I know he did."

"Same words."

She nodded. "Ora Mae said we'd better get back to the ranch. I was glad I wasn't alone. I swear I could feel him watching us. It spooked us both."

"You won't be alone again. Until this guy stops *missing you,* me or one of the men will drive you anywhere you want to go." He glanced her way and saw her open her mouth to argue, then stop.

"Agreed?" he pushed, knowing it sounded more like an order than a request, but he couldn't just talk about her safety, he had to do what he could.

"You're right. If I know Bryce, we won't have long to wait. He had the attention span of a mosquito sucking tequila. He'll either show up soon or move on. I should warn you, he's a master at causing distraction and walking away like the victim. Once when he blacked my eye, Galem taught him a lesson. On the way to the hospital to get a few stitches, Bryce swore he'd see Galem in jail. When I begged him not to, he ran off the road. I was barely conscious when he shoved me behind the wheel and called 911. My injuries, as well as his, were written up as a car accident. The sheriff thought I was driving blind drunk, and he said he'd gone along hoping to stop me." Nevada shook her head. "He put on such a show of begging the sheriff not to book me, even promising to hide the keys on the nights I drank."

"Were you over the limit?"

"Probably, but I hadn't been the one driving. Luckily, we were still on the ranch when the wreck happened. Private property saved me from a DWI."

"You could have told the truth."

"I wouldn't have been believed. It would have been my word against his, and Bryce has this way of telling lies that suckers everyone in. After that night he was the long-suffering husband and I was the wild spoiled brat who had totaled yet another car."

Cord remembered reading about the wreck. Even the local paper had run it more as a "see what the Britain girl has done now" story than a news report. They'd even reported the injuries suffered by the passenger, her husband.

"That where you got the little scar just over your left eyebrow?"

Surprise pulled her out of her depression. "You noticed that."

"I notice everything about you, Babe."

He'd managed to make her smile. "Apparently you do, except that I hate being called Babe."

When he pulled up to his place and cut the engine, he thought his farm looked abandoned. With the farm equipment and the trailer gone, the house and barn looked even more run down. Tumbleweeds were caught along the fence line and one of the chairs had blown off the porch. Far to the right he could see the first crop breaking the soil by a few inches. Thanks to the Boxed B's huge tractors, they'd plowed and planted in days instead of weeks. Cord had even bought mobile irrigation units, almost guaranteeing a good crop. When their marriage ended, he'd haul the irrigation system over to her place.

Glancing down at her finger, he saw the thin band of gold. She was still wearing it, so today wouldn't be the last day. After a month, he'd thought they were working well together, but now he wasn't so sure. After all, he had made love to her just before dawn without them even talking it over first.

She hadn't exactly invited him to make love to her, but she hadn't objected. He'd thought she enjoyed it as much as he had. She'd come home in the middle of the day and pulled him away from work, saying she needed to talk. A note left on a car didn't seem that urgent. Something else was bothering her.

Maybe he'd stepped over that invisible trip wire he'd been looking for since they walked out of the courthouse . . . maybe he'd tripped the switch that was about to blow up everything.

"So, I finally heard what Ora Mae had been trying to tell me. That woman would drive to heaven in a wheelbarrow to get her point across."

"What did she tell you?" He'd dropped out of the conversation at some point. He had enough frightening things in his past. The housekeeper wouldn't have to make something up. Whatever it was, he knew he'd found the real problem that had made her drive across half the ranch to find him.

Nevada huffed as if she'd been asked to say everything again. "She told me that you're not comfortable in the house. She says you go around opening drapes and turning on lights. She says every door you walk through, you leave open, and you're forever roaming through the kitchen looking for something to eat."

Cord relaxed. She was complaining about his habits. He could fix that. "I like light and fresh air. I like being able to eat whenever I'm hungry, but if it bothers you I can change." He could learn to live in the cavelike rooms with their thick drapes and closed windows. He could eat on a timetable; he had in prison.

"It doesn't bother me." Now, after he gave in, she sounded angry. "If you want light and air, we can work on that. I told Ora Mae to leave a basket of fruit and snacks out on the counter and clean the wine cooler out and stock it with individual milks you can take with you or whatever kind of drinks you like. Since our marriage I seem to have given up the habit of wine with dinner anyway."

Now he was confused. She was giving in. He climbed out of the Jeep and ran the few feet to the overhang at the side of his parents' home. "What are we talking about, Nevada?"

She followed him to the corner of the porch and sat down, propping her boots up on the steps. "We're talking about making you happy, you idiot, so stop making a big deal of it and tell Ora Mae what you want her to do. She'll stock up on whatever you like. We'll turn off the air conditioner and keep the windows open as long as the wind is under forty. W—"

He knelt to her level on the thick grass that had always grown on the shady side of the porch.

"One more time. What are we talking about, Nevada? This isn't about me turning on lights or what I want to drink. You didn't drive out to talk about Ora Mae's worries, did you? What are we really talking about here? Say what you want to say, Babe," he asked again, and then waited.

For a while she didn't look at him, and he just listened to the rain playing on the tin porch roof of the old house. He'd grown up in this quiet farmhouse where no one talked out their problems. He didn't want it to be like that between him and Nevada. He'd rather face trouble head on than wonder what was bothering her.

When she finally did look up, her beautiful eyes were swimming in tears. "Why'd you make love to me like that, Cord?"

Of all the things he thought might be on her mind, bothering her, making her nervous and angry, their dawn loving had finally made it to the top of the list.

He cupped the side of her face and brushed a tear away with his thumb. "Like what? Did I do something wrong?" He wanted to scream that he could change, he could get it right next time, only in his life there were very few second chances and maybe she wasn't willing to give him one.

Her hand covered his, pressing his palm against her cheek. "I didn't expect it, not knowing the kind of man you are. I didn't expect you to be so tender." She gulped down a sob. "No one's ever made love to me like that. Like I was special, like I was made of fine china."

He stood and looked down at her, wondering how any man could touch her in any other way. The thought that someone had made his gut knot.

She straightened, lifting her chin. "We agreed to be honest, so here goes. I've had more lovers than I can count. I gave it away to half a dozen on my sixteenth birthday just to show my dad that I could party even if he forgot to say *happy birthday* to me. I've had one-night stands where I couldn't remember the guy's name in the morning. I had three husbands, one who thought that wild sex was an every-night rodeo and one who used it to dominate and control. If I didn't want to, he'd torture me insisting on it and, if I agreed too easily, he'd say that I was a tramp and deserved to be treated like one."

She held to her pride, and he saw all her invisible scars for the first time.

"I've had sex in the back of pickups and penthouse suites, coatrooms and bathroom bars, but I've never, ever had what you offered this morning."

He circled his arms around her and pulled her gently against his chest. "What do you want?"

She pressed her forehead against his chest. "I want that kind of loving again, but I don't want to have to ask or beg for it. I don't want it to be part of the negotiation between us. I don't want it to be a game between you and me. Not this. I need to know that this one thing is real between us."

He turned her head up and kissed her before whispering, "I've never done it in a pickup or a penthouse, or a bathroom bar. In fact, except for a few awkward times before I left for prison, I've never made love at all, so I guess if you put us together we average out to about even."

"But how?"

He laughed. "I dreamed of making love a lot, and always when I did, I dreamed that it was with you."

She pulled away. "You're kidding."

He shook his head. "That's why it came so easy last night. I'd practiced in my mind a thousand times."

He kissed her again, this time with passion. When he finally broke the kiss, his hands still moved over her. "Making love to you was never part of any game. Whenever you want to again, just touch me. There will be no negotiating or bargaining." He kissed her ear. "Or holding back. Any time. Any place."

"Now," she whispered, then laughed when he stumbled backward into the rain.

She wrapped her arms around him and held on tight, not caring that big cold raindrops splattered around her. Her first kiss was almost shy.

He moved his hands over her bottom and lifted

her as she wrapped her legs around his waist. Moving toward the house, they were lost to everything around but each other. Without a word, he kicked in the door, climbed the narrow stairs, and walked into his old room. The storm made it seem like night, and the rain blocked out all the world.

Pulling the dust cover off the bed, he lowered with her still in his arms. "I want to take that dress off you real slow. Any objections?"

He tugged the tie free at the back of her neck. "Then, I'm going to take my time learning every curve of you, Babe, all over again."

She giggled as if it were her first time to be truly loved.

Within minutes their clothes were piled on the dusty floor, but neither noticed. They were too wrapped in each other. As the storm pounded the little farmhouse, passion flowed between them in long kisses and easy strokes. In the shadowy light he watched her face, loving knowing how much he made her feel . . . loving knowing what his touch did to her.

In his dreams he'd hadn't heard the way she sighed softly when she was happy and how she cried out when lost in passion. Now, every sound she made washed over him in sweet melody. Loving her was as easy as breathing, and he never wanted to stop. Even when he was exhausted and she lay sleeping on his shoulder, he couldn't keep from touching her.

As he drifted to sleep, he dreamed of loving her and woke to find her still in his arms.

When they finally got dressed and started home, the rain had stopped and the sun was setting. He turned the Jeep toward his old barn. "Want to go for a ride in my grandfather's old plane?"

She looked worried.

"I'm a safe pilot." He laughed. "I swear."

She slipped her hand in his and nodded, making him feel like he could almost fly without the plane. She was trusting him, something it seemed like he'd had very little of in his life.

They flew over their land with the wind blowing in their faces. They watched the sunset and night move over the fields. The smell of spring brushed past them, making the night seem newborn.

When he set the plane down, she climbed out and into his arms.

"Can we do it again?"

"Babe, we can do everything again, and again, and again."

Nevada laughed free and unguarded.

They talked of nothing when they pushed the plane back into the barn, then held hands as they walked to the Jeep.

He drove slowly, not wanting the world to catch up to them again. Twice, he stopped in the center of the road to pull her close and kiss her.

"I already want you again," he whispered, and

loved the way she laughed as she moved her fingers into his hair.

When she finished kissing him, she pulled away and added, "We'd better get home fast. Maybe we should have flown the plane home."

He saw her need for him in her blue eyes and felt like his heart might explode.

The ranch house was dark when they finally made it home, and he noticed she turned on every light as she walked through to the kitchen. Then, like starving children, they collected everything that looked edible and camped out in the breakfast nook. They talked of nothing and ate ice cream over cereal topped with chocolate sauce.

He felt like he'd gone to prison before he'd finished growing. He never remembered allowing himself to act silly, but tonight the air seemed enchanted. They fought over every cherry he pulled from the jar. She tickled him, then giggled when he refused to tickle her back. Though he wanted to hold her tight against him, he kept his embrace light, easy for her to move in and out.

When they crawled into bed, they settled in the middle, making love one more time as if both knew eventually this day had to end. After she fell asleep on his chest, Cord lay awake thinking that if he had only one day of heaven coming to him in this lifetime, this one day was enough.

He kissed the top of her head. "I love you," he whispered, wondering if he'd ever say the words to her when she was awake. Nevada didn't believe in forever.

She didn't believe in love.

He knew the seven months of married life they had left wouldn't be long enough, but he'd take the time and do all he could to become the one person in her life that she couldn't do without.

He'd become the habit she couldn't break. Even if she never said the words, she'd love him, and when their time was over, she'd remain in his bed. She'd sleep with him through the first frost.

"Sleep, Babe," he whispered as he bumped his chin against her forehead.

She moaned and wiggled closer to him for warmth.

He moved his hand down her back, pressing her against him. "I'm going to make love to you again at dawn."

"Promise," she mumbled, more asleep than awake. "It'd be a great start to the day."

"Promise," he answered, knowing that Nevada already loved him and didn't even know it. "Tomorrow and every morning," he added, smiling.

# Chapter 22

April 5

The doctors warned Ronny that Marty Winslow would have good days and bad, but the good days were always too short and the bad days were growing worse. Sometimes he didn't wake for more than an hour, and when he did, he didn't seem to see the world.

His brother and cousins who had been waiting for him to die seemed content to stay away and let Mr. Carleon and Ronny handle the work of the last few days. With the nurses on eight-hour shifts around the clock and the doctor coming every day, there was still plenty of work to keep both Mr. Carleon and Ronny rushing.

Mr. Carleon read to him from adventure books he knew Marty loved, and Beau would still play for him in the evenings. A hundred times Ronny checked and swore Marty was less with them than he had been the day before. The machines were working, counting off breaths and heartbeats, but he seemed to be leaving an inch at a time.

Ronny found her escape in long walks when

she knew he was resting well. Time lost all meaning. She would move like a ghost through the town in the early morning and again when the moon was high. People she sometimes passed were no more alive than the mannequins in the windows of the stores on Main.

She kept her phone close, knowing that Mr. Carleon would call her if anything changed, but sometimes she feared she wouldn't hear it because she didn't hear anything. The world, her world, was growing silent.

Cord McDowell dropped by on Thursday morning, just to see if she needed anything. He was a quiet man trying to be kind, and she knew being sociable didn't come any easier for him than it did for her. On impulse, Ronny invited him in. Marty was awake and might enjoy the company.

Cord didn't seem to know how to make small talk. When Marty asked him about the ranching business, he told him some of the problems he was having trying to run a ranch after spending most of his adult years in prison.

To Ronny's surprise, Cord and Marty talked with a kind of honesty that few people bother to use. No frills or stories just to entertain. Marty's mind seemed to sharpen. He knew nothing of ranching, but he knew business. Like a man working a puzzle, Marty asked the right questions, drawing Cord down logical roads.

"If you'll bring your books over," Marty finally said, "I'll take a look at them. I stayed in college long enough to get a minor in everything and a major in fun."

"I don't want to be a bother, but thank you for the offer." Cord smiled at Ronny, and she knew he saw what she saw in Marty, not the frail man in the bed, but a bright mind with little tolerance for fools.

"It's no bother," Marty said. "You've given me something to think about besides dying. I'm asking more for my sanity than your need."

"I have to come to town tomorrow. Would that be too soon for you to start answering a few questions? I swear I can't make heads or tails of the books, and I don't know how to figure out exactly what the profit margin is on the cattle. I'd interview for a bookkeeper, but I don't even know what questions to ask."

"Sure." Marty sounded excited. "If I can't figure it out, Ronny might be able to help."

Cord picked up his hat and backed out of the room. She knew without asking that having people be kind to him was still too new for the man to take it for granted. She kissed Marty on the cheek and followed Cord out.

"Thanks for coming. Your visit did him a world of good."

Cord looked embarrassed. "He's a good man. I wish I knew half of what he does."

"He is a good man and you'll learn fast with his help. I think I loved him from the first, even when he was angry and yelling at me. One thing I love about him is that he never stops growing."

Cord reached into his pocket and pulled out a scrap of paper. "This is my cell number. If you need me just call."

She looked at the note. "It's an easy number to remember. With the two sets of thirteen, it's like a double bad luck number."

"Yeah, that's probably what my wife thought when she picked up the phone."

"I'll bet she searched for an easy one to remember."

Cord agreed. "You're probably right, because she calls me several times a day." As if on cue, his phone rang.

Cord pulled it from his pocket. "Hello." He paused for a moment. "Yes, I'm in town. I'll pick you up." He closed the phone and smiled. "She wants to have lunch. Like I have time for lunch."

"You're going, aren't you?"

"Of course. I'll make time. She's meeting me at the diner. Lied and told me she couldn't wait to try the daily special."

Ronny smiled as he walked away. He didn't have to say a word. She knew Cord McDowell was in love.

The next night, Ronny pulled on her black coat and walked along the dried-up creek that crossed through the heart of town. She forced herself to listen to the crunch of leaves and twigs beneath her feet. She was fighting to stay positive, but she knew deep inside she was already grieving what would never be.

Marty had enjoyed a good day. They'd talked and watched the dawn together, and then he'd slept most of the morning. Cord, as he had promised, showed up around one with a pie his housekeeper had made and a folder full of accounts. They all ate a slice of pie while he showed Marty the mess he'd made of keeping books. Marty talked in "big picture" terms of running a business, teaching gently, while Ronny pored over the books. After all her boring finance and bookkeeping classes, she finally saw reason in the lessons.

While Marty slept the afternoon away, she worked on Cord's books, loving having something to fill her mind as she sat next to Marty, watching over him.

After supper, they had their time together. He talked about what life would have been like if they had years and not days. After all his traveling and adventures, Marty saw paradise as living here in Harmony with her. They could open a business. They'd build a funny house with round rooms and a skylight in every ceiling. They'd invite friends in for dinner and go to the movie every Friday night no matter how bad the film. They'd make love on a blanket in the backyard and pretend they were in the Amazon.

He fell asleep holding her hand, and she sat for a long while in the darkness, lit only by lights from the machines, and cried for what might have been and never would be.

When the shift nurse took her place, Ronny pulled on her jacket and went for a walk. Days, even the good ones, were sometimes too sweet to relive. She just wanted to stretch her muscles and feel the night. She crossed the calm darkness of sleeping streets, heading in no particular direction.

As she paused to get her bearings, she heard footsteps behind her. Suddenly her numb body came awake.

Someone was following her.

With quick steps, she ran to the opening between the trees that led her out of the creek. No one was ever out at this time of night. In all the years she'd been walking, she'd never crossed paths with another so late. And this other wasn't just walking, he was following her, for she heard his steps rushing toward her as she climbed.

When she reached the road, she darted across to the park, where shadows layered and no one would see her. The grass was slippery and damp, but she didn't stop running until she passed behind the trees, leaning against an old cotton-wood to listen.

Nothing.

Slowly, she looked around the tree. The foggy glow of a streetlight a hundred yards away showed nothing. For a long time, she stood, listening, waiting.

Nothing moved. Maybe she'd just been hearing the echo of her own steps. Maybe she'd let her imagination run away. When she'd been little, her mother had always filled her head with evil men roaming the world in search of little girls to kill.

Ronny pushed away from the tree. She wouldn't live in fear. She wouldn't base her life on her mother's irrationality. She wouldn't hide.

With sure steps she marched to the road and headed toward Buffalo's Bar. She could just make out the outline of Beau's ancient car. She didn't want to retrace her path back to the duplex. Within minutes she stepped into the old bar.

It looked like it had been packed tonight. Bottles of beer were stacked on the tables along with empty red baskets that had once held wings and burgers. Even the floor was snowy with napkins and the place smelled of aging grease.

"We're closed," the bartender said.

"I just came to see Beau."

"He's—"

The bartender's words were flooded by Border yelling from the cage. "Ronny. You need a ride home? We were just closing up."

Ronny hurried over to the boys who were her

neighbors. "I was just out walking and thought I might catch a ride. It looks like it might rain," she lied.

Beau picked up his case. "How's Marty? I got a new song I want him to hear."

"He's asleep." They'd agreed days ago to stop giving medical reports to everyone who asked.

Border climbed out of the cage of a stage. "You want to go over to the truck stop for enchiladas?"

"I thought they fed you here?"

"Harley does, but that was ten o'clock." Border glanced at Beau. "You coming tonight?"

"Sure," Beau answered as he shoved his black hair out of his eyes. "If Trouble doesn't show up."

Border grinned and interpreted. "Trouble is this girl he knows. She comes in now and then. When she does, he drops me like I was his ugly half sister."

Border was the only one who laughed at his own joke.

They walked out of the bar with both guys talking at once about everything that had happened that night. Border swore he had two women beg him to go home with them. Beau reminded his friend that both bar lizards had been old enough to be his mother. They talked about one woman who got so drunk she started stripping on the dance floor, and Harley had to carry her out with half the bar cheering and the other half booing.

Ronny let them convey her along, needing the

time to just be normal for an hour even though she felt a twinge of guilt at not being home with Marty.

As they drove to the truck stop, she texted the nurse and learned all was quiet. Marty was sleeping calmly through the night.

They ordered three enchilada plates with rice and beans on the side. While they waited, Border showed her how one lady had danced like an upright snake, and Beau claimed another guy always danced like he was a rooster strutting around the yard.

Ronny laughed and breathed and relaxed, but Marty never left her thoughts. By the time they paid, she found herself in a hurry to get back home, and the ghost who'd followed her along the dried-up creek bed was forgotten.

# Chapter 23

April 7

Martha Q Patterson headed up to her study on the second floor Saturday morning before anyone woke. She had a house full of paying guests who were keeping her from doing any writing. Stories bounced around in her head like Ping-Pong balls, and she planned to get a few of them on paper before they dribbled out.

On the third step her left sock stuck to something. She wasn't awake enough to investigate, but when her right foot stepped on something that pushed through the wool to her toe, Martha Q decided to sit down and check it out.

Mud. There was mud on her stairs. Not dirt, but mud. Because she locked the doors after everyone had retired to their room, and she was the first one up, she saw only one answer. One of her boarders was sneaking out. And worse, tracking in mud.

Pulling off her socks to hold the evidence, she tiptoed upstairs. The three widows were on the second floor, but the mud droppings continued up the next flight of steps. Reason told her Mr. Carleon, with his neat habits, would never commit such a crime. That left Bryce Galloway, the well-dressed snob who didn't bother washing his whiskers out of the sink. He was guilty as sin in her mind, and she didn't plan to stand for it.

Thirty minutes later she was waiting when Mr. Carleon came down the stairs. "Morning," she managed with a nod.

"Morning," Mr. Carleon answered with a polite smile.

Martha was so angry she couldn't return his smile. "Is Mr. Galloway awake yet?"

"I didn't hear a sound. I like to be up and out of the bathroom before he wakes."

"I don't blame you. My housekeeper tells me what a mess he leaves. I wouldn't want to be in there after him."

Mr. Carleon smiled. "Sharing a bath is only a slight inconvenience for being so close to Marty. I enjoy the walk over and back every day as well as your company and conversation each evening."

She led him into the breakfast nook, where he and the widows usually took their morning coffee while Mrs. Biggs prepared the dining room breakfast buffet.

"I've something to talk to you about while we're alone, Mr. Carleon."

He waited until she wiggled into the nook, then sat down across from her. "I hope there is no problem with my lodging here?"

"Oh, no, but you may find my question a bit personal."

"Ask away, dear lady. I'll answer if I can."

Martha Q had to fight down a giggle to remain in her innkeeper mode. "May I ask if you left the house last night after I locked the door? I know you might be called back to attend to Marty at any hour."

He frowned. "I did not, but if I'd been called, I would have gone, of course. If that happens, Mrs. Patterson, I assure you I'll lock the door behind me."

"I know you would, Mr. Carleon. Just as I know you would not leave mud on the stairs."

He nodded in understanding. "I stopped to pick up a few chunks that were not quite dry on my way down a few minutes ago." He leaned closer, obviously enjoying the conversation. "You think Galloway went out last night and didn't come in early enough to have his muddy footprints dry before dawn."

"That is exactly what I think. I also think that it is strange for a man to go out after ten at night and not take his car parked in my drive. Bryce Galloway doesn't strike me as the type for mid-night walks."

Mr. Carleon took a slow drink of his coffee. "The man wears Italian loafers. A man who wears that kind of shoes doesn't walk in mud."

"Good point. Just as a man who goes for a walk at night would be most likely to stay on the sidewalks or even in the street, where the lights would be bright enough to show any mud holes."

They both sat in silence. Martha Q wiggled her eyebrows at him, loving that they were sharing something so intimate together. A conspiracy, maybe. A plot perhaps.

Finally, he said, "I'm sure there is a simple explanation for this."

"So am I, but I got a feeling it's not one we're going to like."

She made up her mind. "If he goes out tonight, I think one of us should follow him. I noticed a scrap of paper he carries has times in and times out. I'm guessing he's watching someone who doesn't know he's watching."

"Agreed. But who?"

"Maybe his ex-wife? I heard rumors that she didn't play fair in the divorce. 'Course, that was from someone who played golf with Bryce when he was married to Nevada."

Mr. Carleon shook his head. "Surely he's not bothering her. She's remarried to a nice guy. Cord McDowell's been by the duplex a few times. Judging from the measure of the man, I think Bryce Galloway would be a fool to mess with him."

Martha Q laughed. "It's been my experience that ex-husbands turn into fools quite easily, and you're right—if Bryce steps in Cord's way, he won't be the last one standing."

Mr. Carleon reached across the table and laid his hand over Martha Q's. "What is our plan, dear lady?"

Martha Q almost giggled, and she hadn't giggled in years. At that moment she really didn't much care what the plan was or what Bryce was up to. She loved the game they were playing at the breakfast nook, and she planned to make sure it continued. Her blood hadn't been this warm since the summer it reached 107 and half the air conditioners in town seemed to break at the same time.

"I think we should think all this out. I'll ask my hairdresser. She'll know all the gossip on Bryce Galloway. If you've no objection, I suggest we meet tonight over hot cocoa on the porch."

Mr. Carleon raised one eyebrow. "Should we include the widows in our discussion?"

"Not just yet," Martha Q answered with a sly smile. If she had anything to do with it, the widows would be out for the evening.

As if they'd heard their names called, all three of the women hurried in. Before the good mornings were said, Mrs. Biggs opened the door to the dining room and announced that breakfast was served.

Martha Q closed her fingers over the hand that Mr. Carleon had held briefly and decided she'd have not only her hair done, but a manicure and pedicure as well. She might even have a facial . . . all in the name of gathering information, of course.

# Chapter 24

April 9

"You make her happy, Cord, you know that, don't you?" Galem said as he poured coffee while both men stood in the bunkhouse kitchen. Dawn was just turning the sky. The ranch hands were already gathering around the table for breakfast.

Cord had come over early to check out the day's work schedule with the cook. He looked over at the man who was quickly becoming more a friend than an employee of the ranch. "Who?"

Galem smiled. "Nevada, of course. You make her happy."

"Maybe." Cord hid a smile behind his coffee cup as he remembered the pleasure they'd shared less than an hour ago. "She seems to like the changes around here." He tried to get his mind on the ranch and not the way his wife's body had felt against his in the shower. "I think we'll finish all the roads on the Boxed B today, and I'll send the crews over to work on my farm for a week or so. The crop's coming in, so a good road would help with moving the equipment we're going to need come harvest."

Galem frowned. "She does like the changes, but that's not what I'm talking about. Little Miss has got her share of problems at work, but it does my heart good to see her light up every time she sees you."

Before Cord could comment, the cook added, "Hell if I know why. You never say more than a few words to her. Let me give you some advice. They like that. A woman also likes to be complimented now and then, talked to, even when you don't see a need. They're funny creatures that way."

"I'll work on it." Cord had given up suggesting Galem stop offering him advice. It seemed to come with breakfast, and Galem, having been married for years, thought he had all the answers.

Galem smiled. "Good. Now, next time you see her, be sure and tell her how nice she looks. With all the time she spends shopping, it's bound to be important to her."

Before Cord had to swear he would, the back door of the bunkhouse flew open and a ranch hand, covered in mud, bolted in at a full run.

"We got trouble, Boss." Jackson gulped for air as he took off his hat. "One of your wife's horses is down in the front pasture. I tried to get her up, but . . ."

Both men grabbed their hats and followed the messenger out as he kept talking. "I drove past a few minutes ago and thought the black mare looked strange. I might have just thought she was resting if I hadn't seen the fence down. White wooden planks scattered all over the road."

"Nevada's horses are boarded in stalls at night. Never left in the field." Galem voiced what both Cord and Jackson already knew.

They all three grabbed anything they thought they might need from the tack room as they moved toward the truck. "What happened?" Cord shouted over the noise they made.

"Looks like someone rammed the fence." Jackson picked up a couple of gallons of water and climbed into the bed of the truck. "I could see tire tracks in the mud by the road."

"The horse?" Cord would worry about the downed fence later. He tossed in blankets and a toolbox along with a few ropes and a first-aid kit. Nevada wouldn't be happy if he had to rope one of her horses, no matter how crazy the mare might be acting.

"The mare's alive, but barely moving. I couldn't get her to raise her head, much less stand. When I saw how bad the horse was, I figured running for help was the best thing I could do." Jackson looked tortured. "Man, I hate like hell to see a horse in pain."

Cord glanced at Galem. The cook had read his

mind; he was already talking to the vet as he climbed in the passenger side.

Taking the curves toward Nevada's private horse barn and pasture at sixty with rocks flying everywhere, Cord ordered Galem, "Have him meet us there as fast as possible. Then try to get ahold of the trainer who cares for her horses. Nevada won't want us touching the horse without the trainer there."

"He's usually there by now." Galem punched numbers on his cell. "She likes to stop by on her way to work now and then to talk to him. Joey comes in early, but he seems to think as soon as he finishes, his eight-hour day is over. He's never around when she comes past there after work. But he wouldn't have let the horse out this early. It's not part of his routine."

Pulling his phone from his vest pocket, Cord punched two and waited for Nevada to answer. She'd gone in before dawn, saying she had a meeting over some big problem at one of the drill sites.

No answer. Maybe she hadn't made it in to the office yet. Cord left a message for her to call him, then tried to remember her general office number. He hadn't bothered to key it into his phone, thinking that if he needed her he could always call the cell.

Cord was parked and walking toward the downed mare when Galem got Nevada's secretary on his cell. The cook passed his phone to Cord.

"This is Cord McDowell. Tell my wife to call me," Cord shouted into the phone.

When the secretary stuttered, he added, "Now!"

Then, without waiting for an answer, he handed Galem's phone back and knelt down beside the beautiful star-marked black mare laboring for every breath.

Jackson had been right. Something was very wrong with the horse. Cord pulled off his gloves and slowly moved his hands over the animal. Huge wild eyes watched him as she fought for air. The powerful muscles of her hind legs jerked slightly as if longing to run, but the horse didn't get up.

"It's going to be all right," Cord said, more to himself than the mare. "We're here now. We'll take care of you."

Galem hauled blankets and water. He tried to pour water into the horse's mouth, but she wouldn't take it. "She's burning up," he said.

Cord spread one of the blankets over the horse's head and wet it down with water. He had no idea if he was doing the right thing, but he knew that the dark would calm the horse, and hopefully the cool wet blanket would help.

"The doc's on his way," Galem said as his phone chimed. "He'll be here in five."

Jackson, the rough cowhand whom Cord had rarely seen say more than three words without one of them being a swear word, now sat patting the horse's neck and whispering softly as if he were talking to a baby.

Cord stood, feeling helpless. He didn't know horses. He only knew if something happened to one of Nevada's beautiful animals she would be crushed. For some reason they seemed to mean more to her than people.

The vet drove over the downed fence and hopped out of his truck running, bag in hand. His clothes were wrinkled and he was at least three days away from his last shave, but Doc Freeman was a welcome sight.

Cord felt so relieved he almost hugged the man. Within minutes the doc was shouting orders to everyone and working with the skill of an emergency room specialist. He might look like a down-on-his-luck cowboy, but the vet knew what he was doing.

Other hands arrived, circling around the animal, watching, worrying, whispering guesses of what might be wrong. Cord sent a few up to the barn to check on the other horses, fearing that the mare might be the first to be coming down with something deadly.

But as he paced, he knew no illness had caused what was happening. It hadn't taken much to figure out that the fresh tire tracks had come from the barn, crossed the pasture, and broken out. The shattered remains of the fence had been scattered on the road, not in the grass. Whoever did this was in a hurry to get away.

"Maybe we should call the sheriff?" Galem asked.

"Let's see what we're dealing with first. We take care of the animal, then call. When I worked at Parker Trucking I used to pass the sheriff heading for work a little after seven thirty. If we wait a few minutes we'll get her and not some deputy who's been up all night."

Whoever did this knew the property, and he knew how much the act would hurt Nevada. Cord could think of only one man who might have done it. Any fired hand could have slashed the tires on his car, but hurting a horse would cut deep. Bryce Galloway crossed his mind, and he decided that whether Nevada liked him in her business or not, he planned to find out more about the trouble between his wife and her last husband.

Moving among the men, Cord asked each one what time he'd driven by the fence. Was it down when they passed? Did they see lights heading toward town?

A few didn't remember noticing because it was dark, but three swore the fence had been intact when they turned onto the road about fifteen minutes before Jackson had discovered it. He'd been running late. He was the last cowhand to head in from the main road. If he hadn't overslept, they might not have found the horse for hours.

Cord also knew the fence had been up when Nevada drove past to go to work. She would have noticed. He'd seen her look toward the barn every time they passed, no matter the hour.

As Cord walked back, the doc stood. "No maybe about it. This horse has been poisoned. If we'd reached her ten minutes later, we'd be looking at a dead animal right now."

"But that barn is kept locked with the horses inside every night," Galem said. "Since the day it was built, I don't ever remember a single horse left in open pasture."

The vet lifted his bag. "If someone will stay with the mare, I'll go check the other horses. By the time I get back, the shot I gave her will be working and she'll be in less pain." He walked toward Cord, scrubbing hair that hadn't been combed in days. "Someone needs to notify the sheriff, and Cord, I'd appreciate it if you'd get a trailer up here for me to transport the mare to my clinic. Pad the sides as heavy as we can. I've got a strap in my pickup that will keep her standing once we get her in."

Cord nodded at the doctor as he ordered several men to follow the vet. Galem and Jackson went for the trailer.

When all were busy, he walked back to his truck and spread his hands out wide on the hood, trying to calm down. Nevada hadn't called, but she would. When she did, she'd panic at the news.

Several minutes passed as he waited for Nevada to call and the sheriff to arrive. The vet reported that no other horses seemed to have been poisoned, and the mare had managed to stand on her own. When he helped Dr. Freeman load the mare, he realized the trainer was late. As the vet drove away, Cord pulled Zeb and one other man he trusted aside.

"Either of you have any idea where the trainer lives?"

Zeb nodded. "I was working here when he first came. Nevada wanted him to live on the ranch, but he insisted she rent him a house in town. Her husband at the time sided with the trainer. Me and another fellow were ordered to go help him move in. I think I can find the place without much trouble."

"Good. Go find out why he didn't show up for work this morning. If he's not sick, he's fired." He paused, then added, "Check his car for damages by a fence." Cord doubted the trainer would run the fence; whoever did this must have known he had little time before being spotted where he didn't belong.

When Zeb was out of hearing distance, Galem said, "I'll wait for the sheriff." Everyone knew Cord hadn't called in a crime when his tires had been slashed.

"All right," Cord answered. "You stay, but right now, I've got to get to Nevada before she hears about this from someone else. Tell the sheriff I'll be happy to give a statement. She's welcome to investigate anywhere on the land she needs to, and she'll have full cooperation from every man."

Galem walked with Cord toward the door of his truck. "If Nevada's not in her office, you might try the rig site out by Rattler Creek. Ora Mae said she wore her boots this morning." Galem frowned. "She always wears her boots when she heads out there. She's hated snakes ever since her big brothers used to tease her with little garden snakes."

"I'll do that." Cord climbed in his truck. "Keep me informed on anything here. I'll be back as soon as I can."

He headed toward town, trying to think how he could break the bad news to Nevada. She didn't have to tell him how she loved the horses; he knew. He'd seen the way she patted them and cared for them. They were her children, her family.

When he pulled into her office parking lot, he'd decided telling her straight out would be the only way.

He walked in beneath a six-foot-tall gold plaque bearing the Boxed B brand. This was her world, all business and professional. The day he'd picked her up for lunch, it had taken her ten minutes to relax and talk at a normal speed. She might complain about it, but her father had groomed her to take over this business. Cord couldn't help but wonder what the old man had done to make sure she knew oil. He must have thought she was his last chance after failing to make any of his sons ranchers.

Cord rushed toward the main set of offices. Her office door stood dead center among them. The huge double doors had the Boxed B brand burned into the wood. Everything reminded him that she was a Britain, yet when they'd married, she'd insisted on taking his name.

A receptionist jumped in his way with the look of a startled rabbit. "May I help you, sir?" she said, near panic when he didn't slow. "These are private offices."

"I'm here to see my wife. I'm Cord McDowell."

"Yes, sir," she said, trying to get ahead of him. "Miss Britain is in an important meeting, but I'll tell her you're here."

When she glanced at a closed double door, Cord knew he'd be wasting his time bothering with the receptionist. "I'll tell her myself and her name is no longer Britain, it's McDowell."

He opened the door and walked in before he changed his mind or the rabbit thought of pouncing on him.

Half a room away, Nevada stood talking to two men in suits. All three held papers in their hands, but the gray-haired suit looked like he'd paused in midsentence.

Cord made it three more steps before he heard security rushing toward him from a side door. For a blink, they reminded him of the prison guards, beefy and determined. Only now, Cord wouldn't back down. He stood his ground as they advanced.

Nevada raised her hand before they reached him. "It's all right. Don't touch him."

Every one of her employees looked confused.

"Gentlemen," she said calmly, "this is my husband, and if he's here, I'm sure it's something important, so I'll have to ask you all to step out for a moment."

The older lawyer looked bothered, but he walked out, closing the door behind him with a bang.

Cord stood, facing Nevada from five feet away. Here in her tailored pantsuit and her hair tied up in a knot, she looked hard as stone. *This* woman could handle anything he had to tell her. It crossed his mind that he would have never fallen in love with Nevada if this were all he knew of her, but Cord knew the woman inside all the polish and ice.

"What is it?" She seemed impatient, but not unkind. "I've got a full schedule this morning, but you obviously have something to say that can't wait. So tell me."

He stared into her eyes, wondering where the woman he'd made love to only hours ago had gone. Maybe she was always like this at work.

He'd stepped into her world. He'd stepped into where he didn't belong and hadn't been invited.

"One of your mares was found down this morning. She'd been poisoned."

For a heartbeat, she didn't move. She just stared at him.

He forced it all out, knowing the blow would be no lighter if delayed. "Someone broke into your barn about dawn."

Color drained from her face. "Is the mare dead?"

"No. Not yet. The vet says she's got better than a fifty-fifty chance, but there may be internal damage."

He hadn't realized he was moving toward her until he reached to brush her arms. "We loaded her up and sent her to the vet's. He'll watch over her. Galem called while I was driving in and said whoever did it didn't know horses. He bloodied the mare's lip forcing down the poison."

She backed away from Cord and gulped for air, then raised her arms at him. At first, he thought she was trying to block his words, but then she swung at him.

Cord didn't move. Didn't try to defend against the blows as she pounded on him. The pain in her eyes was so great, he barely felt the hits. She was lost in a horror she'd always feared would come true.

"I told you never to move my horses."

She sobbed so deeply he could barely understand her. He knew the blows were not aimed at him, but at the world. "No one touches my horses. No one hurts them. My daddy promised. Never again."

Engulfing her in a bear hug, he held on tightly as she struggled against him and swore, calling him names. As she cried, he knew her pain was bleeding through an old wound that had never healed. All he could do was stand and let her rage.

After a while, she stopped and, leaning her head on his shoulder, cried.

"It's all right, Babe," he whispered. "It's going to be all right." His hand pulled the pins from her hair and dug his fingers into the golden strands. "I didn't want you to hear it from anyone but me. I couldn't let the horse die without a fight. You've got to trust that we did all we could, and the vet is still working."

She pushed her forehead against him. "You came because you didn't want me killing any messenger you sent."

He relaxed a bit and smiled. "Well, there was that. I figured you could kill me and no one would care. Hell, no one likes me anyway." He kissed her forehead. "Besides, I had a pretty good idea how you'd react, and if my wife is going to pound on anyone, it better be me."

"That part of the 'for better or worse' section of our contract?"

"Something like that." His hold gentled and she rocked slowly in his arms, letting her breathing slow to normal.

"Now that you know what's happened, we can go over to the vet's together. I'm right here, Nevada. We'll figure out who did this in time, but right now we'll worry about the horse."

She nodded and stepped away to blow her nose. The office door opened.

"Are you all right?" The gray-haired lawyer was back. "I heard crying and shouting. I've got security out here and we've called the sheriff."

"I'm fine," Nevada said, as she pulled herself together as calmly as she straightened her jacket.

Cord stepped in front of her. "My wife is upset. One of her prize horses was hurt this morning." He forced his fists to relax. "I appreciate your concern." Now that he knew Nevada was back in control, there was no reason to keep the facts a secret. "I called the sheriff before I left the ranch." He looked at the rabbit of a receptionist. "If you'll call her office and tell her we'll meet her at the ranch, I'd appreciate it."

The girl jumped to the door and vanished. The old lawyer, if possible, looked even more angry. "Nevada, you know who did this. You know."

Nevada moved to Cord's side and leaned into him. He widened his stance to brace her.

"We don't know for sure. Bryce is too clever to leave any clues. Even if he's doing it, he's planning on me firing up and doing something stupid. This time I'm not falling into his trap."

She slipped her hand into Cord's. "I want to check on my horse and then talk to the sheriff. If you gentlemen will excuse me, I'll reschedule this meeting for later today."

Nevada held it together until they were in his truck, and then she leaned against him and cried all the way to the vet's clinic.

# *Chapter 25*

Nevada sat beside Starlight as Doc Freeman talked about the damage done by the poison. Tears fell unchecked when he said the mare had already lost the colt she carried. Between the loss of blood and the injuries, it would be an uphill climb.

"I don't usually suggest this," the vet said, "but she's in a great deal of pain. If you want me to, I'll put her down."

Nevada couldn't speak. She just shook her head and heard Cord telling the doc to do all he could first. "We don't want her to suffer, but if she's got a chance to pull through, we want to give her that chance."

Starlight hadn't been her first horse, but Nevada was more girl than woman when she bought her. At first her mother had insisted that only the trainer ride the horse, but within two weeks Nevada was sneaking away from the house and taking Starlight for midnight runs in the pasture. To her the horses were her friends, each very different, each loved for different reasons.

When she was eight, her father moved her first three ponies to the back pasture with the cattle. During a storm, two had frozen to death. Only one had survived, just barely. Nevada had cried for weeks. She swore at the time she would never care that much again for anything or anyone, but she couldn't stop herself. She loved horses. And now, someone hated her enough to hurt her again by hurting one of them.

Nevada pressed her face into Starlight's mane and felt as if she might lose an old friend. People always let her down, but her horses never had.

When Cord offered his hand to help her up, she shook her head. "I'll stay awhile. I don't want to leave her alone."

"We need to talk to the sheriff." Cord's voice was low and calm. Not an order, just a fact.

"You go. I'll be here when you get back."

He touched her shoulder. "Call if you need me. I'll be back as soon as I can."

She nodded and laid her head down next to the mare just as she had once before when she was

250

eight. The last pony was still alive when they found him that winter, but her father shot him, claiming the pony wasn't strong enough to make it back to the barn. The first bullet hadn't killed the animal.

Nevada dropped to the pony and hugged him as if she could help.

When her father saw the damage he'd done to his daughter, he'd pulled Nevada off the animal, angry both at himself and at the child for making such a scene.

She'd heard the second shot as Galem carried her away from her pet. She cried for days and refused to eat. Her mother promised her another horse, then a barn of her own. But it was her father's promise never to go near her horses again that finally stopped the crying.

He hated that he'd given in to his tiny daughter, but he kept his word. Even let her put up wooden fences in her pasture and breed her horses. By the time his wife died and he could have gone back on his word about the horses, Nevada had her own money for their care and her father had other worries to occupy his time.

Kneeling down close she brushed the mare's warm neck. Through all her life she'd known that she was only a play toy to her mother and a bother to her father, but to her horses, she was a friend. She loved them and they loved her back, without question. Without judgment.

She closed her eyes and envisioned herself riding Starlight across the midnight pastures.

"Nevada?" The vet's voice woke her.

"Sorry, I didn't realize I'd fallen asleep."

"Your mare's resting easy now. If she holds on, I think she might just make it."

She smiled up at the doc. He was one of the few people she knew who loved horses as much as she did. "You mind if I stay a little longer? My husband will be back for me soon."

Dr. Freeman smiled. "I have no doubt. I never saw a man look so worried when I pulled up to the mare. It took me a while to figure out that it was you and not the horse he was worried about. You might love this animal, but that man loves you. He couldn't stand the notion that something might hurt you."

Nevada shook her head. The doc was wrong. She almost told him that all they had was a pretend marriage. But they'd agreed to play it like it was real, and she'd keep that promise.

"He was just afraid of how angry I'd be. He says I tend to storm, and I guess he's right."

"Nope. He's not afraid of your anger. A man don't walk right into what he's afraid of. As soon as we'd done all we could in the field, he said he was headed to you. He didn't want anyone telling you but him. That doesn't sound like a man afraid."

# Chapter 26

Cord drove toward the ranch while he got an update from Galem on the phone. The cook told him that Zeb had reported back that the trainer, Joey Mason, wasn't at home. They pounded so hard on his door that the neighbor came out to say that if his car wasn't in the drive, they were probably wasting their time.

So far the trainer's only crime was coming in late to work, and he'd like to keep it that way.

As soon as he closed the phone, Cord swung the truck around in the center of the road and headed toward the old part of Harmony. An idea had been dancing in his mind since he first thought that Bryce Galloway might have something to do with not only the horse, but other trouble they'd had lately. He needed help from someone who'd walked both sides of the law all his life, and Cord could think of only one man who might fit the bill.

Minutes later he pulled up in front of the duplex where Ronny Logan lived. She was taking groceries out of her car when he arrived. Cord jumped out and hurried up to her.

As he neared, Mr. Carleon stepped out of the house and took the grocery bags.

Cord couldn't hear what Ronny said, but the man nodded a hello and vanished back inside.

"How's Marty?" Cord asked as he neared. He didn't know Marty well, but he liked the man. Plus, anyone Ronny obviously loved so much had to be worth liking.

"About the same. Addison gave him something new for the pain and he seems to be resting easier this morning." Ronny smiled her shy smile. "But you look like hell, Cord."

"It's been a hard morning." He didn't have time to explain, but he did try to dust a little of the dirt off his jeans. "I came to ask a favor if you've got a minute for me to pick your brain."

"I'll help any way I can."

Cord started with the facts. "The first few months, when I was in prison, there was another guy in my unit who said he was from Harmony. He was only there awhile, but I remember one of the guards saying that once he was free he'd disappear. They called him Cam and I don't remember his last name."

Ronny shook her head, telling Cord he might be wasting his time, but he pushed on.

"One of the cons claimed he'd left Harmony to work a crew on a small-time movie production company. He ended up settling down in the Dallas area and between working on film crews, he turned to crime. He would move into a nice neighborhood, blend in with everyone, rob the houses one by one in daylight, and then disappear without anyone being able to give the cops a good description of him. The guy said he never got caught because he was the most bland, plain-vanilla person who mixed into a crowd. No marks, no scars, no accent, nothing stood out about the man."

Ronny smiled. "What did he look like in prison?"

Cord shrugged. "I don't really remember. Not tall or short. Medium build. Nothing specific. The guy hung around like faded wallpaper. When I met him, he had his earlobe bandaged because he said his new wife had ripped out his earring in the fight before she called the cops on him. Mumbled something about living a life of crime and ending up in prison because the one woman he loved forgot to love him back.

"He was only there for a few months, so everyone figured she must have dropped the charges against him. But, like some guys do, he bragged about the jobs he'd pulled to the other cons."

Ronny waited, listening to every word.

"I was wondering if there is any chance you know where Cam Whatever might be. Doesn't the postal service know everyone? I'm guessing he didn't go back to Dallas to reconnect with his wife, and if he's gone straight, he's probably working around town. The one time I talked to him he told me he loved Harmony, so I figure he might have come back."

Ronny frowned. "The sheriff might know, but I can't think of anyone. Lots of people look like that, I guess, just customers on the other side of the desk. I don't pay much attention sometimes."

She shrugged. "There's one guy who comes to mind that I've waited on a few times. Only thing about him I thought strange was the round sunglasses he wore. You know, like he thought he was Truman Capote. Sorry I couldn't be of more help."

"If you think of more, let me know." He started to walk away, then paused. "If you need me—"

"I know. I'll call." Her smile was sad, as if she knew the time was coming.

Cord climbed back into his truck and headed for the ranch. He'd deal with the sheriff and help any way he could and then go back after Nevada. He hated thinking about her lying in the hay beside the horse. He'd never seen her like this. Broken. He had no idea how to help.

When he reached the barn where she kept her horses, several cars he didn't recognize were clustered around the front. One was a sheriff's cruiser. The silent flashing lights brought back bad memories of ten years ago when the lights had flashed in the dark stillness of midnight.

It had been hot that night and the air so dry it

seemed to suck the moisture out of everything. A dozen of what had been Harmony's wild crowd in high school had gone out to celebrate the Fourth of July by setting off fireworks at the lake. They knew it was illegal in the drought of summer, but they all figured they could see a cop car coming from far enough away to vanish before they got caught.

Cord didn't remember much about the night. A campfire. Couples scattered around in the dark. He was two weeks away from being eighteen and thought he was bulletproof after half a bottle of whiskey. He must have passed out after complaining to anyone who would listen that his dad was going to make him go to college.

What he thought was a stick woke him with a hard poke in the stomach. Someone was yelling at him, screaming for him to get up and shining a flashlight right in his face.

He came up swinging and connected solidly with the intruder's jaw. The stick that had stabbed Cord turned out to be the barrel of a rifle. When the shadow's head flew back from the blow, the rifle fired wild, lighting the night. For a blink Cord watched a man in a uniform fall on the rocky shoreline.

For months after that, through the trial and going to prison, Cord would relive that one moment over and over in dreams. The cop shouting in pain. The night so black. And then always in the background the voice from several feet away whispering into radio static. "Officer down. Send backup with an ambulance." Finally, a flashlight's beam passing back and forth across the camp as if on guard until more help arrived.

The rest of that night was a blur. He'd knelt beside the downed cop trying to see where he was hurt, but it had been too dark. The voice that had radioed for help ordered him to raise his hands or he'd shoot. Cord felt warm blood on the cop's face and threw up while he felt his hands being cuffed behind him. The other cop grabbed him by the shoulder and shoved Cord down into the dirt spotted with vomit and blood.

"Cord?" A woman's voice drew him out of his nightmare. "Cord McDowell."

He cut the truck's engine and climbed out. Despite the sun, he removed his hat. "Sheriff Matheson. I'm sorry. I was thinking about something."

The slender sheriff walked closer.

She smiled. "You looked a million miles away. I haven't seen enough of you lately to recognize you, but my message box was full of people telling me you wanted to see me. I came as fast as I could and we're already working the crime scene."

He had to make himself raise his eyes from the ground. Too many years of not looking at guards directly made it a hard habit to break. "I know this was just a horse—"

"Stop right there, Cord." The sheriff started walking toward the barn and he followed along beside her. "I'm from ranch folks and am married to a man who loves horses. There is no such thing as 'just a horse.' You and I come from generations of people who know the importance of horses. In fact, it wasn't so long ago when stealing a man's horse was a hanging offense, so don't you think we're going to take this lightly."

"Thanks," he said, feeling good that he'd had Galem call her. Sheriff Alex Matheson was as good an officer of the law as he'd ever seen. When he'd first gotten out, she'd been the only law officer who hadn't threatened to keep an eye on him.

She paused and turned to look at Cord. "We've brought in a Texas Ranger to help with the investigation. He's a brand inspector and knows cattle and horses better than most. He's been working a rustling problem nearby and offered to help."

Cord saw a stout man dressed in a tan shirt and pants heading toward him. He was a few inches shorter but seemed all business. His Stetson shadowed his face as he offered his hand to Cord.

Cord took the offered hand in a strong grip as the ranger looked up and said, "Ranger Travis Salem."

For a moment both men froze.

Cord hadn't seen *Deputy* Salem in almost ten years. Memories of a young cop in his late twenties with a bandage over his eye were nothing like the ranger in his late thirties with graying hair and fifty pounds added to his build.

"Cord McDowell," the ranger said without emotion. "I wouldn't have recognized you."

The sheriff seemed unaware of the two men's past as she watched the movements of her deputies and the cowhands still surrounding the barn. "We've found a few clues, but your boys didn't make it easy, tromping all over my crime scene before I got here. One even picked up the bucket of poison, ruining any chance of finger-prints."

Travis Salem moved closer to Cord and lowered his voice before he loosened his grip and the handshake died. "We've got a man killing horses to deal with right now, McDowell, but when this is over, I'd like it if you and I could talk."

Cord didn't move. This man's testimony had sent him to prison. He said Cord had attacked, and there were no witnesses to stand with Cord when he said he swung wild without knowing it was an officer of the law. The patch over Salem's eye had been a constant reminder to the jury of the damage Cord had done.

"You don't have to talk to me, Cord," Ranger

Salem added. "I can't order you to, but I think it's something that needs to be done."

All the times guards had ordered him around or asked him to do something when he knew he had no choice in the matter piled up in his throat. There were no *yes, sirs* left in him. "I'll think about it," Cord answered. "Right now, all that's on my mind is protecting my wife's horses."

The ranger seemed to understand. He pulled out a notepad and began rattling off facts. The sheriff joined them.

"I've got two of my deputies out looking for the trainer," she said. "He may have just left for a day off, but it seems strange that he'd go missing on the same day someone tries to kill a horse."

"My wife has a standing order that if the trainer takes a weekday off, he calls in to Galem. We've got the third key to the barn hanging in the bunkhouse and Galem comes out to feed the horses if Nevada has to stay late in town. Other than them, no one is allowed near the barn."

"What about you, McDowell? Don't you have a key to the barn? You run the ranch, don't you?" Salem wasn't too friendly.

"I do run the ranch as well as my farm to the south, but we've only been married a few weeks and I've never needed to get in here before." He felt the need to add, "When we ride together, I always come back here and help Nevada brush her mount down, then we ride double back to the main barn. So I know where everything is in here and I know the horses are all well taken care of. At least until today."

"So these horses are not part of the ranch?"

"They belong here. Nevada breeds and trains them. Most of the colts go for several thousand. They're fine show horses."

"Seems like a waste of time and money on a working ranch," the ranger said, as if talking to himself.

Cord didn't miss the fact that a few of his hands, including Jackson and his brothers, were standing behind him as if ready to back him up.

The ranger paced, then twirled as if he planned to say something dramatic. "Any of your cowhands come to work in shoes and not boots?"

"No."

Salem held one finger up. "Your wife. Does she have big feet and wear loafers?"

"No, she doesn't. She wears heels to her office and boots on the ranch."

"Are you sure about that, McDowell?"

Cord tried not to let any anger show, but he stood his ground. "My wife is afraid of snakes. If she walks the land, she has boots on."

Galem, never a quiet man, broke from the crowd growing behind Cord. "I can back the boss up. I've known her for near twenty years and I've never seen her without her boots if she goes beyond the shadow of the house."

"You telling me your boss is an honest man and I can trust his word?"

Cord heard the men behind him shift as if widening their stance.

Galem did the same. "He is, mister, and I'll fight any man that says he ain't, including you if you'll take off that star on your pocket."

Alex Matheson obviously had had enough of the tough talk. She stepped between the men and stared at the ranger. "I brought you here to help, Ranger Salem. This is McDowell's land. He's got a right to be here. You, however? I'm not sure this case is even in your jurisdiction."

The ranger smiled. "You're right, Sheriff, I was out of line. I just needed to know fast what kind of boss we were dealing with. Most of the time when something like this happens, it's one of the hands trying to get a dig in at his boss." Salem looked at Cord with his men standing firm behind him. "I got my answer. To the man, they stand with him. So I'll tell you what I know."

The tension in Cord's shoulders relaxed and the men gathered around to listen.

"First, we're dealing with someone from the outside who knows the ranch. He's walked this land at least once before today. He knew what time the men arrived and that there would be time to drive in, poison the horses, and leave before anyone passed down the road again. My guess is, he waited somewhere along the road to town for

Nevada to pass, then counted the cars of cowhands coming to work. Only somehow he missed
Jackson."

"That's because I usually ride in with my
brothers, but when I wasn't ready, they left
me."

Ranger Salem took notes, then added, "The
man we're looking for also knew the barn was
locked and brought a key along. I saw no sign of
forced entry. My guess is if we check we'll find
one of the three keys missing."

"I got mine right here," Galem offered, now
willing to help the ranger, since he appeared to
finally be making sense. "Nevada keeps hers on
her keychain. That only leaves the little trainer's
key."

The ranger nodded his approval of Galem's
logic. "Third, I found a few prints of a man's
size shoe among all the bootprints. One in the
soft dirt by the door and another near the first
stall. Whoever poisoned the mare wasn't wearing
boots."

Everyone began offering possibilities. No one
had ever seen the trainer, Joey Mason, in anything
but the polished riding boots he must have worn
during his days as a jockey.

Cord's phone sounded, and everyone paused.

"It's my wife," he said as he looked at the ID.
"I have—"

Before he could finish, all the ranch hands

chimed in with what he always said, "to take this call."

Cord would have sworn he was too old to blush, but he stepped a few feet away and didn't bother lowering his voice when he said hello.

No one made any pretense of not trying to listen. When he said, "That's good news. Starlight is out of danger," the men were cheering and only the ranger heard Cord add, "Come on home, Babe. I'll be at the barn."

Fifteen minutes later, when one of the vet's assistants dropped her off and Nevada ran into Cord's arms, no one on the ranch doubted how dearly he cared for her. He lifted her off the ground into a hug.

Salem stayed around to ask her questions, but he was polite, calling her Mrs. McDowell and thanking her for her time.

Cord walked the ranger to his car. "What was between us was between us. It has nothing to do with the ranch or my wife."

The ranger nodded. "We'll talk maybe, if you agree, but right now you'll have my best effort to help find this guy."

"Thanks," Cord managed. "And when this is over I'll meet you for coffee one morning at the diner." Cord was making it plain that whatever happened between them would be aboveboard and in daylight. There'd be no two versions of the story this time.

He noticed the long, thin scar just above the ranger's eyes as Travis offered his hand. "Fair enough."

As he drove away Cord knew they'd never be friends, not in this lifetime, but hatred no longer festered between them.

He walked back into the barn as men left. Nevada was moving among her horses, touching each as if reassuring them.

Galem was the last to leave. He'd made it to the door when Cord yelled, "Mind asking Ora Mae to bring my supper out here? I've decided I'm sleeping in the barn tonight."

Galem nodded. "I'll drive her out. She goes nuts on that four-wheeler. I don't trust her more than ten feet in that thing. How about you, Little Miss? You want me to give you a lift to the house?"

"No, if Cord's sleeping here, so am I." She smiled at Cord, as if knowing he was doing this just for her.

Galem walked away mumbling something that sounded like, *Why am I not surprised?*

An hour later they'd eaten dinner on paper plates and were sitting in the loft opening watching the sunset. Nevada had been so quiet, Cord began to worry. He wanted to pull her close, but he guessed she needed time to let her nerves settle.

"You still mad at me for moving the horse?"

"No."

He decided she wasn't going to say anything, but then she whispered, "If you found out I did something to hurt you, would you hate me?"

"I didn't move the horse to hurt you, Babe."

"I know. I was just thinking. Cord, if I hurt you, would you forgive me if I asked you to?"

He thought about it a minute and pulled her against his side to whisper, "I don't know what you've got on your mind, but I've already forgiven you. No matter what. You can stop worrying about it right now." He'd done a few things he wasn't proud of. He'd ended up in prison, and not once had she held his past against him. "If you're thinking the pounding you gave me hurt, forget about it. Seeing you in pain was far more torture."

"I wasn't thinking of that," she said, "but now you mention it, I shouldn't have taken it out on you. Give me a little time, Cord, I've never learned to rein in emotion."

He kissed the top of her head. "I know, Babe, that's why I'm looking forward to rolling in the hay with you tonight."

She pulled away. "We're not having sex in front of my horses."

"I'll blindfold them all if you like." He laughed. "But, Babe, we are having that roll in the hay."

# Chapter 27

Ronny knelt beside Marty's bed, wishing she could talk God into trading her life for Marty's. He was so smart. He had so much to offer the world and she had nothing. No one would miss a postal clerk, but everyone who met him thought he was brilliant. Even ill, he'd helped Beau handle his finances and begin savings. Marty had given Cord advice about making a better profit at the Boxed B. He'd changed her life—no, he'd started her life, because the years before him all ran together into dull days of just existing.

She curled back in her chair and began to think of the little things she used to do at the post office to help pass the time. She'd sign up folks who never got mail for free gifts and secretly help people out when they didn't pay the right postage or forgot to forward their mail. When she'd mailed Cord the Harmony paper, she guessed he would enjoy it, but he'd told her it kept him sane some days.

As she turned through the people in her mind, an average-looking man in his forties who sometimes came in to ask about his mail crossed her thoughts. One magazine about the ins and outs of Hollywood wouldn't fit in his box. She'd always leave a note and he'd ask for it, not by his name, but by the box number.

She thought it was strange that he took that magazine until one day the postmaster told her he worked at the old movie theater down on Main. "The waitress over at the diner said he must love movies if he watched them all day. Said he told her he once worked on a film set."

Ronny could almost see the name on the magazine, not Cam, but Cameron. He might be the man Cord was looking for.

She pulled out her phone and remembered the way she'd thought of his number as double bad luck, two sets of thirteens.

Foster Harrison, one of the nurses, came on duty just as she moved to the kitchen to talk to Cord. Foster gently touched her arm, silently telling her not to worry, Marty was sleeping easy tonight and he'd take the midnight watch while she slept.

Ronny thanked the kind nurse with a nod.

"Hello," Cord snapped, as if he were in the middle of something important.

"I remembered someone," she whispered.

"Ronny?" he lowered his voice. "Good."

"There's a man who runs the movie house. If it's him, and I'm not saying it is, I might have an idea of where he lives. Years ago the Palace used to do live performances, and there were rooms behind the stage. You might find your Cam there."

"Thanks."

She hung up before he could ask about Marty and she had to try to think of something to say. Waving at Foster, she pulled on her jacket, thinking she'd take a walk before she went to bed. The day had been hard and endless.

Unlike a few nights ago, she stayed to the street, walking down the center and heading toward the old downtown area. Since the night she'd heard someone following her, she hadn't felt safe, but she needed the exercise and there seemed to be no other time. So she kept to the pavement where she could see. Buffalo's Bar would still be open, and the men would be hanging out at the fire station if she needed to run for help. This way wasn't as quiet a walk, but it was safer.

When she turned down Main, she thought she saw movement half a block away. Someone else was on the streets tonight.

She rounded toward the fire station. If someone else was out walking, they were keeping to the shadows. The night didn't feel right. Something or someone was out there watching her. A few times she'd passed Beau walking home from the bar, but even dressed in black, they'd both seen each other.

As she reached the firehouse, she glanced upstairs, where a few firemen usually slept. The windows were dark tonight, but the bright lights over the huge doors out front lit the street.

Ronny jogged across to the sheriff's offices and relaxed when she saw Deputy Phil Gentry sitting outside on the steps talking on his cell phone. He waved and called, "Any problem, Ronny?"

"No, sir, just walking."

He shoved his phone into his pocket and stood. "How about I walk a block with you? I'm on a break and this time of night it's either eat or exercise. Some nights around town are so calm I think I'll have to lock myself up to keep from going crazy."

She was happy for the company. Phil had been around for as long as she could remember and liked to visit. Some folks said if he ever retired, the paper would have to double to keep everyone up on what was going on.

As they walked, he told her what had happened at the Boxed B that morning, and Ronny understood why Cord had looked so upset when he stopped by. He must have thought she had her own share of problems, so he hadn't mentioned his.

Phil reached the bridge that crossed onto her street. "You can almost see your house from here. I think I'd better be getting back." He handed her his flashlight. "Take this. You can bring it back to the station on your next walk."

Ronny didn't really need a flashlight, but she took it just because Phil always wanted to help. So she thanked him and shoved it into her pocket.

As she strolled the short block to her duplex, her mind was full of all that had to be done. Taking care of Marty was far harder than she thought it would be and she couldn't forget, or leave out a single detail. His life depended on it.

A tear bubbled over and dripped down her cheek. If she did everything right he might live one more day, or maybe one more week. He'd already beaten the odds the doctors at the hospital had given him. But nothing she could do would change the fact that his body was shutting down, turning off like old Christmas lights left up until spring. One light burning out at a time until one day soon there would be no light left in the world.

She stepped to the side of the duplex so she could circle around to the back entrance. Ronny caught a movement out of the corner of her eye. More reaction than action, she ducked as someone reached toward her.

Instinct took over. She moved away from the house as she pulled the flashlight out of her pocket. The shadow moved again, reaching but not willing to step out of the blackness. She fumbled with the flashlight switch but couldn't make it work. As she took a step backward, the uneven ground tripped her.

She fell, hitting the side of the ramp with her shoulder and crying out in pain.

Fighting the need to curl into a ball, she lifted

the flashlight and threw it toward the shadow above her.

It hit the mark and Ronny heard a muttered oath. The back door rattled open. Foster clicked the porch light back and forth trying to make it come on. "Ronny," he whispered, not wanting to wake Marty. "Ronny, is that you? Is something wrong?"

The shadow vanished in the dark behind the house. Bushes along the dry creek bed rustled as he ran.

"Ronny?" Foster tried again as he moved down the back ramp.

"I'm here," she said, standing slowly. "Someone tried to attack me."

Foster helped her into the house and insisted on checking her shoulder as she called the sheriff's office.

Phil Gentry was at the back door before she finished talking to the dispatcher. While Foster wrapped her shoulder, the deputy asked the same questions the dispatcher had. "What happened? What did you see? Tell me everything that happened. Every detail, no matter how small."

Ronny went slowly through every detail she could remember from the first movement to the sound of the weeds when he ran. Phil took notes and asked that no one go in or out the back door until sunup and he had a chance to look for evidence.

This wasn't a chance happening. Someone

knew she was out walking and waited for her in the darkness.

"Whoever did this has been watching you." Phil finally stated the one fact he knew.

Ronny told him about having the feeling that she was being followed a few nights before.

"I'll ask the sheriff to come out first thing," the deputy said.

Since Mr. Carleon and the nurses always entered through the front door, Ronny knew there would be no problem. She'd muddied her hands when she'd tumbled, so there might be a chance they would find something out back.

After the deputy left, Ronny sat with Marty and tried to calm down while Foster cleaned up in the kitchen. The deputy had wanted to take her to the hospital to be checked, but she trusted Foster's care and she couldn't leave Marty. Not now.

When she'd fallen, her shoulder had been cut. A thin line now ran along her arm, and the place where she'd hit the ramp would leave a bad bruise, but no bones were broken. She'd been lucky.

A few hours before dawn Marty woke and asked about the bandage. Ronny told him every detail calmly.

"You shouldn't have been out there," he said, sounding more worried than angry.

"No," she smiled. "He shouldn't have been out there."

"Right," Marty agreed. "In another world I would have rushed out there and beat the guy to a pulp."

"In another world Gentry wouldn't have given me his flashlight and the attacker would have gotten in a few more blows. Then I'd be buried beside you." The words were out before she could stop them. After no sleep, the filter on her thoughts no longer worked.

With effort, he took her hand. "In a perfect world we'd live long lives and then lie side by side in a garden of stone. Only we both know the world's not perfect. I want you to live, Ronny, really live, and then someday when your hair is white and your bones are brittle, I want you to go to sleep beside me. I'll be waiting."

Ronny laid her cheek against his hand. "I love you so much. I never said it, but I felt it."

"I know. I love you too. It doesn't matter how much time we have. Tonight we have time, and I want to spend every waking minute talking to you. We'll make up memories that will stay with us forever. You'll have them here and I'll have them in the next life to think about while I'm waiting for you."

She cried softly as he began to talk of taking her down the Nile and getting lost in a rain forest. He talked as if they'd had their time and all he said were shared memories. "Remember when I had to kick you out of the sleeping bag so you'd make coffee, because you know I can't make coffee that's fit to drink on a campfire?"

Slowly she began to see what he was doing. Marty was weaving together his adventures to include her.

"Remember that time we got lost in the subways of New York? You wanted to go to the Bronx Zoo, and between us we couldn't read the map on the subway car. I was never so glad to climb out of that hole and see daylight. Even the New York air smelled good."

She smiled. "It wasn't my fault; you said you could read the map. You're the great adventurer who knows every continent."

He laughed. "I can read a map. Well, usually I can. My favorite part that day was buying hot dogs in Central Park and ending up feeding the buns to the squirrels."

"A few of those squirrels looked like huge rats." She laughed, remembering that once he'd told her about the rats in Central Park.

"I like the times we went skiing in the Alps. Remember the Black Forest and how you wanted that stupid cuckoo clock, but I knew I'd have to make room in my backpack for it? After we lugged it around for days, it never did keep time."

"We threw it away in Paris, didn't we?"

"Yeah, in that little village we found when we were biking. Remember the one where no one spoke English and we had to get by on what little

I learned in one semester of French back in high school?"

"Your French is terrible."

"I know; I'll work on it before we go again."

"I hated the cold, but I loved the lodge." She smiled, remembering a picture she'd seen of a farm in France. "Didn't you say the place we stayed was three hundred years old?"

"Four, I think, and judging from the bed we slept in, the mattress was the same age."

Ronny raised her head. "I can't remember, Marty, did we make love there?"

"We did, great passionate love. The kind that left both of us mindless for a while. Your body was made for loving, Ronny. The best part of loving you is spooning with you afterward when you're all warm against me, like we're not two people but two parts of one."

"Like salt and pepper shakers that fit together."

He laughed. "The next time we travel let's buy some of those funny sets. They'd look great on that shelf in the kitchen, and they'd be a lot easier to get home than that damn clock."

She nodded, not telling him that she'd taken the shelf down to paint two years ago and forgotten to put it back.

He fell asleep telling her that when he woke they'd remember the time they took a train from Chicago to Albuquerque and made love in every empty private car along the way.

Ronny sat in the silence with the blinking machines surrounding her and realized she'd never gone more than a few hundred miles in her life, but she'd carry the memories of everything they'd talked about as if they were the only memories she possessed.

A little before dawn, she fell asleep thinking of the other adventures he'd tell her that they'd shared when he woke. She'd ask him to describe how they made love and if they ever fought. She'd ask him about the food they ate in the jungle and in Paris when they slept beside a bridge because he lost his wallet. That would be a fun memory to build.

Only Marty never woke. He left her while she slept, holding his hand.

He left her with the memories of a perfect world.

# Chapter 28

April 10

Tyler Wright woke Martha Q before eight the next morning to ask her if Mr. Carleon would mind coming to the phone. He said he didn't have the man's cell number or he wouldn't have bothered Martha Q.

She trudged up the stairs and knocked on Mr. Carleon's door, then waited in the hallway when he took the call.

She listened to Carleon talking to the funeral director long enough to guess what had happened, then rushed to her room to dress in one of her best jogging suits. When Mr. Carleon came back down the stairs to leave ten minutes later, Martha Q was ready.

"If you've no objection, I'd like to go with you, Anthony." It was the first time she'd used his Christian name, but she thought it was about time. "Tyler wouldn't have called you unless there has been a death, and I can think of only one that would concern you. I'd like to go to help, if you've no objection. Ronny is as dear to me as a daughter." Since she had no daughter, Martha Q had no idea how dear that was, but it sounded good.

"That's very kind of you, Martha," he said. "I'm sure Ronny can use a friend right now."

"And you," she added. "Marty was your friend too. I want you to know I'll be there for you as well if you need a shoulder to cry on."

"Thank you. I'll miss him, you know. We've been talking of this day for months. Marty Winslow was a brilliant man who never seemed to plan his life, but he did plan his death. I have many details to put into action before I have time to grieve the loss of a friend and an employer."

As they walked out the door, Martha Q added, "I'll do whatever I can. Ronny will take this hard, I'm afraid. I was there when she thought she lost him two years ago." She handed Carleon her keys. "I hope you don't mind driving?"

"Of course not." He opened the car door for her. "Should we call her mother to be with her at this time?"

"No, there's no need to make it harder than it has to be. Dallas Logan complains she's dying every few months. If we ask her to come over, all she'll talk about is her funeral. Says she has no reason to live now that her Howard is gone and her daughter ran away. I try to tell Dallas that daughters who are twenty-seven don't run away, they just leave, but she doesn't listen."

Martha Q knew Mr. Carleon couldn't be counted on to keep up the conversation, so she'd help him out by talking as he drove. "If you ask me, Howard Logan is up in heaven on his knees every single morning praying that the Lord will let Dallas live a long life so he'll have a little more peace in the hereafter."

Mr. Carleon didn't say a word. He just drove the few blocks to the duplex.

Tyler and the sheriff were already there sitting on the front porch.

Martha Q greeted them with a nod and asked if she could see Ronny. She really didn't feel like she needed permission to enter a place she owned, but it pays to be respectful at times of grief.

When she went in, Ronny was sitting beside Marty's bed. He looked like he was sleeping, but all the machines were off.

Martha Q waited until Ronny looked up at her and then whispered, "You said your good-bye to him, child?"

Ronny nodded.

"Well then, there's much that needs doing. How about I walk you through the beginning until you get your footing?"

Ronny stood, moving so slowly she looked like she'd aged overnight. She leaned over Marty and kissed him one last time, then went with Martha Q to her bedroom.

Without a word Martha Q helped her into the

shower and stood waiting until she finished. Then, wrapped in a towel, Ronny sat and let the older woman comb her hair. She looked hollow, as if someone had carved the insides out of her and left only the shell.

Martha Q talked about how pretty Ronny's hair was and how the day would seem endless, but the night would come just as the morning would tomorrow. She had no idea if Ronny heard her, but it didn't matter.

The morning nurse came in and rebandaged Ronny's arm. The cut was no more than a thin line of scab; bruises ran from shoulder to elbow. Both women helped her dress in a simple navy dress.

"You can do this, Ronny," Martha Q whispered as they moved back into the living room. "Death knocks on all doors whether we want it to come or not. The only advice I can give you is to not think about anything but putting one foot in front of the other. You'll make the hard climb one step at a time. That's what survivors do."

Tyler Wright had taken Marty's body away and most of the machines had been shoved against the far wall. Someone had set up chairs around the fireplace even though it wasn't cold enough to light the fire. Coffee percolated in the kitchen.

Mr. Carleon took Ronny's hand and sat beside her, explaining all the details Marty had already taken care of concerning what he wanted at his funeral. He insisted that he wanted to be buried here in Harmony in a simple graveside service. Marty had instructed Mr. Carleon to buy two plots in the Harmony Cemetery the day after he arrived.

"He said"—Carleon picked his words carefully—"that you could leave the space beside him empty. If you married and wanted to be buried elsewhere, you might consider putting up a bench so you could sit beside him now and then. He said he liked the idea of watching you growing old and knowing that you hadn't forgotten him."

Ronny nodded, but she didn't ask questions. When she looked up at the silver-haired man who'd been with Marty for years, he seemed to read her mind.

"I'll stay for as long as you need me. He would have wanted me to, and I find I've grown very fond of you and this little town. I'll make sure everything is taken care of before I leave."

Finally, Ronny seemed to wake from her trance. "Where will you go?" she asked, as if suddenly her family were falling apart.

"I don't know. When I left with Marty to come here, the Winslows terminated my employment within hours, but don't you worry, I've got enough money saved to live comfortably just about anywhere in the world."

Martha Q, who was listening, suddenly realized that if Mr. Carleon left, she'd miss him. The fact shocked her. She hadn't missed a man in years. In fact, the last few husbands she had been looking forward to missing for months before they finally left.

Throughout the morning people came and went from the duplex. The preacher. The postmaster, who'd heard the news. The boys next door. As the word spread around town, people came bringing food and flowers as if they'd known Marty for years. Even the three widows Martha Q was boarding came. They'd never met Marty, but they cried just the same.

The only person who didn't come was Dallas Logan. Her only child had just lost the love of her life, and Dallas couldn't set aside her anger long enough to comfort Ronny.

It made Martha Q so mad she hugged Ronny every chance she got while she plotted to thump Dallas Logan a good one if she ever saw the woman again.

In the evening, the cook at the funeral home stopped in with her baby. She asked Ronny to come back to her apartment in the back of the funeral home. The girls had shared it once before, and Martha Q guessed it was as close as Ronny had to a home that she'd want to go to.

Autumn talked Ronny into taking a walk, leaving Martha Q and Mr. Carleon alone in the little duplex apartment.

"It's been a long day," she said as she sat next to him on the porch. "And tomorrow won't be any shorter."

Anthony nodded. "You were a great help today, Martha."

"I try to be," Martha Q lied. Help was rarely something she tried.

"I feel a bit lost," he admitted. "I don't think there has been a minute I haven't had Marty on my mind in two years. Most of my energy has been spent taking care of him, and now I'm not sure what to do with myself."

She'd been watching Anthony Carleon all day. He was organized, always thoughtful, and as pure a gentleman as she'd ever seen, but the man lived on coffee and nothing else. "It's been my experience, Anthony, that the only cure for feeling lost is home-cooked food. How about we go back to my place and raid the fridge?"

He offered a tired smile. "That sounds like a good idea, my dear."

A few minutes later when they climbed the steps of the bed-and-breakfast, the three little widows were waiting for them. All three were so angry they looked like they'd been wound up too tight and couldn't stop jittering.

The trio had been told by the sheriff to quit following Bryce Galloway, but they were determined, even if threatened at gunpoint, to continue their quest. They'd followed him into the cleaners and asked to see the jacket he turned in.

The little lady behind the counter didn't understand why. Joni Rosen, the leader, made up a story about being Bryce's mother and said she'd put something in his pocket at church and he must have forgotten it was there.

Martha Q thought the story lacked her own natural creativity, but she nodded and encouraged Joni to continue. "And did you find your missing valuable?"

Joni smiled. "No, but we found this."

She held up one piece of straw. "Talk's all over town about how someone tried to poison one of Nevada Britain's horses. Well, ladies and gentleman, I have the proof right here."

"You mean Nevada McDowell's horses. She's married, you know." Martha Q liked to use the right name. She always hated it when people called her by the wrong last name. Usually when it happened, she had to fight down the urge to hit them up the side of their head and tell them to read the paper now and then. She'd made the front page in her wedding dress all seven times.

"Whatever," Joni said. "Back to the find. A clue. Horses hang out in barns. This proves Bryce was in a barn, therefore he was probably the one who tried to kill the horse."

Martha Q doubted one piece of straw would do the trick, but she decided to do all she could to keep the widows off spying and out of the house. "This is great, ladies. Keep up the good work."

About that time Bryce pulled up out front and the widows scattered.

Martha Q and Anthony remained on the porch.

Bryce whistled as he walked up the steps. "Good evening," he said, obviously in a good mood.

"Evening," Martha Q offered in return. "Had a busy day?"

"Not particularly." Bryce passed them without stopping to talk. "Just looking over some investments."

He'd disappeared inside before she could ask any questions.

Anthony leaned close and whispered, "My friend in Houston checked on him. Nothing. He'd been questioned twice about fights he'd been in, but charges were never filed."

"Money bought him out of trouble," she whispered back, loving being so close to Mr. Carleon.

They stood, listening to Bryce run up the stairs. Finally, when the third-floor door slammed, Anthony offered his arm. "I believe, Martha, we have a date waiting in the kitchen."

"A date?" Martha Q grinned as she curled her hand around his arm. "Does it come with a good-night kiss?"

Anthony looked more relaxed in the porch light's glow than she'd ever seen him. "It just might, dear lady. It just might."

# Chapter 29

April 10

Cord left Nevada sleeping on the blankets in the hay and moved to the door of the barn loft. It was sunup and he should be at the bunkhouse giving the men orders for the day, but he didn't want to leave her. Even after he'd held her close all night, he was still hungry for the feel of her against him. She was quickly becoming an addiction that went all the way to the bone. It occurred to him that if he'd known her, really known her, before he went to prison, he would have died of starvation for the feel of her in the six years he'd been behind bars.

She'd teased him about having a girlfriend when Ronny called concerning the man Cord was trying to find, but Nevada would have to be blind to not see that she was the only woman he looked at. Cord was falling hard for his temporary wife. He already knew that when their time was over and he had to leave, his heart would be staying behind.

He'd held her all night long. He'd always

thought of her as headstrong and wild. Only yesterday he'd seen her broken, and he never wanted to see her like that again. Whoever poisoned the horse must have known how it would hurt her. Someone wanted her shattered, unable to fight, but why? Surely not over land? If Bryce was to blame, he wouldn't have needed to break her to get her to sell the land. His family was rich enough to buy half the ranches in Texas.

He pulled out his cell and called Galem, passing along what needed to be done on the ranch. Then Cord asked if Galem would tell Jackson and his brothers to wait for him in the bunkhouse kitchen. When Galem confirmed his order, Cord added that he wanted Zeb to pack lunch and a rifle and be at the horse barn in ten minutes. Cord was taking no chance of anyone who didn't belong stepping foot in the place again.

"If Zeb sees a stranger's car turn off the county road onto the ranch, tell him to fire off a couple of shots. I want no one stepping on the Boxed B that doesn't belong."

"Will do," Galem answered. "He'll be on his way to act as guard in a few minutes."

The horse barn was a good place to station a guard. From the loft opening one man could see the land all the way to where their road hooked up to the county road. The only other entrance into the ranch was eight miles farther down, and Cord planned to bust the dam at that end. Within an hour the dirt road would be so muddy not even a tank could get down it.

"You know, Galem, this trouble isn't over." Cord needed to be honest, with himself and the cook. "We may have hard times coming."

"I know. We all know, Boss. Only I'm thinking you may be wrong about Bryce Galloway being behind all this trouble. He ain't got the balls. I think he wants Nevada back, but he won't face you."

Cord hadn't met the man, but from what Nevada had told him, he didn't like Bryce. Maybe Galem was right; the ex-husband did seem to be more the type to bully Nevada, or even frighten her, to get what he wanted, than to come straight on. "I'm not taking any chances."

"I agree. Nevada's old man made his share of enemies, and even you made a few when you fired men those first few days. In Harmony you'll be hard-pressed to find a dozen people who like the Britains, and most would question your sanity for marrying one. They'll wonder why you'd want to step between Nevada and her ex."

"They don't know me." Cord grinned, thinking no one would ever understand how he felt about Nevada.

Galem laughed. "You got a point, but the men here are with you."

"Then we make our stand here."

Cord walked to where Nevada slept. When he

290

tried to wake her with a touch, she only curled deeper into the blanket.

He gave up and lifted her, blanket and all. He carried her to his truck and nestled her beside him as he drove the short distance to their house. Without trying to wake her, he walked into their bedroom and placed her in the middle of the king-size bed. She'd had an emotional day yesterday, and maybe she'd sleep the morning away.

When she didn't move, he closed the curtains for the first time since he'd moved in with her and left the room dark. As he walked through the kitchen, he told Ora Mae not to wake her.

Cord hesitated a moment and added, "When she does wake up, tell her I have one of my boys at her barn and he's staying."

"She won't like that." Ora Mae never stated more than the facts.

"I don't care. If she's got a problem with it, tell her to talk to me." He checked the phone in his pocket. "Of course, she'll have to find me first."

By the time he was out of the house, Cord's mind was focusing in on what had to be done. A few minutes later he was eating breakfast as Jackson filled him in on every detail he and Zeb could find out about the trainer. He'd been hired while Nevada was married to Bryce. He wasn't from Harmony, and as near as they could find out he'd made no attempts to fit into the community. He was a loner who liked it that way, but Nevada had never complained about his work.

When Jackson finished the report, Cord simply said, "Find him."

Jackson smiled. "That's the same thing the sheriff said she planned to do."

When Jackson left, Galem poured himself a cup of coffee and sat down across from Cord. "You can't afford to do anything illegal. You know that ranger and half the cops in this part of the state are watching you. Waiting for you to make one wrong move."

"I know, Mother." Cord smiled.

Galem got the hint. "I'm just saying that if you're planning anything the least bit shady, you got to let me do it. I've got this innocent face. Everyone trusts me."

Cord almost choked on his coffee as he laughed. Galem's face was weathered and pockmarked. He'd admitted to having his nose broken once by a bull and then straightened with another break in a fight. A few of the men kidded him once, saying they were surprised Galem ever found a woman willing to marry him, since he was so homely even the cattle noticed. Galem had answered that great lovers are always handsome in the dark.

"I'll stay legal, I promise." Cord set his cup down. "Watch over the ranch for a few hours; I need to go to town and set a few things in motion."

Galem raised an eyebrow but nodded.

Cord drove to town, pulled through the bank's drive-through window for cash, and headed to the movie theater. He couldn't believe Cameron had been in town and he hadn't noticed him, but then, no one ever noticed the man. Plus, Cord hadn't been on this end of Main more than a dozen times in the three years he'd been back, and he'd never gone to the movies.

He found Cameron, older but still as bland-looking as ever, emptying the trash out back of the theater. His hair was gray and in need of a cut, his clothes baggy.

"Remember me?" Cord said as he walked up.

"Nope." The man turned to go back inside, showing no interest in talking.

Cord was a long way from the kid he'd been when he met Cameron in prison. Cord had grown a few inches since then and put on fifty pounds. "We met once almost ten years ago. You told me you were from Harmony and would be headed back as soon as you got out. I probably said I was never coming back here if I ever got out of prison."

Cameron stopped and slowly turned around. He took the time to study Cord, from his expensive boots to the monogrammed initials on his cuff and the western-cut leather jacket. "I've tried to forget that time in prison, and I'm guessing you have too. I thought you looked familiar, but I'm trying never to remember anyone I met behind bars."

Cord guessed he had about thirty seconds to make his point. "It doesn't matter if you remember me. You interested in a job that pays good money?" He pulled the cash from his pocket. "Nothing illegal. I just need someone watched and I don't want him to spot you. A few of the guys used to say you were good at moving around without folks noticing. All you got to do is tail him."

"I used to be good at not being noticed." Cameron straightened a little taller with pride. "I could shadow anyone right into their own house without them spotting me. I'm strictly legit now, but there's no harm in watching someone, I guess. I could really use the money. My boss wants to sell this place, and if he closes I'll have trouble finding another job. You want them tailed day and night, I'm your man—Cord?"

"You do remember me?"

Cameron smiled. "Nothing slips by me. I've seen you around town a few times; surprised you noticed me."

"I didn't, but I hoped you were here. A friend helped me out with your address, but that's not the problem. I'd like to hire you starting now and going until I get the information I need. I'm guessing it won't be more than a two- or three-day job, with a bonus at the end if you learn something helpful."

"It'll cost you three hundred a day, and all I

do is watch and report. Nothing more. I'm too old to get in the middle of anything."

"If you're spotted, you're fired."

"Fair enough, but if I get what you want, the bonus is a thousand. I can work till Friday, then if you still want me, I can call in sick here. I got a kid who can fill in and run the projector. I stay on this guy until you call me off, or get what you want in the way of information."

Cord nodded. "Be ready in thirty minutes. I'll pick you up here in the alley."

Cameron disappeared into the theater and Cord drove over to the mall. He bought a phone with prepaid minutes, a camera with extra batteries, and a pocket tape recorder from a secondhand shop. When he circled back by the theater, Cameron was waiting for him with a toolbox and a clipboard in one hand and a work jacket in the other. The old guy had changed into dark blue trousers stained on one knee and a denim work shirt.

As he climbed into Cord's special-edition Ford, he whispered to himself, "If I'd known you drove a 450, I would have doubled my price. You've done well for yourself since prison. Heard folks talking about you and some rancher's daughter marrying. I don't have to take the paper; I just listen to folks talk before the movies."

"I married money," Cord answered flatly.

Cameron laughed, like he thought Cord was kidding.

The little man took notes as Cord rattled off the facts about Bryce Galloway. "He's probably eating over at the bed-and-breakfast about now. From there I have no idea where he goes or who he talks to"—Cord glanced at Cameron, who had started playing with all his new toys—"but I will after today. I'll expect details for my money."

"You'll get them." Cameron shoved everything into his toolbox. "I'll need all your numbers and I might call at any hour. I can't step away to talk to you until I know this guy is set somewhere."

"I only have one number, and it's already in the phone. Don't talk to anyone but me. Don't call me until you have something important to say. I'll call you if I hear anything you need to know about this guy."

Cameron nodded. "If I don't answer, I'll call back as soon as I can. This ain't the kind of job that allows visiting."

"I understand." He handed over the five bills. "I'll pay the balance when the job is over."

"Drop me off a few houses from the Winter's Inn. I don't want anyone seeing me with you." Cameron shoved his notes into his vest pocket.

Cord pulled to the curb. "You planning on just walking in?"

Cameron smiled. "No, I'll be invited in. I may have given up crime, but I still watch what's going on. The old lady who owns the B&B drives a boat of a car. I see her cruising Main like some of the kids do. Since it's not parked in the drive, she's not home. I'm guessing there will be a cook or housekeeper to let the gas inspector in." He pulled a faded ID tag from his pocket and clipped it to his coat. "Folks never read the tag; just having one is all you need if you smile and act all polite."

"Be careful, Cameron. This guy could be dangerous."

"I figured that or you wouldn't be hiring me." The little man winked like he was about to have the time of his life.

Cord let him out, then pulled across the street and watched Cameron walk straight up to the front door. He talked to a lady who looked like the housekeeper for a minute, and then she opened the door to let him in.

Smiling, Cord noticed a rental car parked to the side. He'd bet it was Bryce's, and Cameron was probably watching him eat breakfast right now. The con man might just be worth the money.

On his way over to the sheriff's office he called the house and wasn't surprised to hear Nevada was still asleep.

Circling by Ronny's old duplex, he noticed Tyler Wright wheeling a body down the ramp he'd made. Marty had passed. He'd finally used the ramp.

A boat of a car was parked beside the under-taker, so Cord didn't stop. He had his share of trouble today, but he couldn't help worrying about his friend. He hoped she'd remember to call if she needed him.

Alex Matheson was out of her office when Cord walked into the sheriff's station, but Travis Salem had taken over the small conference room next to the sheriff's office. Cord tried to back out without the ranger seeing him, but Salem looked up.

"McDowell," he yelled. "Come on in. I need to talk to you."

Cord didn't bother taking off his hat as he stepped a few feet into the room. He didn't like being this close to Salem. He didn't trust him, even if he was a Texas Ranger. His memories were washed in whiskey from the night they'd first met out by the lake, but Cord didn't remember going at the man in a wild rage like then-Deputy Travis Salem had testified.

One of the older sheriff's deputies saw Cord and offered him a cup of coffee. Cord was glad when the deputy stayed in the room to hear what the ranger had to say. Cord didn't know Phil Gentry very well, but he couldn't start avoiding folks he didn't know or he'd have to be a hermit.

Ranger Salem pointed to a pile of papers. "The way this is stacking up, McDowell, we don't have enough hard evidence to charge anyone, even if you and your wife think you know who poisoned the horse. That ex-husband of your wife's could just say he dropped by the barn one day for old times' sake. Even if we could prove it was his footprint, we don't have enough to charge Bryce Galloway."

Cord wasn't surprised. He hadn't expected Travis Salem to help him.

"Galloway, you say," Phil lowered his coffee. "I just took a complaint from him. He claims he's being stalked."

Cord froze. He'd left Cameron fifteen minutes ago. Surely he wasn't already caught? He hadn't earned a dollar of the five hundred.

Phil laughed. "Yeah, the guy claims three little widows staying at the bed-and-breakfast tail him everywhere he goes. He says losing them usually takes half the morning, but he's tired of the hassle."

Cord relaxed. Just for a minute. Until he realized the women's interest in the man might mess up Cameron's tracking possibilities.

"Why would they be following Bryce?" Travis asked, without showing much interest.

"I don't know. He's a good-looking man. Maybe they're all three in love." Phil poked his cheek with his tongue. "Come to think of it, if I go over there they'll take one look at Bryce and start following me around. A man with a little gray in his hair is far more attractive to the widow types." Phil shrugged. "Don't see how we can charge them with anything. Eating at the same café as Bryce or driving down the same street isn't a crime that I know of."

Travis Salem looked like the deputy was interfering with important police work, but since he was a guest in the office he probably figured he shouldn't start giving orders. The ranger stood politely and waited for Gentry to finish his one-sided conversation.

Cord listened to the deputy while he watched Salem out of the corner of his eye. The ranger didn't seem any more comfortable around him than he was around the ranger. Surely the guy wasn't afraid Cord might swing at him again. More than likely, he decided, Travis Salem worried that the lie he'd told ten years ago that had sent Cord to prison might somehow surface.

Only no one had believed Cord's side of the story back then, and if Cord was guessing, he'd say no one would believe it now.

Cord finished his coffee and headed out. "Let me know if you find anything," he said to the ranger, then smiled at Phil Gentry, deciding he liked the old deputy. After all, Gentry was one of the few lawmen who hadn't suggested he leave town permanently. "Good luck with the band of widows. You might think about arresting them to keep them out of trouble."

Gentry nodded as if he were considering the idea.

Cord made it to the bottom of the front steps before Gentry caught up to him. "Mr. McDowell, you're a friend of Ronny Logan, aren't you?"

"I am."

"I thought I should tell you she was attacked out behind her house last night. Someone hiding in the shadows tried to grab hold of her and she fell backing away. Luckily, she was only bruised, but I tell you, I can't think of why anyone would do such a thing. The poor girl's got her basket full of troubles already. With Marty dying, she's got other things on her mind today, but I'm filing a full report."

Cord asked a few details, but Gentry didn't know any more.

"It don't make any sense." Phil shook his head. "Everyone likes Ronny, except maybe her mother, and I can't see that old witch trying to kill her only child. Who would she have to complain about?"

Cord climbed into his truck. Gentry was right. No one would go after Ronny. Unless . . . unless they thought by hurting her they'd be hurting someone else.

When he made it back to the ranch, Nevada was dressed and reading the paper as she nibbled on a muffin. He stood in the kitchen doorway for a moment watching her. When she finally looked up he asked, "Should I run?"

She smiled. "No, I've decided to let you live."

"I'm not backing down on the guard at your barn. I want a man I can trust there." He figured he might as well face the problem head-on. "The guard stays no matter what you say."

"Okay," she said, shocking him.

"No storm?"

"No storm," she answered. "I think after a month of living with you I've figured out that, for the first time in longer than I can remember, I've got someone on my side."

"Want to go with me to make a round of the ranch? I want to check fences and change the codes on all the locked gates going to where your oil rigs are. If someone's out to cause hell on the Boxed B, I plan to make it as hard on them as I can."

To his surprise she said yes and pulled on her boots. "Let's take the old Jeep; I haven't driven it in a week. If I go much longer it won't start."

"Fair enough, but I drive."

He rested his arm lightly on her shoulder as they walked out behind the barn, where she always parked the Jeep in an old shed that looked like her grandfather had probably built it. More boards were missing from the sides than on it.

"I'm doubling the security at my office. Everything else that has happened lately could be written off as an accident, but not Starlight."

Cord agreed. "I feel like we're under attack."

She smiled up at him. "And we fight, right?"

He kissed the top of her head. "Right, Babe."

As she moved beside him, he fought the urge to kiss her again. She was becoming a part of him. Everyone he'd ever cared about had turned their backs or died on him. Cord knew she'd do the same when their bargain was finished. She had her secrets and she'd leave before she'd let him any closer, but right now she needed him.

Nevada always left the keys in the ignition and the windows rolled up. Most of the paint was gone on the roof of the Jeep, but Cord guessed it had once been blue, or maybe army green. He couldn't be sure.

He pulled the driver's door open as she smiled and swung into the passenger side.

Everything happened in a flash, like lightning hit several places at once.

Nevada screamed.

Cord heard the familiar tick-tick-tick of a rattler's tail. He'd already extended his hand toward the wheel and felt the hard sudden stab of fangs going into his wrist before he could pull back. When he did step away, the snake came along, attached to his wrist.

The rattlesnake had to be near six feet long and held on as Cord tried to swing it free. His skin ripped when he finally slung the snake a few feet away. More out of instinct than logic, Cord slammed his boot straight down an inch below the snake's head, pinning it in the dirt.

The body of the snake whipped and coiled around his legs.

Nevada continued to scream for help. She'd managed to climb out of the Jeep, but he couldn't tell if she'd been bitten.

Cord ground hard, but the dirt around the shed was too soft to kill the snake.

He couldn't move. If he did, the snake might try to strike again, or worse, slither off. Tightening his fist, he could already feel the numbness moving into his wrist. This was not a dry bite. The snake had injected venom.

Ora Mae came running from the back door of the house as two cowhands rushed from the barn. Like a warrior of old, Ora Mae raised her garden hoe and swung.

Cord closed his eyes, figuring if she missed he would not only have a snakebite to deal with but also a few missing toes.

The hoe hit the rattler just behind the head and severed the body.

Cord stared down, afraid to move. He had no idea if his heart was pounding in his throat because of the venom pumping in his blood or because, for the first time since he got out of prison, he was terrified.

The cowhands reached them just as another snake slithered from the open door of the Jeep. One of the men borrowed Ora Mae's hoe and killed the second snake with one whack.

Cord moved to Nevada's side. "Are you bit?" he yelled.

She shook her head as she gulped for air and moved closer to him.

They watched silently as four more snakes were pulled from the Jeep. All were longer than four feet. This was no nest. They'd been planted in the hot vehicle and they didn't look too happy about it. The windows had been rolled up. Towels for them to hide in had been piled in the backseat.

When Cord pulled off his belt and tied it around his forearm, Nevada saw the bite marks as blood stained his cuff. "We need to get you to the hospital."

"You drive. I'm not sure I won't pass out."

They headed to his truck. He'd only seen one man with a snakebite before. He was a day laborer on his dad's farm. Cord had been about seven, but he remembered how sick the man looked before they got him to town.

Nevada stopped shaking as anger built in her. She drove so fast he figured a poisonous snakebite might be the least of his problems. Neither talked. They both knew what was at stake.

She pulled into the emergency room drive before either said a word.

"Can you make it in?"

"I can." Cord was giving serious consideration to a prayer of thanks for surviving the drive. One good thing, she'd taken his mind off the bite. He'd read in books that anyone bitten should remain calm. Fat chance of that. He took a deep breath, testing to see if he had any trouble breathing. No problem, but his arm was starting to swell and he had no feeling in his hand.

She jumped out of the truck and ran around to help him out, then pushed him into the empty emergency room.

While the nurse took him back, Nevada stopped to fill out paperwork. He could tell she didn't want to leave him, but she was starting to make him more nervous than the dripping blood from the two bite marks.

"I'll be fine, Babe," he yelled over his shoulder as they led him away.

"You'd better be." He could hear the anger in her words and knew if he died on her she'd never forgive him for breaking their bargain.

Dr. Addison Spencer was waiting for him with shots ready and a list of instructions taped to the wall.

He took one look at the shot and said, "I didn't know you were a gunslinger, Doc."

She smiled in that *this is going to hurt you more than it does me* kind of way as she pulled his already unbuttoned shirt off his shoulder and shot him.

Cord flinched. "Hey, Doc, aren't you supposed to say 'Make a fist' or something?"

"I didn't want to waste time. Snake venom can restrict your air passages."

"After that shot, it's going to take me a while to

breathe normal." Cord watched her carefully in case she reloaded.

While she worked, a conversation passed through the curtain that acted as a door to the emergency area. One woman's voice said, "Strange couple, if you ask me."

Another said, "I've heard he's violent. Almost killed a deputy about ten years back."

The first laughed. "Well, I heard she tried to kill her last husband, so they're probably evenly matched."

Cord growled.

The first voice from the hallway added, "I'm surprised a rattler would even bite him. They usually don't attack their own."

Dr. Spencer laughed, drawing Cord's attention. "You that mean, cowboy?"

"Probably," he answered, realizing she was far too bright to buy into gossip. "I'm working on it."

"My fiancé, Tinch Turner, was over at the vet's this morning working with your horse. He said the vet told a different story. Said he heard you and your wife slept with the horses to make sure they were all right."

Cord frowned. "Don't tell those ladies, you'll ruin my rep."

"Your secret's safe with me, cowboy." Without another word, she began cleaning the wound.

Cord decided he liked this no-nonsense doctor.

When Nevada found him fifteen minutes later,

he'd already had two shots and the wound had been cleaned and bandaged. He'd been ordered to wait on the examining table, and the nurse would be back to check his heart rate.

He felt like a fool with his feet swinging off the table and his shirt open. They'd offered him a hospital gown, but he told them he'd as likely wear pink PJs as a gown. In truth, he felt fine. He hadn't even wanted to lie down. Once the fear wore off, Cord felt like everyone was making a big deal over nothing. His arm ached, but it was no longer swelling and he had most of the feeling back in his hand.

For the first time he realized how frightened Nevada looked. "I'm all right, but they cut up the sleeve of the shirt you bought me. I really liked the way you put my initials on the cuff. I'm sorry about messing it up."

Nevada pressed as close as she could get to him. "I don't care about the shirt, Cord. I care about you, you idiot."

He looked up into her beautiful blue eyes and smiled. "You do?"

The meaning behind her words seemed to hit them both at the same time. Somehow during the past month they'd changed from two almost-strangers who'd made a bargain to something different, and neither really knew what it was.

She leaned down and kissed his lips softly. "Don't you dare die on me. I didn't really think

I would, but I like having you around, Cord McDowell."

It wasn't exactly a declaration of love, but he'd take it. He slid his unbandaged hand into the hair at the back of her neck, pulled her close, and kissed her soundly, then whispered, "I thought about it, but I figured you'd really storm if I cut out on the bargain."

Her hand moved through the hair on his chest as her cheek rubbed against his. They didn't know how to say the right words about how much the other meant to them. He'd never used a word like *love* much, and she'd used it so often it no longer held any meaning.

She moved between his legs and wrapped her arms around his neck. He circled her waist with his bandaged wrist and pulled her close enough to feel her heart beat against his. When he caressed her soft breasts beneath the silk of her blouse, he decided if the poison wasn't out of his system it was probably running double time through his veins about now.

"I thought I'd die when I saw that snake; then when you were bit I swear my heart completely stopped." She gulped for air. "I think I finally found something more frightening than snakes. It's thinking about you hurt and knowing that it's somehow all my fault." She pulled his face close to hers. "This is my fault, Cord. I know it."

"No. It's not. Whoever's doing this may want to

hurt you, but it's not your fault. We're going to get through this. Me and you, Babe." Any doubt that they were in this fight together was gone, and they both knew it.

She leaned into him and kissed him softly on the mouth. A thank-you kiss. A promise. A bonding of their own special kind of loving.

Cord forced the words. "As soon as my heart slows down a few hundred beats a minute, how about we go back to those blankets in the barn?" He could think of one place where they had no trouble communicating. "Or, I think it looks like rain. We might want to take a nap over at my farm."

"I don't want to sleep." She smiled.

"Me either," he answered.

She tortured him by wiggling against him again. "Are you saying you want my body?"

"I want all of you." *Including your heart,* he thought as his hand moved over her hip. "It'd take more than a snakebite to slow me down." He needed to be alone with her more than he needed air right now. "How about we go back and send Ora Mae home? We could tell her the doctor ordered bed rest."

Nevada kissed him tenderly, but her body seemed to be begging to be handled with passionate touches. They'd made love enough to know what the other liked, and right now Cord was thinking he liked everything about her. Something about being scared half to death made him feel totally alive. He could read every move she made, and he had no doubt he could give her just what she wanted.

Cord was almost lost in pleasure when he heard boots stomping their way down the hall and knew their time together was about to end.

He managed to push her away a few inches before the room filled with half a dozen of his men. They were all talking and cussing at once. Most had been out working cattle when they heard about the snakebite. Cord swore the smell of cows followed them into the hospital room.

Jackson slapped his hat against his leg. "Someone's trying to kill you, Boss, and we're not going to stand around and let that happen."

"No, not me," he answered. "They weren't trying to kill me."

He looked at Nevada, who paled seeing the truth in his words. "No one drives the old Jeep but me," she whispered as her hand gripped his shoulder. "The snakes were meant for me."

If she'd taken the Jeep by herself, it would have been midmorning and no one would be around to help. Two or three bites and she might not have gotten to help in time. Before, everything had seemed like accidents, but no longer.

"The snakes had to be brought in from somewhere else," one of the men volunteered. "We haven't seen a rattler that big around the ranch in years. And four of them together. It wouldn't make sense. Someone took the time to catch them and put them in there."

Everyone started talking at once about what needed to be done. Cord listened as he thought. They were right, of course; the snakes had been planted, but by whom? Again the same facts came back that he'd faced yesterday after the horse had been poisoned. Whoever did this knew the ranch, knew that Nevada drove the Jeep, maybe even knew she was afraid of snakes. If she hadn't noticed the rattlers for a few minutes, she might have been driving; fast, of course. Then the Jeep would flip on the narrow road and kill her. The snakes might even crawl away before anyone reached her.

He made his mind go through all the men who'd been fired the first day he came. They'd been mad at him, not at her. A few had cussed when he'd fired them, but none looked like he wanted a fight. What would be the point? Cord wasn't likely to hire them back.

That left only one person: Bryce Galloway, or maybe someone he'd paid to plant the snakes. Galem had mentioned once that Bryce said once that he'd never let her go. Maybe he'd always thought they'd get back together eventually. When Cord married her, that option vanished.

Cord thought about how Nevada had asked him to marry her. She hadn't wanted a husband; she said she wanted his last name. Could she have been that afraid of Galloway? Was that the real reason she'd married him? The reason she said she wouldn't explain?

Only Bryce came from a wealthy family. He had relatives in the state senate and an uncle who was a judge. Everyone in the state thought she married up on her third try, and half the people in town still thought that Nevada and her wild ways drove Bryce away. Maybe she thought Cord was the only man who'd be on her side if a fight came. Remembering the way the cowhands had ignored her when she'd walked into the bunkhouse that first Monday after they married, Cord decided maybe Nevada had guessed right.

But why him? She could have hired bodyguards and lawyers. Even though the ranch was losing money, she still had resources. Why marry the dirt-poor farmer next door? What had made her take a chance and believe that an ex-con would stand with her when trouble came?

If she knew it was coming at all?

He looked at Nevada, knowing that sometime soon he was going to have to ask the one question she'd told him never to ask. Why'd she marry him?

Dr. Spencer came into the examining room and demanded that all the cowhands leave. They were polite, even respectful, but reluctant to move. When she finally promised she'd let Cord go as soon as she was through examining him, they wandered off. Two offered to take his place if she'd examine them, and one asked her for a date before Cord reminded him that the doc was engaged to Tinch Turner.

All the town knew of Tinch's ability with his fists. The hospital had seen its share of his sparring partners after a bar fight. Only Tinch had settled down once he met the doctor. The cowboy and the city-girl doctor were an odd couple. Almost as odd as Cord and Nevada, Cord thought.

Finally only Cord, the doc, and Nevada were in the room.

"He'll need to take it easy for a few hours," Dr. Spencer said. "If his arm starts to swell or he experiences chills or sweats, I want him back in here."

"You treat a lot of snakebites, Doc?" Cord asked, just so she'd stop reading from a printout he felt sure she'd hand him when he walked out.

"You're my first. Most people who see snakes walk around them."

Cord reached for his hat. "I'm fine, Doc. You did a great job and I'll take your advice from now on, but I got to get back to work."

She looked like she might argue with him, but then she smiled as if she'd dealt with stubborn fools before. "Get some rest, Cord."

He put his arm around his wife and said, "I'll do that, Doc. My wife is taking me straight home to bed, aren't you, Babe?"

# Chapter 30

April 11

Martha Q didn't like the idea of leaving Ronny in her grief, but the girl was in good hands with Mr. Carleon watching over her. They were busy notifying all of Marty's friends and relatives that the graveside service would be at dawn tomorrow. After his accident and long stays in the hospital, most of those he knew had drifted away. Except for three men, all others made excuses as to why they couldn't come. But the three friends who'd carried him off the mountain after his fall said they were on their way. Mr. Carleon called them Marty's knights.

Ronny looked like she was moving through water. Her face was pale and her hand shook now and then. Only she kept busy, as though if she were to stop and take a deep breath the sorrow would catch up to her and smother her completely. Nothing anyone said or did would take the pain away. Mr. Carleon was doing what he could. He walked with her through the hardest day of her life.

Martha Q had never known great love like that,

and as she watched Ronny, she felt both thankful and cheated. She'd known passion and lust, but *love* was mostly just a word she used. She hadn't cried when her father died until she found out her sister inherited everything. Her mother passed on after ten years of swearing she was "about to." Martha Q felt like she'd been holding her breath for years waiting for death to show up, so when her mother stopped breathing it came as no surprise. Two of her husbands had died after long illnesses, leaving her more relieved than heart-broken. She had no children or pets she liked. So grief was something usually a few pounds of sweets could cure.

And there was certainly no time for a great love in her life now, Martha Q decided. She needed to get back to her place and have a talk with the three little widows. The sheriff had told her about Bryce's complaint, and it was only a matter of time before one of the widows broke and spilled the beans that Martha Q had come up with the idea to follow Bryce Galloway.

Martha Q's part in the plot would be exposed. Bryce would probably sue her, or worse, kill her. After all, he had to start somewhere, and she was always around. She still had the feeling he was secretly a serial killer in training. He might act all sweet and polite, but she wasn't fooled. She'd played that part herself now and then and knew all the lines.

It would be an even greater crime if he killed her right at a point in her life when she'd found a man who might be interested in her. It had been years since her last real flirtation. Her pen pal in prison really didn't count, since half of his love letters were blacked out. She thought about asking if they could send the deleted half to her anonymously so she could at least dream, but she doubted the correctional system had much interest in her longings.

Martha Q knew she was getting ahead of herself thinking that Mr. Carleon might be interested. After all, all he'd ever touched of her was her hand and, at her size, that didn't amount to even five percent if she measured interest by the pound. The kiss he'd hinted at after their almost-date in the kitchen was no more than a peck on her cheek.

She knew she shouldn't, but she just had to drive over to the funeral home and talk to Tyler. He was busy planning all the details for Marty's graveside funeral, but surely he'd have a few minutes to visit with her. First, he was the only man who would listen to her problems, and second, she wanted to check on Kate. The woman must be insane to get pregnant in her forties. Didn't Kate realize that Martha Q was too old to have a friend who was having a baby? Hell, as her best friend, Martha Q should probably give her a shower.

She was thinking about having a stay-at-home

shower when she pulled up to Wright Funeral Home. She'd invite women over forty and tell them if they didn't want to come, they could send two gifts and stay at home. Kate would get a ton of gifts and Martha Q wouldn't have to waste time thinking of dumb games to play.

She climbed out, already making her list of who wouldn't come to the shower. Of course, she would leave Dallas Logan off the list, even if they did go to high school together. There was no excuse for Dallas disowning her only child, Ronny. The woman had always had rocks for brains, and now they were mold-covered.

Not feeling like the climb up the front steps, Martha Q went around to the kitchen door and tapped. Autumn, the housekeeper and cook, answered the door, a fat little baby in her arms.

Martha Q grunted. The world was exploding. If people didn't stop having kids, Harmony would have to change the population sign again.

"Morning, Mrs. Patterson. How can I help you?"

The girl was just too cheery for Martha Q's liking. People in funeral homes should at least look respectfully sad, not like they'd just been laughing.

"I need to see Mr. Wright." Martha Q pushed her way in. The smell of warm gingerbread made her offer a quick smile to the cook.

"He's not here, but you could talk to Kate. I

was just about to make her lunch, and I know she'd be happy if you joined her. It's no trouble to make an extra plate."

Martha Q decided she always did like Autumn. Even if she did have a baby, at least she had the good sense to be able to cook. "What are you having for lunch?"

"Chicken salad, made with walnuts and grapes, on homemade wheat bread with a slice of red velvet cake I made this morning for dessert. It's still too warm to cut, but by the time lunch is over, it should be ready."

"I thought I smelled ginger?" Martha Q examined the organized kitchen. They'd added a baby cage in the corner. She knew people called them playpens, but she'd never seen a child actually playing in one.

"Oh, you did. I'm making cookies for the fire department meeting tonight. You're welcome to have a few as an appetizer with lunch."

Martha Q reevaluated her opinion of the girl. Perhaps Autumn should breed; after all, she was obviously brilliant as well as talented.

Martha Q plopped her purse down on one of the stools. If the designer purse got any bigger or heavier, it would need rollers on the bottom; but fashion was fashion and the shopping network claimed orange went with everything this year. "Well, I guess I could keep Kate company for a while." She'd decided years ago that food she

319

hadn't made or paid for was calorie free. "I might even have lunch just to make sure she eats. She needs to keep up her strength for the birthing due next week."

Five minutes later she sat in the breakfast area of the warm kitchen eating with Kate and told her of the problem with a full house at the bed-and-breakfast.

Unfortunately, unlike Tyler, Kate wasn't one to just listen. She talked, asked questions, made suggestions. Martha Q liked the woman, but she often found her exhausting. Tyler listened to her problems, but Kate tried to solve them.

Finally, as if she were no match for interrogation, Martha Q told Kate of her worries about Bryce Galloway and, to her surprise, Kate said that if a woman who knows men as well as Martha Q did thought there was something wrong with the man, it was worth investigating.

Then Martha Q told her about the widows getting caught trailing the man. It seemed he wasn't willing to believe they just happened to eat at the same place he did for lunch and walk in the park at the same time of day. He not only noticed them, but he'd tattled on them to the sheriff. Everyone in town knew the sheriff had more important things to do than haul in three widows for interrogation.

When her water broke, Kate lost interest in Martha Q's story. All at once Martha Q's problem was pushed aside, and everyone rallied around Kate like there hadn't been a few billion babies already born in the world. Tyler was called and told to meet them at the hospital. Autumn ran out with two baby bags and said she had to drop off her little girl with Willie at the fire station, and then she'd meet Kate at the hospital. The secretary, two guys from the basement, and Kate all piled into one of the vans and disappeared without even waving good-bye.

To Martha Q's surprise, she was left in charge of the funeral home. She felt like she hadn't been invited to the party. No one needed to go except for Kate, and she'd looked plenty calm enough to drive herself the few blocks. The two guys from the basement didn't need to go, or the secretary. And Autumn probably had snacks in the second baby bag. Everyone was over in the waiting room laughing it up, while Martha Q was alone in a building full of rooms where dead people normally hung out.

After waiting by the phone for fifteen minutes, during which no dead people called needing business, Martha Q locked up the front and let herself out the back door. She'd go to the hospital when all the screaming and blood was over.

She headed home, needing a nap after all the excitement.

When she pulled into her drive at the bed-and-breakfast, Beau Yates sat on the steps to her porch looking like the ghost of a young Johnny Cash in his black clothes and hat.

Martha Q swore. Lobbies in this town got less wear than her front porch. Every time she left, someone seemed to be waiting for her to return. It was downright nerve-racking.

Rolling down her window, she yelled, "Can you drive?"

Beau stood. "Of course."

"Well, get in. I need a cherry lime from Sonic to wash down all the ginger cookies I ate at the funeral home." After everyone left, Martha Q had been nervous about being in charge and munched the firehouse cookies down from three dozen to two.

Beau took off his cowboy hat and climbed into the driver's side like he was saddling up for a wild ride while she tried to slide across the bench seat. All her body parts didn't seem to follow willingly. Once on the passenger side, she had to take a few moments to regroup her layers of fat.

Beau put the car in reverse and pulled out of the drive. "You should get you a new car, Mrs. Q. This one rattles worse than Leon's old ice cream truck."

She ignored his insult. "My name is not Mrs. Q and you know it. I swear it's hard to believe you're the brighter of that nest of bums living in my duplex. If I didn't happen to talk to Border now and then, I'd find it impossible to believe.

His bulb's not only dim, someone forgot to flip the switch on. I have a feeling his reading list consists of only his tattoos."

Beau smiled. "Having a good day, are you, Mrs. Q?"

She glared at him. "No, I'm not." She glanced up and noticed Dallas Logan, Ronny's mother, coming out of the bank. "Run that woman over, would you, Beau? It'll cheer me up."

Beau gunned the engine. "All right, if you say so."

Dallas Logan saw him coming, squealed like a pig before jumping to the curb, and then started yelling like she'd been robbed, raped, and run over all at the same time.

"You nitwit," Martha Q swore. "You missed her by a mile. Turn around and try again."

Beau looked at her as if he thought she might have finally lost her mind. "Come on, Mrs. Q, you can't be serious. Who was that woman anyway?"

"That was Ronny's mother."

"Oh, why didn't you say so?" He turned the car around in the middle of Main Street.

By the time they got back to the spot, Dallas Logan was gone. Martha Q laughed so hard she cried, and Beau seemed to catch the disease from her.

As soon as she could draw a breath, she yelled, "Damn if that wasn't the most fun I've ever had with my clothes on. It was worth risking prison to see her mouth open so wide her whole face turned into wrinkles."

"You're not thinking of taking your clothes off, are you?" Beau paled.

"No, I think you'll have to settle for a float at Sonic. I'm not putting on any show. Those days are over."

When he looked relieved, she thought of hitting him, but since he was the one driving that might not be a good idea.

They sat at the drive-in and had their drinks with Tater Tots and mustard. Then she asked him to drive her out to the cemetery so she could see where Marty was going to be buried.

The drive cheered her up. Martha Q liked the Harmony Cemetery. The very air seemed peaceful and most of her enemies rested there below ground.

Beau held her arm as they walked through the grass to the empty grave along the north side where tall cedars grew. Tyler Wright and his crew had everything ready. The fake grass over the mound of dirt. The folding chairs beneath a flapping green tent. The empty racks for flowers.

She sat in one of the chairs while Beau stared into the hole and frowned like he thought he might see right into hell.

Martha Q guessed Beau was lost in a song that played in his head. Much as she teased him, she knew talent dripped off him like sweat. She wanted to tell him to go for the dream he always talked about. Don't let anything stop him. Don't back down. Don't make promises or fall in love or be dishonest even with himself. Head straight for his dream and don't let any roadblock get in his way.

Only, maybe it was the things that got in the way that mattered. Maybe it was the turns in life that made it worth the living, not the goals or the dreams.

She pulled a tissue from her pocket and blew her nose. She was getting way too deep. Maybe it was this creative energy running through her. If she'd given up sex ten years earlier, she could have had the energy to outrun Nora Roberts on the charts. She would have a limo driving her around, not some kid who couldn't remember her name. She'd have so many servants she'd have to call them by number because, after all, a great writer couldn't be expected to remember real people's names.

"You ready to go?" Beau broke into her daydream.

"Sure. I'll be renting space in this place soon enough."

They walked back to the car.

"Why were you waiting on my porch? Mrs. Biggs finally wise up to you guys and lock you out of her kitchen?"

"No, I came to see you." He opened her car

door. "I need to ask you what you think I should do."

Martha Q wiggled into her seat. "So many people want advice from me lately, I'm thinking of moving to a mountaintop and becoming a sage. If it wasn't for having to wear robes and put up with eagles flying low, I'd probably be gone tomorrow."

Beau slid behind the wheel. "Can we make this about someone else besides you for a moment, Mrs. Q?"

"Of course." She thought of pouting, but at some point her round, plump face started to look pumpkin-fat when she even thought about twisting her lips together.

Beau turned so he could face her when he said, "I think whoever reached for Ronny last night wasn't going after her, but he might have been wanting to talk to me."

"What?" She was sure her eyebrows went so far up they moved into her hairline. "How in the world did you come up with that? Even people who hate country music don't want to grab the singer."

"No. Hear me out. We live in the same place, just different sides. Ronny's tall, almost exactly my height. We both wear black coats. In fact, we got them mixed up the other night when Border and I took her out after we played."

"Okay, black coats. Same height. It's not exactly a *CSI* plot."

"We both walk at night in the shadows. She does it even more, I think, since Marty came back. Last night, when she was walking, it was about the time I usually take my break. I sometimes walk for a few minutes just to enjoy the clear air and the silence from the bar."

"You both walk. Not much to make me believe your theory, Beau."

"All right, how about this? Can you think of one reason anyone would want to hurt Ronny Logan?"

"No, I can't."

"Well, Harley, the guy who owns the bar I play in, said he saw two beefy types hanging out behind Buffalo's Bar late one night last week. He said they were staring at my old car. He tried to talk to them and they claimed they just needed to talk to me. When he started to ask more questions, they disappeared."

"Maybe they wanted your autograph?"

Beau tried again. "Not likely. Harley said they were sober. If they were fans, wouldn't they have been inside listening?"

Martha Q studied him. "Be honest with me. Are you seeing some woman? Maybe another man's wife or a rich rancher's only daughter? These guys could have just wanted to tell you to get lost."

Beau shrugged. "Yeah, I kind of am seeing someone, but nobody knows about it."

"If what you're saying is true, then I think there is a good chance someone does know about it. They might not want you seeing whoever you're seeing. Maybe the rich daddy hates the thought of long-haired grandsons, or the husband just hates. You might ask this secret lady if she's married and her husband wants you beat to a pulp. It's been my experience that affairs usually stop about the time the couple starts to talk."

Beau nodded. "So you're agreeing with me that maybe these guys did want to talk to me, and I'm thinking they got Ronny last night instead."

"Maybe. Anyone else you know who might be waiting in the dark to have a talk with you?"

"My dad. He tells everyone I've gone over to the dark side. I've heard his sermons usually have me in them somewhere as the bad example."

Martha Q's head was starting to pound from too much figuring. She didn't even like mystery shows. She was always worn out by the time they solved the murder. Sometimes she'd flip channels during the commercials and miss the show's ending. Then she'd stay up half the night wondering who did it.

"We'd better get home, Beau. You probably need to practice, and I need a nap. We'll worry about this tomorrow. Problems never seem so bad when they're warmed over."

# Chapter 31

April 12

At half past midnight the fifth generation of Wrights in Harmony came into the world. He weighed six pounds, fourteen ounces, and his daddy, Tyler Wright, thought he was the most beautiful baby ever to be born.

McAllens, Mathesons, and one Truman filled the waiting room. The three families who'd built Harmony stood ready to welcome Jonathan Henry Wright to town, just as they'd welcomed his great-grandfather almost a hundred and fifty years ago.

Tyler walked through the double doors of the delivery room with little Henry in his arms, knowing that they all wished the first Wright born in forty-six years well. He also hoped that "Hank" would grow up to watch over the people just as he had, and his father, and his father, and his father.

"My Kate says if you want to hold the baby, you got to wash your hands and put on a mask first."

Noah McAllen shouted, "The kid'll think he's

been born into a band of outlaws. Come on, Mr. Wright, we just want to look at the little fellow."

A few others grumbled.

"That's Kate's orders. She says when he cries I'm to bring him right back, so some of you better get to scrubbing." Tyler looked down at the bundle. "Now, son, try to remember everyone's name when I introduce you. You'll be needing to know."

He passed the baby over to Adam McAllen, the oldest of the McAllen family. The tall, lean cattleman had silver in his hair but was smiling wide. They'd brought a saddle to the hospital for little Henry Wright.

The Matheson women made a quilt for the baby, and the sheriff and her husband gave him his first spurs. Tyler lost track of all the trucks and baby clothes. It didn't matter. He was thankful for the friends more than the gifts.

Reagan Truman hauled a five-foot apple tree right into the hospital foyer for her gift. She said by the time he could climb, the tree would be ready for him.

Tyler was glad a few minutes later when Hank let out a yell and the doc said visiting hours were over. He wanted to take the baby back to his Kate.

All the people in the waiting room waved the newborn good-bye, as if he'd notice. Tyler fought back tears of joy.

If a man's heart could burst with love, he knew his might. He'd never considered himself good-looking, or smart, or talented in any way, but he always tried to be kind. Maybe that was the secret, because he could ask for no more in life than what he had.

In the morning, a little after dawn, there would be a funeral for Marty Winslow. Tyler would leave Kate and go by the home to change clothes, and then he'd do his job as he had all his adult life. But his family would never be out of his thoughts. From now on, no matter how sad the day, he'd be heading home smiling. Kate would be waiting, and they planned to spend their days watching Jonathan Henry grow.

Maybe that was how his great-grandfather had felt when he'd nailed a hand-painted sign on the fence by the road after his crops failed. The sign said simply: WILL UNDERTAKE ANY HONEST WORK. The first Henry Wright hadn't set out to become an undertaker; he'd just wanted to feed his family, and he'd found a way to help the entire community.

"Tyler," Kate whispered as she held the baby close against her. "Now, we begin."

"Yes, my Kate, now we begin."

# Chapter 32

April 12
Harmony Cemetery

Cord stood stone still as he watched the hearse winding slowly up the hill. He couldn't remember attending a funeral before he went to prison, and he hadn't been able to attend either of his parents' burials. This was his first time.

He'd expected only a few people, but there were at least forty. Most folks didn't know Marty, but they knew Ronny and they'd stand beside her this day.

The long black funeral car stopped in the middle of the road and Tyler Wright climbed out. He opened the back and six men slowly pulled out a plain wooden casket. Three tall businessmen in their early forties on one side and the Biggs brothers on the other, with Beau Yates sandwiched between them.

As they moved up the hill the last few feet, Cord felt Nevada's hand slip into his. He wondered if she had any idea how much he wanted to run. He was twenty-eight and staring eye to eye at death for the first time. When he'd been told his mom and then his dad had died, he hadn't reacted at all. He'd been too hard by then to care. Nothing changed. The next day was the same hell as the day before. So Cord guessed their deaths didn't seem real. Nothing did back then. He'd shut down, turned off all emotion. After a few months in prison, a light went out that he thought would never turn back on.

Only it had. One thing had happened that made him care if he lived or died. Cord felt like he was standing in death's garden coming alive again cell by cell.

He tried to remember the exact moment it happened. Not when he got out of prison. Not when he went back home. Cord McDowell had come alive the day that Nevada had driven up on his land and asked him to marry her. He couldn't name the exact moment his heart started beating again, but it was around the time he realized he was going to take her offer no matter what the conditions.

Before that day he should have been taking his pulse every morning just to make sure he was among the living.

Nevada tugged on his hand and they began to follow the others toward the grave. Ronny sat in the front row with Mr. Carleon on one side and Martha Q on the other. Cord had no problem telling which were Marty's family and friends and which were there for Ronny.

City folks and country folks, he thought. Someone had said that Marty's brother had been in London and told them to go ahead with the funeral without him. There were a few fashion statements there who looked bored and antsy to leave. They must have been his cousins from Oklahoma City. Ronny's friends looked truly sad as they huddled near her; most had their work clothes on because as soon as the funeral was over they'd head back to work.

Beau opened his guitar case and pulled out an old Gibson. He began to play. For a while the music filled the dawn air like a scented breeze, and then his low words blended with the notes. He sang a song about the "never weres" in life, the things we never do, the words we never say, and how we pile them up over the years we walk this earth so we'll have something new to do in heaven. When he finished, everyone had tears in their eyes. There didn't seem a need for any eulogy, any prayer. Beau's song had done it all.

Cord didn't hear most of the rest of the service. He was too wrapped in his own thoughts. The bad thing about coming alive after ten years was that now he thought about dying. He'd never been afraid of dying. First he'd been too young, and then in prison he hadn't cared. He'd seen more than one inmate carried out on a stretcher with a blanket over him, and all he'd thought was that the guy was free.

When everyone stood and began hugging, Cord pulled Nevada to him so hard she whispered, "Let me breathe, Cord."

He loosened his grip and kissed the top of her head. "Sorry. I thought this was the hugging time."

Last night had been the first time they hadn't made love in a week, and somehow the night had been sweeter. She'd fretted over his snakebite and been worried about her horses. He was sad because of Marty and frustrated that Cameron hadn't reported in. So they crawled into bed and just held each other.

She'd whispered about how she wanted to change the locks on the barn and what time she needed to get to work and a hundred other things Cord didn't really care about, but he loved listening to her whispering in the darkness. It was almost like she was singing him a good-night song.

He also liked the way he could put his hand on her and she didn't pull away. Sometimes, while she talked, she would reach up and move his hand from one place to another as she wiggled into just the right spot beside him. He didn't care; touching any part of her felt just as good. He'd never be able to tell her how much her sleeping next to him meant to him.

Hoping to clear his mind, Cord tried to focus on where they were, but it was impossible. Nevada was branded into his thoughts and heart too deep.

When people began to head back to their cars, Cord walked her to her car and asked if she wouldn't mind waiting while he told Ronny to call if she needed anything. He had no idea what was proper to say, but he needed to talk to her.

To Cord's surprise, Nevada pulled a card from her purse and handed it to him. "Tell her the same goes for me. I'm in town. If she needs me I could run over to her place."

Cord winked at his wife. Maybe he wasn't the only one coming alive.

As he glanced down the line of cars parked in single file all the way to the gate, he noticed a round little woman storming the hill like an invader.

Looking back, he saw Ronny curling down in the grass beside the grave. Crying. Beau knelt beside her, trying to offer comfort, and the three friends of Marty's stood behind the grave looking sad and helpless.

Border Biggs and his older brother were headed toward Cord, but most others who attended the funeral were pulling away in their cars.

"We got to stop that woman." Border's words were low, deadly serious as he reached Cord.

"That's Ronny's mother, and she's here to cause trouble."

Cord noticed a few other people trying to delay the woman's climb, but she didn't stop to talk with them. She kept coming. He stood his ground, not sure what was going on, but if they were somehow protecting Ronny, he'd join the brigade.

"Get out of my way," the woman shouted as she reached the path leading up to the grave. "I got to get to my daughter. She's making a fool of herself lying in the grass."

Cord moved, blocking the woman. "I don't think anyone needs to bother her, Mrs. Logan. Maybe later when she's rested."

Border's brother brushed Cord's shoulder on one side; Mr. Carleon was on the other.

"If Ronny wants to mourn beside his grave all day, I'd say she has that right. You'll not disturb her." Cord wouldn't touch the woman, but he wouldn't move out of her way either. He doubted she'd climb the uneven grass just off the path, even in her practical two-inch heels.

Dallas Logan took a step back and looked like she planned to fight. She obviously was a woman used to bullying her way through life.

Cord had no idea what he'd do if the old woman stormed the line. Marty's three friends in suits joined behind him, looking like they felt sorry for Mrs. Logan, but still they couldn't let her hurt Ronny. Others backtracked from their cars as if hearing a call to arms. The postmaster, two mailmen, a waitress from the diner, two men who wore fire department shirts, a sheriff's deputy in a suit too small for him. An army of friends stood between Dallas and the grave.

A standoff. Dallas just glared at them.

To Cord's surprise, the undertaker walked around them all and reached Dallas Logan.

"I'm so very sorry you were late for the service, Mrs. Logan," Tyler said, as if he'd just noticed Dallas in the crowd. "I know you wanted to be with your daughter in her time of sorrow. It was a beautiful service and a fine morning to walk into heaven, I think."

Dallas looked shocked as Tyler took her elbow with one hand and wrapped his free arm around her shoulder. "Why don't you ride along with me? I'd hate to think of you walking all that way back down to your car. If you took a fall, I'd never forgive myself." He started moving, leaving her no choice but to follow. "These old roads can be slippery in the morning dew. I've got a thermos of hot coffee in my Cadillac. It'll warm you up and give you time to think about what you need to say to Ronny to help her get through this hard time."

When the dragon lady halted, he continued, "I remember when your dear husband died. It was such a nice service and all those yellow roses the postmen sent from all over the state made the chapel look so grand. He was much loved, I could tell that right away."

Dallas broke into sniffles and Tyler patted her.

Everyone watched in amazement as the chubby little funeral director guided her off without stopping his account of the funeral long enough for her to get in a word.

"Man," Border whispered, "that Mr. Wright is my hero. Did you see how he walked right into the mess that I don't think most bomb squads would have tackled?"

"It's his job," added someone from behind Cord.

"No," another said, "he's truly gifted."

Cord broke from the others and climbed back up to where Ronny lay in the grass. He could hear her sobs even as she tried to keep them inside. The sound hurt his heart to listen.

"She won't get up," Beau whispered. "She says she wants to stay here with him."

Border and Big Biggs joined them as all others moved away, maybe because they couldn't bear to see her pain or maybe because they didn't know what to do. Marty's three friends seemed to be finding their purpose in shuffling Winslow relatives back in their rented cars.

Cord knelt down and put his hand on her back. "Come on, Ronny. Marty would have wanted you to lean on your friends. Maybe that's one of the reasons he came home, knowing he was dying.

He wanted to be with you and he didn't want you to be alone when his time was up."

She didn't seem to hear him.

Cord didn't know her well, but he couldn't stand to see her so shattered. He tried to think about what a friend should do, wishing he'd had a little more practice in being one.

He waited as the cemetery cleared of all cars except for a few. "Ronny, it's time to go. Marty's not there, he's gone to another world."

She looked up. "There is no perfect world, you know."

"I know."

Without a word, he lifted her off the ground. She came to him like a child, too broken to protest.

With the Biggs brothers on either side, Cord walked toward the cars still parked along the road. He turned away from the black funeral car with Ronny's mother inside talking to Tyler.

"I'll take her home," Big volunteered. "Put her in my truck." He pointed to the nearest pickup.

A tall young woman waited by the old white truck. She opened the door to the passenger side as Cord walked closer.

He lifted Ronny inside. The woman crawled in beside her and wrapped Ronny in a blanket. Big climbed in the other side while Border swung into the bed of the truck.

Big slowly drove away.

"Don't worry, mister," Beau said when he neared. "We'll take care of her. Big's girl said she'd stay with her tonight after Mr. Carleon leaves if she needs someone to."

Cord smiled. "She's lucky to be surrounded by friends."

"We're just strays nobody wants, but when we get together we make a pretty good family." Beau waved and headed to his old car.

Cord walked back to Nevada, thinking he fit in that category too, or he would in a few months when the marriage was over. He had no one, and Nevada only had her brother Barrett, who she said called once last year just to tell her he was never coming back. He'd cleaned out all the accounts, sold the ranch to her for all she could raise, and vanished, saying he never wanted a sister anyway.

"Let's go home," Cord said to her as he slipped into the passenger seat of her car, very much aware that her place wasn't really his home.

How would it be to look across his fields and see Nevada's land after he'd moved back to the farm? She'd made it plain that she'd only wanted him and his name until the first frost. By then the crops would be in, the cattle sold for a good profit.

Then, like she had after every marriage ended, she'd go back to being Nevada Britain. She'd be back in her world and he'd be back in his. Suddenly the money he would walk away with didn't seem nearly as important as the fact that he'd have to sleep alone again. The clear difference from before would be that he'd miss her every night for the rest of his life.

How could he tell her that he didn't want this marriage to end? She'd think he was just playing her like the three husbands before. He couldn't break the bargain they'd agreed on. He'd have to live each day as they'd agreed until the day he walked away.

That day, he'd be just as dead as Marty Winslow was now. They might as well put him in the ground.

"You going into town to your office?" Cord had to concentrate on what had to be done. He forced his entire body to harden because if he didn't, he'd fall apart. "I've got work in the south pasture. I told the men to start on it after breakfast and I'd be out as soon as I could. I'd like to have the fence ready to hold about a hundred head by next week. Sooner we get the cattle on the land, the fatter they'll be for winter."

"I don't want to go in," she whispered, almost like a child begging. "Take me flying, Cord, please. If you can spare the time?"

"Of course." He lifted his arm and stretched it behind her shoulders. "I'll be happy to. Maybe it will do us good to get away for an hour. I'll take you up where the air is pure. I need to clear my head."

Neither said a word as she drove to his place.

He was surprised how clean the yard looked on his parents' old farm. The road crew must have carried away some of the weeds and trash that had blown up with the last storm. The house almost looked lived in and not abandoned. Someone had even replaced the missing boards on the porch steps. The place had been his only home growing up, and he'd fought like hell the past three years to hang on to the farm, but nothing about the house drew him. No sense of coming home. No longing to be there. It was just a place where two quiet people lived with a son who never asked for much, even love.

Nevada parked beneath the old oak halfway between the house and the barn.

They pulled out his grandfather's old plane and flew, crossing back and forth over their land. Now and then she'd tap him on the shoulder and point to something below she wanted him to see. The crops coming up, the cattle, her horses.

When they flew along the back of Britain property where the land was rocky and uneven, Cord noticed black spots in places, like shadows of clouds. Only the sky was clear. When he flew lower, he could tell the grass had burned. Maybe fires set by lightning and put out by the rain. Maybe not. Nevada didn't comment on the charred spots, so Cord didn't say anything, but he made a mental note to drive out as soon as the earth dried enough to cross open field.

His mind and body slowly relaxed as childhood memories of flying with his granddad drifted back. He'd let Cord fly the plane when he turned twelve and by sixteen he'd had his license. The old man moved into a home the next year, his body crippling with arthritis, his mind dulling.

Cord felt his grandfather's loss. School, the farm, even his horse didn't really matter once the old guy left. A few times Cord tried going to the nursing home to talk, but his grandfather was too drugged up. Each time less of the man he'd loved was there and only a shell remained.

Cord began to run with a wild crowd looking for excitement, looking to feel alive. He wasn't old enough to understand why, but he knew he had to run fast because he'd seen what was coming at the end. One day his grandfather could fly and it seemed the next he couldn't even feed himself.

Part of Cord was glad his grandfather didn't know where he'd been headed that last summer. Gramps wouldn't have been proud of him, and it would have torn Cord up to know he'd discovered his only grandson had gone to prison. Cord's parents hadn't even written to tell Cord of the old man's death. Cord had read the Harmony paper's obituary to learn the truth.

He'd written asking his father to save the plane for him.

His father had sent a note saying simply, "Will do."

They'd never talked about it again, but the plane was waiting in the barn when Cord came home, the only thing that welcomed him. Flying now was like drifting through time, weightless among memories of the past.

When they finally touched down, he helped Nevada from the plane and couldn't resist pulling her against him. He needed to hold on to someone, to her, to one spark of happiness in life while it still burned.

"You feel so good, Babe," he whispered as he smelled the wind in her wild hair.

When he kissed her, it occurred to him that this was one less day they'd spend together.

The kiss deepened, not out of passion, or need, but just with the pure pleasure of knowing that she welcomed his touch. He knew she'd had many other lovers, but it didn't matter; right now she was his.

When he finally lowered her feet to the ground, she smiled as if she understood how he felt. "Thanks for taking me away. It was nice."

"You're welcome. Anytime." He took her hand and they headed toward the car.

A picnic basket sat on the farmhouse porch when they walked close. He wanted to keep her beneath his arm even though the day was more cool than cold, but Nevada laughed when she spotted the red basket and ran to open it like it was the first gift Christmas morning.

"Ora Mae must be getting used to the idea that she might need to find us now and then to feed us." He watched Nevada pulling out food wrapped in plastic. "I feel like I'm a free-range diner around this place."

"She probably didn't notice we were back, since she's always in the house, but I'll bet Galem did. He's the one who guessed where to leave the basket." Nevada grinned. "I'm starving. Want to eat inside or out here?"

Cord didn't care. He wasn't ready to go back to the world just yet. Work, his and hers, could wait an hour. He liked having her all to himself. "It's dusty in there."

"Not on the bed," she said, smiling as if she knew a secret.

He picked up the basket and followed her in and up the stairs to his old room. He moved through the shadows, watching her drop clothes as she rushed toward his bedroom. Her jacket, her shoes, her blouse. He barely noticed that someone had cleaned his room, adding fresh linens and a colorful bedspread.

"You been in here?" he managed to say as she unsnapped her skirt.

"I wanted to surprise you," she said, stripping down to her bra and panties. "I thought we might want to use your place as our getaway cabin. Since we spent the afternoon here the other day I think of it as special, like an enchanted cottage where we are just ourselves and the world can't interfere."

He knew how she felt. The ranch house of hers seemed heavy with unhappy memories and stale like old velvet flowers in a winter window box.

She pulled the covers back and climbed in, standing on her knees to tell him, "I want to paint this room blue and maybe take out that wall so the upstairs area is one huge bedroom. Since college I've never had the opportunity to redecorate more than my study, but I didn't figure you'd mind if I had some fun with your place. It's a wonderful old house that's got great bones."

"I don't care what you do around here. Knock yourself out." He thought of his closet full of clothes he'd never have time to wear and figured he was releasing a monster. But she was a cute monster, especially in pale blue underwear with lace that almost wasn't there.

"I've been thinking this place could be great with a few coats of paint and a dozen carpenters hammering away. We could knock out part of the roof and you'd have skylights over your bed. Then I'd start on the kitchen. Really could use some—"

"Hush, Babe. Talking time is over." He pulled her to him as he popped the last button on his shirt. He needed them skin on skin. "We'll talk while we eat, and we'll eat later." The sight of her body was driving him crazy.

Nevada giggled. "I thought you'd never take the hint."

Hours later, Cord lay back watching moonlight drift through the cloudy sky. Nevada was curled against him fast asleep, wearing one of his old T-shirts they'd found in his drawer. They'd made a slow kind of love that drifted like a song, beautiful. Then they'd taken a shower together in the tiny bathroom off his room and eaten everything in the red basket as if they were starving. Still on the bed, huddled in blankets, they talked about everything and nothing.

All afternoon they touched, unable to get enough of each other. Maybe it was the fact that they'd been to the funeral, or maybe he was growing on her the way she was on him. Neither talked of love or forever. They wanted the now to stretch as long as it could.

Like a windup toy, she fell asleep in mid-sentence, not even noticing that he was still touching her, moving his hand beneath the covers and over her body.

"I can't give you up," he whispered as he kissed her hair.

He saw right through her tough-girl attitude and her temper tantrums. He saw the beauty of her, inside and out. The only problem was he couldn't seem to figure out why she'd picked him. Right now *he* was the one thing in her world that didn't make sense. She could have hired a foreman and bodyguards if she thought she needed them. Hell, she probably could have found a better lover than him.

He grinned suddenly, remembering how she couldn't have had any complaints today. She'd dropped back on her pillows after they'd made love and demanded, "Just kill me now because it'll never be any better than that."

He'd laughed and promised to work on making her statement a lie.

Once she'd asked him if he'd forgive her anything, and he hadn't known what to say. Now he knew he would. No matter how wild she'd been. No matter what she'd said or done. He'd forgive her. She didn't even need to bother to ask. The lives they'd lived before didn't matter, not when they were together like this.

Cord watched her sleep, wishing he could wake her and relive the afternoon. But the cell phone in his pocket buzzed before he could carry out his plan.

Rolling from the bed as carefully as he could, he pulled on his jeans and moved to the hallway.

"Hello," he whispered.

"Cord," a gravelly voice said. "I got some information."

"What is it?" Cord moved down the stairs, wondering what Cameron had managed to find as he followed Bryce Galloway. Whatever the news, Cord knew it wouldn't be good. Nothing about the guy was.

"I'll show you if you can meet me at the theater after midnight. Come alone to the back door. I don't want anyone to even know I know you."

"I'll be there," Cord answered, and hung up knowing that his time in paradise was over.

He carried his sleeping wife home. He stayed in bed with her for more than an hour to make sure she was sound asleep, then finished dressing in the bathroom off the kitchen without waking Nevada. He had to handle this alone, and he knew he'd touch her if he went back in the bedroom they shared.

Cameron's information might change everything. If Bryce Galloway was hurting Nevada, Cord wasn't sure he could hold his rage.

# Chapter 33

April 13

Beau woke Friday morning to the smell of rain and the constant beat of thunder rumbling in the background like a low drumroll.

"Beau?" Border yelled from the other bedroom. "Is it raining in your room?"

Beau sat up in bed and felt drops drip on his head and shoulders. "Yeah," he said, knowing that Border could hear him through the thin walls. Indoor rain was one of the thousand complaints he had about this place.

Border showed up with their only two good pots. "I already used all the bowls for my room."

They moved the bed and began to catch water in every container they could find. By eight the place had a tinkling sound like the opening to a children's ballet. Beau covered the equipment with tarps, dressed in sweats, and talked Border into running across the creek to Martha Q's place. It might be muddy, but Beau reasoned that it was half as far as using the road, so they'd only get half as wet.

Martha Q looked at them like they were two homeless wet dogs at her back door, but she let them in. "Take off your shoes and just drip there till I get some towels."

"Thanks," Border said, then took a deep breath as if he could smell a few hundred calories of breakfast cooking.

"I've been meaning to get that roof fixed, but I don't think of it till it rains." Martha Q looked like she'd been out partying all night. Her lipstick had slid off one side of her mouth, and one fake

351

eyelash was missing. Surprisingly, she had the nerve to look at them as if they were the ones who looked strange.

"If you boys will clean up and dry off I'll let you eat with my guest. Mrs. Biggs can add a little water to the gravy and we'll have plenty. We always have hot biscuits on Friday."

After she left to go put her face on, Border whispered, "She's just feeling guilty because she doesn't fix our roof. If we never, ever mention it, maybe she'll forget again and we can guilt her out of a few more breakfasts."

Beau accepted a towel from Border's grandmother and tried to dry off without taking his clothes off. "I hope she never marries again. If she does, and forgets to take her makeup off again, her husband will wake up and think he's on a *Night of the Zombies* rerun."

Mrs. Biggs tried not to smile at the comment. "I've got a couple of old raincoats that workmen left here a year ago when crews came in to build a fast-food place over by the mall. You boys can wear them home. They'll cover you from head to toe."

"Thanks, Granny." Border kissed her cheek.

Beau did the same even though he found it hard to believe that such a sweet lady could be related to the Biggs boys. Must have been grandbabies switched at birth.

She waved them both away. "Go sit down in the

dining room, but no eating until all the guests have filled their plates. If we run out, it should be you two who have to wait until I can scramble more."

Beau moved into the formal little dining room with one wall of windows facing east. Normally the place was sunny this time of day, but this morning it was gray with water tapping against the glass.

One man sat drinking coffee at the end of the table. Dressed in a white shirt and plum-colored sweater, he looked out of place among the mismatched table and chairs Martha Q must have found at a secondhand store.

"Morning," Beau offered. "Nice day." The guy was in his thirties. He stared at Beau with a bored expression that must have taken years to practice.

"Morning," he finally said. "Don't tell me you're other guests. I thought the place was packed."

Beau poured himself a cup of coffee and sat down as far from the man as possible. "No. I was just invited to breakfast. Heard it's biscuits and gravy. I love the way Mrs. Biggs puts those big hunks of sausage in her gravy."

The man sighed as if talking to call waiting. "I don't eat flour, or milk products, or pig."

"I'm sure the chickens are sorry to hear that."

The stranger just stared at him. "I don't eat any meat products." He had that why-am-I-telling-this-idiot-anything look about him.

Border backed his way into the room with cookies in both hands.

While he set his appetizer on the tablecloth, Beau thought he'd try the introductions. "Border, this is one of the guests. He's a vegetarian."

Border smiled. "That's great. My grandmother is a Presbyterian."

Beau grinned. Border had figured out people often took one look at his tattoos and assumed he was dumb. He played it up to the hilt.

Border smiled at the guy. "I'm Border Biggs, mister. I was just pulling your leg."

"Bryce Galloway," the man said, without offering a hand. "I've heard about you two. You play in a band over at Buffalo's Bar."

"That's right," Beau said. "You should come hear us some night."

Bryce lifted his cup. "I might drop by tonight. It's been a long time since I've heard that country twang."

There was no more time to talk. The three widows, staying at the place, hurried in. They'd all met Beau and Border, so they made a fuss over them like they were company and ignored the strange man at the end of the table. When all were seated, Beau didn't miss the fact that the seats on either side of Bryce Galloway remained empty.

Joni, the chatty one of the three, chimed in as if she'd raised her hand and it was her time to talk. "Are you gentlemen aware you all have names starting with *B?* Border even has two. Would one of you consider changing?"

All three men said no at the same time, and the room went back into silence as if a sign had dropped down demanding it.

Martha Q came in as they were finishing up and said she'd drive the boys back to their place because she planned to take breakfast to Mr. Carleon and Ronny. He'd gone over early to help with the moving of all the medical machines remaining in the duplex.

Beau was glad for the ride and happy to be out of the same room with Galloway. Something about the man bothered him. All his appearance was polished, but Beau had to fight the urge to check and make sure his wallet was still in his pocket when he walked away from the man.

As the day aged, he couldn't get Bryce Galloway out of his mind. He didn't feel like practicing, so he slept and read one of the books Marty had lent him.

Ronny invited them over to eat some of the food that folks had dropped off. She looked heartbroken, but at least she'd stopped crying. Beau had heard her most of the night and wished the walls were thicker. It seemed to him that sorrow always passed through thin walls, but joy never did.

When they left for the bar just after dark, it was raining so hard they wrapped the guitars beneath their thick raincoats and ran for Beau's car.

The mood of the day filtered over into the night. Few came in for drinks or food, and those who did seemed more in the mood to talk than dance. Beau missed watching the people who usually tried to dance.

About eleven a girl with a blond ponytail walked in and sat at the last booth closest to the band cage.

"There's your girl," Border whispered.

Beau lifted his head and winked at her, then continued to play.

She watched them for a while. When Beau took a break and walked by her, he whispered, "Hello, Trouble." He had no idea what her real name was, but she'd been driving over and picking him up now and then for months. They never talked, they just drove through the night.

"My top's up on the convertible," she said with a smile, "but you still think you'd want to go for a drive?"

"Sure." Within ten minutes he'd talked Border into taking his car home and convinced Harley that the band should quit early.

When she left, she pointed to the front door, telling him where she'd be waiting.

Border pulled on the oversized slicker his grand-mother had given him that morning. "Go ahead. I'll load up. You parked so close out back I won't get anything wet. I can load everything, drive home, and have most of the food Ronny left us eaten before you can say good-bye to the little lady."

"Save me one slice of the chocolate pie." Beau knew if he didn't pick something, Border would finish off everything. They had no use for a garbage disposal at the apartment.

Border was tangled in the cords when he looked back. Beau ran to the front. He couldn't remember when he'd needed a ride with Trouble more than tonight. Between the funeral and the rain, sunshine seemed a long way away.

# Chapter 34

Cameron waited for Cord at the back door of the old theater like a leftover ghost of movies past. Cord didn't even see the man until his headlights flashed across him. Without bothering with a greeting, they walked through the narrow theater aisles that smelled of stale popcorn and dust. The seats were in poor shape and the floor sticky, just as Cord remembered it from when he was a kid.

The little guy had made living quarters out of three dressing rooms off the stage. Cord saw into one that looked like a small apartment kitchen with a table and a single chair. He walked into another that must serve as the office for the theater. It had a huge old scarred desk that took up half the space and a file cabinet so full the drawers wouldn't close.

"I thought I'd better tell you what I found. You need to see the whole picture here." Cameron jumped up on the desk and smiled, as if delighted to have a guest in his place.

Cord remained standing. He wasn't afraid, but he felt his whole body go on guard as if from some primal instinct. "Go on," Cord said, wanting to get the meeting over with.

"I followed Bryce for two days, learning only that he was scum. Both days he left the B&B after breakfast and wandered around like he had no purpose. Coffee shops, bakeries, bookstores, diners. All he bought in each was coffee, and he didn't even buy that in the used bookstore. The owner of the store talked to him, asking questions. Galloway never gave him a straight answer."

Cameron rubbed the bridge of his nose with his index finger. "That rented Rover wasn't too hard to follow. He'd stop at each place and usually strike up a conversation with whoever was around, like he was building an alibi. Then he'd sit somewhere, the park mostly, and make calls. I couldn't get close enough to hear, but I could tell he was frustrated, and even angry, at whoever was on the other end."

"Have any idea who he was talking to?" Cord asked.

"Nope." Cameron lit a cigarette with nervous hands. "The first day he had these three ladies following him. I was so busy watching them tail him, I lost him for a few hours. Picked him up at the bar out by the truck stop. You know, the one with three *X*s on the roof. He parked in the back, but so does everyone who hangs out in that dump. Of course I followed him in, but I didn't have to worry about him spotting me. It was so dark I could have picked his pocket and he wouldn't have seen me.

"He mostly just drank and flirted with the ugly girls who were over-made-up and underdressed. I saw him go back behind the curtain with a few of them for a private dance. He always came back smiling like a goon, and they came back looking disgusted. I heard one girl say she wouldn't give him anything extra no matter how much he paid."

Cord thought he could guess what was happening. Nevada had mentioned once that her ex liked to hurt her where the bruises wouldn't show.

Cameron continued, enjoying himself. "When he left there, he drove back to town by way of the road running next to your ranch."

"My ranch isn't on the way back from the truck stop."

"I know. I thought that was strange, but it got

stranger. He ate at the diner, making a point to talk loud enough for everyone in the place to notice him. Then he headed over to the show at the mall. After that, he returned to the bed-and-breakfast. The guy seemed to have no purpose, no friends, no life. He's drifting."

"Did he go out later?"

"Nope. I slept so close to his car, he couldn't have started it without waking me up."

"He could have walked," Cord snapped, tired of the rambling.

"He could have, but he didn't seem the type. I thought he was the most boring guy I'd ever followed until this afternoon, when he bought a ticket to the same movie for the third time. I followed him in instead of waiting outside."

Cameron smiled. "I know my way around dark theaters. He never saw me even when I sat three rows behind him. About halfway through the movie, some guy came in the rear door and sat down beside him. For a second I thought it might be you: same tall build, comfortable in his western clothes. They whispered for a few minutes and then left out the back. I followed them across the alley to a little dump of a house behind the mall. I could see them through the dirty window and took a chance moving closer to hear what they said, but it was muffled."

Cord fought not to shake the man to get facts. "What happened next?"

"When the stranger opened the front door, I was so close to them the door almost hit me in the nose. I heard Bryce say something about how the guy's paycheck would never happen because Bryce said he had to do the dirty work himself."

"Did the man answer? Any clue what it was he didn't do?"

Cameron shook his head. "The stranger just swore and walked off cussing."

Cord couldn't help but wonder, since the man was dressed western, if killing a horse was the one thing he wouldn't do. "What happened next?"

"Galloway picked up a book, big like a photo album, and walked out the back door. He went straight across the alley and back into the theater. When I followed five minutes later, I took the time to take the tape off the lock. Nothing bothers me more than people sneaking in without paying."

"What next?"

"Oh, Galloway watched the movie, drove by a takeout place, and went back to the B&B. I hung around until ten, but he never left the place. I thought of driving back to the dump of a house, but I figure it was just where they met to talk. Then I remembered Bryce hadn't taken the album in. It took me a while, but I unlocked the rental car door and found it under the front seat."

Cameron pulled an old photo album out from under papers on his desk. "I thought you should see this. I'll get it back before dawn so Bryce will never know."

Cord slowly opened the book and began to turn the pages. Photo after photo. All of them were grainy, but he had no problem seeing that they were of Nevada. Riding. Swimming. Walking. Smiling on the steps of her home. He couldn't see much detail. They were probably taken with a cell phone and blown up on a computer before being run off on plain paper. In a few she looked younger by a few years and her hair was shorter than it was now.

"Bryce is collecting pictures of my wife?" Cord whispered after a few minutes. The last one in the book was of her standing next to him at Marty's funeral. In the center of the picture, where her arm linked his, someone had cut a hole in the picture.

Cameron frowned. "Someone is obsessed with her. I heard that her ex-husband was in town to try and buy her ranch, but he doesn't want the ranch back, he wants her."

"But why would he be causing trouble around the ranch?"

"Maybe he thinks she'll turn to him?" Cameron shrugged. "If the ranch fails, are your pockets deep enough to bail her out?"

"I don't even have pockets." Again the reason she'd married him drifted across his thoughts. She'd said she was low on money and needed a good season or she might lose the ranch. Cord had a feeling that if she'd gone to Bryce, she would have given up far more than the land.

Bryce Galloway wanted her back, and he seemed willing to do whatever it took to get her.

"My only question to you is, which one of these guys do you want me to follow tomorrow?"

"Bryce. The other must be just working for him, and from the sound of it Bryce tried to push him too far." Cord flipped back through the book, noticing there were pictures of Nevada in every spot on the ranch. "But why the pictures? He was married to her. He knows what she looks like."

"Not part of my job, figuring out nutcases, but if I was guessing I'd say Bryce is waiting for her to be in the wrong place at the wrong time. He wants her in his sights. That much is obvious. Maybe he just wants to talk her into leaving you and going with him. He strikes me as the type who's always gotten whatever he wants, when he wants it, and you are pushing him, making him go to extremes."

"Maybe he'll get tired and quit?"

Cameron shook his head. "He's like an addict and your wife is his drug. Maybe she's the only one who ever said no to him. Maybe he thinks she belongs to him. I've been around a lot of druggies in my life. If he thinks he has to have your wife, he's not stopping."

Cord nodded and moved to the door.

"One other thing," Cameron added. "I found a couple of high-powered rifles hidden in the trunk of Bryce's car. They were new, looked like they'd never even been tested."

"Lots of men in this part of the country hunt," Cord said, without turning around.

"Yeah." Cameron's answer wasn't reassuring.

Cord walked out of the old downtown theater with more questions than answers. He drove around for a while after he left Cameron. He even stopped in front of the house Cameron had described behind the mall. It was easy to guess which one it was. Just an abandoned house with an old dirt bike parked among the trash near a crumbling carport, a perfect meeting place. No one passing. Not any occupied houses close enough to see a light.

An hour later when Cord slipped back into bed, Nevada rolled in his direction. He held her to him until dawn, knowing that trouble was riding full out toward them and he couldn't do anything to stop it. He didn't have enough proof to go to the sheriff, and Cord knew without asking that Nevada wouldn't run for cover.

But what Bryce didn't know was that he'd have to go through Cord to get to her.

At dawn, while she dressed, Cord kept his voice casual. "What are your plans today?"

She wiggled into her jeans. "I'm staying around the house this morning."

He wondered if she was trying to act normal, the same way he was. "I've got to go check a few things. If you'll wait here, I'll go into the vet's with you in an hour."

"Make it two or three hours. I want to start a painting of Starlight for my study. Then we can go check on her and have lunch in town. I'm starting to like the daily special at the diner."

She moved into his arms, laughing as she kissed him lightly. "I'm getting used to a lot of things lately."

He tightened his arms around her, wanting to keep the conversation easy but unable to hide how much he needed her close. Part of him could almost understand Bryce being obsessed with her. The woman was addictive. He wasn't sure that leaving her wouldn't break him as well. Only, unlike Bryce, if she said good-bye to him, Cord would walk away. He didn't want to own her or control her; he only wanted to love her.

"I'll be back before noon," he whispered against her hair. "Wait here for me."

"You'd better be back." She pulled away so she could smile at him. "I'm already starving."

He could tell by the look in her beautiful blue eyes that her starvation had nothing to do with the special at the diner. He grabbed his hat to stop himself from undressing her. "Bye, Babe."

He ran from the house, not in a hurry to be away, but in a hurry to be back.

Cord drove out to where he'd seen the dark spots on the earth when they'd flown over. The sun had dried the ground, but he knew he was still leaving tracks an inch deep. Whenever he crossed open land he hated the way his truck tires scarred the earth, even temporarily. The only good thing seemed to be that the land always went back to nature.

Cord spotted burn spots in what had been tall natural grasses. Too many circles of blackened grass for it to have been lightning strikes.

When he walked the burned area, he found a charred pack of matches, as though someone had struck them all aflame and dropped the pack. The grass must have caught fire and burned across the rocky uneven ground, and then stopped suddenly. The only reason he could think of was that rain had put the fires out.

As Cord drove back to town he went over the details. All he knew was that whoever set the fires had done so on a stormy night, hoping the fire would be blamed on the lightning, only they hadn't planned on a rain coming so soon. Cord grew up with prairie fires. On backland like this they could spread for miles before anyone noticed, and by then they'd be so wide a hundred men couldn't stop them from spreading. Someone might have noticed Bryce's rental roaming over the land, but no one would have paid much attention to a man on horseback. Maybe the man Cameron had described as a cowboy had set the fires. He could have parked his truck and trailer on a back road and ridden in from the border of the property.

He drove into Harmony hoping to talk to the sheriff but found Travis Salem in her office instead. The ranger looked the same as he had when he'd investigated the horse poisoning, but Cord no longer found him frightening. For a second when Cord first saw him that day, he stepped back to being seventeen again, but now he remembered who he was. The boy no longer existed.

"McDowell," the ranger yelled when he saw Cord walk past the dispatcher's desk. "Glad you came in."

Cord couldn't think of any person he wanted to see less. But other than being rude, he couldn't turn and leave. "Salem. I thought you'd be back in Fort Worth by now."

"I was just packing up. No leads on your wife's case. I'll let you both know if anything turns up. We did find Joey Mason, the trainer, last night. I was planning to call you before I headed back. The trainer showed up on a flight passenger list at DFW and about panicked when he found out everyone was looking for him."

Cord waited for Salem to get around to the facts.

"Security talked to him but didn't hold him. He said he'd gotten a letter firing him as of last week. It was on Boxed B stationery and included a thousand in cash if he'd go quietly. Joey said he went over, cleaned out his gear, and left. The security officer faxed me the letter if you want to see it."

"Who signed the letter?"

Salem dug in a box and handed him the fax. "You did."

Cord glared at the paper. "Not my—"

"I figured that. I asked to have the original sent, but it's probably been handled so much there won't be any fingerprints on it that can help with the investigation."

"I understand."

"Joey Mason didn't question it. He claimed he never fit in on the ranch and was glad to leave. You said you hadn't gotten around to meeting him."

Cord didn't argue. "I should have. I'd seen him from a distance several times." If he hadn't listened to Nevada's rule, he would have ridden over to her barn and met Joey.

"We never had that cup of coffee," Travis Salem finally said as he folded his glasses and slid them in the case clipped to his vest pocket. "Any chance you got time for it now?"

Cord wanted to say no, but he hoped somehow he could let go of some of the anger that had kept him breathing all the years he'd been locked up.

"I'll be at the Blue Moon Diner as soon as I leave a message for Sheriff Matheson. If you want to talk, I've got time for one cup of coffee."

Salem nodded and returned to boxing up papers.

Cord walked away. He headed straight for the dispatcher and asked if Alex would contact him as soon as she had a few free minutes. No emergency. He wasn't sure what he could tell her. Cameron had stolen the photo album, and the letter to Joey still didn't make enough to arrest Bryce.

Cord drove to the diner and parked out front. When he walked in, the breakfast rush was over, so the place looked deserted except for dirty tables. He took a seat in the first clean booth and ordered a cup of coffee. If the ranger wasn't there before he finished, there would be no next time.

Cord's cup was half empty when Travis Salem entered. Even though he'd put on a stomach the size of a basketball, Salem looked so much smaller than he had that night at the lake. That night he'd had a rifle in one hand and a flashlight in the other. That night Cord had been more kid than man.

"Thanks for waiting," the ranger said as he slid in and motioned to the waitress that he'd have a cup.

Cord was silent. He had nothing he wanted, or needed, to say.

Salem took a few deep breaths. "I've been needing to say something to you for a long time. It took me a while to figure everything out. I was madder than hell at you for years. When I finally got up the nerve to talk, I drove out to the prison and they said you'd been released. After that, I guessed I'd be the last person you wanted to see."

Cord held the coffee cup so tightly he was surprised the mug didn't shatter in his hands.

Salem thanked the waitress for his coffee and waited until she walked away. "I lost ninety percent of the sight in my left eye that night. I thought my life was over. All I'd ever wanted to be was a deputy sheriff, and you ended that dream."

Cord stared at the man, not knowing whether to feel guilty or angry. Did he think he was the only one who lost something that night?

"I sat at home recovering and feeling sorry for myself for months. One day, out of the blue, your parents showed up at my door. I figured they were going to beg me to help get you out early, but all they wanted to do was give me your college fund. Said they'd had an argument with you over going to college, and that was probably why you were drinking that night."

Cord didn't breathe. Memories poured like liquid lead over him. His parents not listening to him, the argument, the feeling that they didn't care what he wanted.

The ranger continued, "I took the money and, more out of anger than want, I decided to go back to school and use every dime of it. Four years of school and two eye surgeries later, I walked out with a master's degree and enough sight in my left eye to pass the test to try out for the Texas Rangers. They saw me as a hero, injured in the line of duty. I got a job I never would have worked my way up to on my own. It's more business and paperwork. Not the fun of being out there fighting crime, but I've settled into it and surprisingly I'm good at it."

"You got a point to this?" Cord asked. "I'm almost finished with my coffee."

"Yeah." Salem stared at his cup, still untouched. "One of the first things I did after becoming a ranger was go back and look at the file we had on you. I listened to the tape of your testimony and heard something I hadn't heard before. You sounded scared. I ran what you said over and over in my mind. I remember walking into the camp of drunks and kids high on who knows what. It was dark and the smell of fireworks reminded me of the army when I was nineteen and deployed straight into hell. That same kind of terror filled my mind that night at the lake. I must have been yelling as I headed toward you."

"What are you saying?"

Salem straightened, and Cord knew no apology would be coming. He didn't expect one. He didn't want one. What good would it do now?

The ranger's voice hardened slightly. "I found a note in the file. Apparently, a teenage girl had come forward, to one of the other deputies, after

I was sent to the hospital and you were arrested. She claimed I came at them with a bright light and in charge mode like I was ready for a fight. No one knew who I was. They didn't even know it was the cops. She said she thought I either stepped on your leg or kicked you, and you came up swinging wildly."

Cord froze. Exactly the story he'd told. The story no one believed.

Salem shrugged. "The deputy who took the statement told her to come by the station the next morning, but she never did. When they checked on her, her father swore she'd never been out of the house that night. Since she was a minor, her statement was dropped."

"Why tell me now?" It was too late to change anything. "I don't care who she was or what she said. She didn't help when it counted."

"Oh, I figured you knew who she was." Salem raised his eyebrow in surprise. "You married her."

Cord didn't remember saying good-bye to the ranger. He sat in the diner for an hour in the dungeon of his thoughts.

When he drove back to the ranch, he went straight to the bunkhouse, gathered up equipment, and headed for the south pasture.

At sundown, he was still working as hard as he could, pounding in fence posts across the uneven ground when Galem found him.

"Putting in a hard day, aren't you, Boss?" the cook shouted, without getting out of his pickup.

"Shouldn't you and Ora Mae be gone to the lake?" Cord stopped long enough to wipe the sweat off his face with a shirt he'd ruined hours ago.

"We decided to stay here this weekend. Ora Mae says she don't think she can eat another bite of fish or one more hush puppy for a while. I took her into town for Mexican food, and when we got back I noticed your truck was still gone. If I hadn't seen your headlights shining out here, I never would have found you."

Cord pulled the next fence post from his truck.

"You plan on stringing barbed wire in the glow of your headlights?"

"I might." Cord didn't want to talk any more than he wanted to think. "You want to help?"

"Nope." Galem shoved his hat back. "You want to talk about what's bothering you?"

"Nope," Cord answered.

Galem took the hint and shifted into gear. "Well, I'll see you back at headquarters. I'm guessing if your battery don't run down, you'll be finished about dawn. Anything you want me to tell Little Miss?"

"Nope."

Galem pulled his hat back down almost to his eyebrows. "Well, nice talking to you."

Cord didn't stop to wave as the cook drove off.

# Chapter 35

Several hours later Cord didn't have to look up to know his wife's Jeep was flying across the land at twice the speed she should be driving. He could hear her coming, and dread filled him to the core.

He watched her as she shot out of her seat without turning off the engine or the lights. She headed right toward him. Storming, he thought, there was no doubt.

"Cord, what do you think you're doing out here in the middle of the night? The wire is dangerous enough to pull from post to post in daylight."

"There's work to be done," he said, without stopping the pounding. "That's what you married me for, isn't it? To work your ranch. Don't worry, you don't have to come out to sleep with me, because I don't plan on sleeping. In fact, I'm thinking I might just work until I drop dead. Then you could be a widow for a change."

She stormed around in and out of the beams of light like a moth. He guessed she had to be pretty confused right now. The last time she saw him, he'd kissed her good-bye so deeply she'd tried to tug him back to bed. She didn't know about the pictures or the trouble she might be in or that someone was setting fires in the back pastures hoping to burn the entire ranch down. She didn't know what Salem had told him. She didn't know that he knew she hadn't bothered to even try to keep him out of prison. Her silence had ruined his life just as Salem's lies had.

His whole body and mind were being drawn and quartered into pieces. Six years he'd sat in prison because not one person had come forward to back up his story. Of course the jury took the deputy's side. Cord had known there were others around the campfire, but he'd figured they all ran. Nevada must have stayed long enough to see what happened to him. She even talked to the other deputy, but she hadn't said a word when he needed someone to back him up.

She marched back to her Jeep and pulled out something, then marched back. "Galem said you ruined your shirt. I brought you another one. At least take the time to put it on."

"You spend too much time worrying about what I wear. Don't you have anything better to do?" He twisted the wire around, nicking his hand for the tenth time. Cord barely noticed. "What difference does it make anyway?"

She waited for him to take the shirt. He could hear her pouting like she always did when things weren't going her way.

He stuck the wire cutters in his back pocket and reached out for the denim shirt. In the lights he could see her face and hated himself for making her so unhappy. She'd grown up on a ranch. She knew he was putting himself in danger to be out here alone after dark. She'd probably worried for hours before finally coming out.

"You got a gun with you? There are wild hogs on this back land."

"No. It's been my experience that people are far more likely to hurt me than wild animals."

She walked halfway back to the Jeep, then turned to face him. "I hate it when you're like this, Cord, all closed off and cold."

He almost said he hated it when she wasn't honest. She played him and he didn't even know the rules.

Hell, he hated them both. What kind of game were they playing anyway? If she wouldn't stand up for him, why would she marry him?

Suddenly, he remembered one detail about the night at the lake. One fact he'd stored back in his whiskey-washed head drifted forward. Cord remembered the cop who'd cuffed him and shoved him down in Salem's blood and his own vomit. When he jerked him up to frisk him, he had ripped Cord's shirt. By the time they made it to the office it had fallen completely off.

Cord forced his anger to settle. Before he said a word, he saw panic flash in her eyes. She was afraid of him. He'd never hurt her, never raised his hand to her. But her blue eyes couldn't hide the fear as she stared at him. She thought she was watching a wild animal. Maybe she thought he'd snap and hurt her like all the folks in town seemed to think he might. After all, he was an ex-con.

Slowly, he took the shirt and pulled it over tired shoulders. "Thanks." His voice sounded hoarse even to him. "You were there at the lake ten years ago, weren't you, Nevada? You saw the cop tear off my shirt, because he was certain that I had a weapon. That's why you buy all those shirts. You're trying to replace that one from ten years ago."

She didn't answer.

"I talked to Salem this morning. He told me a girl told the officer left at the scene about what happened, but she wouldn't testify. The next day, her father swore she wasn't there." Cord let out a long breath and felt his muscles relax. "It was his word against a cop who'd seen her in the dark, and nobody thought to question your daddy's word; after all, he was a big rancher."

Nevada crumpled, disappearing from the lights of his truck and her Jeep. For a moment it was as if she just vanished.

Cord stepped toward where she'd been. On the third step, his leg bumped against her. He knelt, feeling her shoulders as she crouched, curled into a ball. His grip was rough as he pulled her up, needing to see her face. Her body was stiff in his grip, as if she were preparing for a blow.

Her tears cracked the wall of anger he'd been building inside all day. He circled her with his arms and pulled her close. All the times when she'd talked to him. All the nights she'd rattled on about nothing and suddenly his wife couldn't say a word.

"We're going to talk about this," he finally whispered as his hands stroked up and down her back. "It's not going to stand between us any-more. We're going to get it all out, right now."

He felt her nod against his shoulder. Before all the wrong words came between them and the fragile peace they'd known was forever broken, he kissed her one last time. Her lips were salty with tears, but she kissed him back. He felt her lip tremble and her hand rest hesitantly over his heart, but she gave him what he needed, one last kiss.

When he finally pulled away, he lifted her and walked to the bed of the pickup. It was dark there, but maybe what they had to say needed to be said in the shadows. After all, that was where it had happened.

He set her down and rested his hands on either side of her knees. "Tell me the truth. I've got a right to know. Did you marry me out of guilt? Was it some kind of sick joke?"

She gulped back a sob, and he understood.

"Before you start, let's get one thing straight. I'm not going to hurt you, Babe. No matter what you tell me, I swear, I'm not going to hurt you. I'm not going to leave you either. No matter what is said here, I go back with you and we finish what we've started. We make it to the first frost. We make the ranch pay."

She nodded, but he couldn't be sure she believed him. He fought the urge to touch her, but he knew if he did, they'd never work this out. The attraction between them was the only thing he knew was real.

She wrapped her arms around her sides, making the shadow of her seem smaller. "I saw what happened that July Fourth. I tried to tell the cop writing down names of who was there, but I could tell he wasn't buying my story even if he did write it in his notes. He kept asking if I was with you and would I lie just to help you."

Cord waited, giving her all the time she needed.

"When I got home, my dad exploded. He slapped me so hard my ears rang. He said everyone already hated the Britains, and if I got mixed up in your problem it would only be worse. He threatened all kinds of things if I spoke up again and convinced me that they wouldn't take my statement anyway. All the time he was talking, he was jerking me around, slapping me just to make sure I got the point of every word he said.

"If my mother hadn't stepped in, I think he

might have beat me senseless that night." She stared at her fingers twisted together in her lap. "My brother Barrett was there. He just stood watching and smiling, like it was about time someone taught me a lesson. I knew that night I was nothing to my dad, and my brother would never come to my rescue. I wanted to help you, but I couldn't fight them all, and I didn't believe a drunk minor's statement would be of much help."

Cord knew she was probably right. He waited for the rest.

Finally, she said, "For years, even after you got out, Barrett teased me that you were going to come over and kill me some night. He said if you weren't a bad guy when you went to prison, you would be when you got out. He had me afraid to drive down the road past your farm."

"How do you know I'm not?"

"I didn't, but that day you worked on the Jeep, I was at the end of my rope. Another year of poor management and I would lose the ranch. My ex had been promising to come back. When my father was dying and Barrett was packing to make his break, Bryce grew tired of all the problems and took off, thinking that I'd be begging for his help in a few months. He didn't take my calls or answer my mail. By the time he found out about the divorce it was almost final. He couldn't stop it, but he swore I'd come back to him begging for his help one day. Even after the divorce was final, he whispered that when I begged him to take me back, I'd have to come on his terms."

"So you married me before Bryce could get to you?"

"No. I needed your name to prove I'd moved on. I don't know, maybe I was tired of fighting him alone. I thought he'd back away if you were in the picture. I told Bryce that if he stepped foot on my land I'd shoot him, and I meant it. I married you because . . ." She hesitated, then put her hand on his arm. "When I saw how you took care of the Jeep that day and how no one gave you any credit for doing it, I wanted to make you the man you would have been if you hadn't gone to prison. The man you should have become."

Cord pulled back. He hadn't expected her to say something like that.

"I saw it in you, Cord, and I was right. You were a good man, broken and hollow, forced into a hard life. I thought I was helping, but I'm not sure if I haven't brought you more trouble than you had before."

He didn't touch her when he whispered, "Don't you know? You brought me to life." He couldn't lie to her, couldn't play any games.

He brushed his fingers over her hair. "I told you once that I'd forgive you anything, but this, it's nothing to forgive. I fell into hell, but you were going through it too."

"You don't hate me?"

"How could I hate someone I love so much? Somehow you crawled into my heart, and I'd have to cut the thing out of my body to stop caring."

He lifted her up and swung her into the light.

She smiled, seeing him open for the first time. All at once she was crying and laughing at the same time.

As he lowered her in front of him, a shot rang out in the night.

Cord reacted on instinct, taking her with him to the ground between the two sets of headlights.

Another shot. Then another as Cord pulled her deeper into the darkness.

"Follow me," he whispered. "Stay away from the light."

He heard one of the bullets kick up dirt. Another hit a rock three feet away. Whoever was firing was guessing. They were too far from town or the ranch to make it on foot, and it was unlikely anyone on the ranch would hear the shots. Their only chance was to make it to the Jeep.

He pulled her close, trying to shield her as much as he could with his body. "Move toward the Jeep and slip into the driver's side," he whispered. Another shot rang out. The shooter was spraying the area between the two lights, hoping to hit something.

Silently, he pulled the wire cutters from his back pocket and tossed them toward his pickup.

They hit the roof and rattled off onto the hood.

Three rapid-fire shots shattered the night air. All hit the truck. One smacked a light. Another broke the windshield.

Cord ran for the Jeep, hoping Nevada had made it before him.

When he climbed in the open window, he heard her shift and gun the engine. Like a rocket the little Jeep went backward for a quarter mile, then spun around and flew toward the main road.

He heard a few more shots, but he guessed they were out of range by the time whoever was shooting at them figured out what was happening.

"Where?" Nevada yelled.

"Straight to town. If we head to the ranch house, we might be followed." As she drove faster than he thought the old Jeep could possibly go, he dialed Galem and told him what had happened.

"Stay inside until light. Tell anyone at the bunkhouse to do the same. I don't want him picking anyone off. Call all the guys and tell them not to come in tomorrow until I send the order. We have to know it's safe before we step out."

Cord listened, then hung up. "Galem thinks the shooter might have followed you out to me. He said he passed a car on the county road that looked abandoned. When you went past, the shooter could have left his lights off and followed you. This Jeep makes so much noise neither of us would have heard another car."

"But he would have to know this ranch very well to know where I turned off the road onto the land. There's only a ten-foot hole in the fence."

Cord thought of the pictures. "He does know the ranch well."

Nevada turned onto the main road, and within a few minutes they saw the lights of Harmony.

When they got to the sheriff's department, the night shift was still working. Phil Gentry took all the notes but wanted to wait for daylight and the sheriff. "Not much we can do for a few hours. Alex will be in about eight if she doesn't get a call on the way into work. As long as you've got your people inside and safe, there's not much we can do about a shooter on your land. It would take a few dozen men to even find him, and we'd never be able to round them up this time of night."

"Once it's light, I can fly and tell you if he's on my land." Cord was already forming a plan.

"That might work. Alex and a few of us can be on the ground. We'll get the highway patrol to block the roads in and out of your place. If you spot him, you can direct us to him."

"I can do that." Cord fought down a yawn.

Phil shook his head. "You folks look beat. Why don't you go over to the diner and get some breakfast and a pot of coffee? I think they open at five."

"I could use a few hours' sleep if I'm going to be flying soon." Cord's muscles were sore from the hard work he'd done and he hadn't had anything to eat since breakfast yesterday, but most of all he needed to sleep.

"I got a couple of empty cells. You're welcome to your pick."

"No, thanks. I'll sleep standing up before I step foot in a cell. How about that couch in the sheriff's office?"

Phil waved them into her dark office. "It's not much better than the bunk in the cell, and with the glass door there's no privacy. What about you, Mrs. McDowell? What can I get you?"

"I stay with Cord," she whispered.

"I understand. You've both had quite a night, but don't worry, I'll be right outside on duty. You're safe here. You won't need an alarm clock. When the day shift comes on they make enough noise to wake even the dispatcher."

Cord tugged off his boots as she closed the door and found a blanket folded in a corner. He stretched out on the couch and she moved in beside him. The milky glass on the door made the pale light in the room almost moonlight.

"There's not enough room," she whispered, pushing him over.

He tugged her against him, already half asleep. "Where I sleep—"

"I know," she answered.

After a few minutes, she whispered, "Did you mean what you said back there?"

"When?"

"Before the shots were fired. Did you mean what you said about loving me?"

He took a deep breath and answered, knowing that there would be no going back, "I did. I think I always have, but Babe, I've got to admit, you're not an easy woman to love."

She rested her head on his shoulder and wrapped her arm across his chest. "I know. Haven't you heard that nothing worth doing is ever easy?"

He kissed the top of her head. "Well, at least it's not boring."

# Chapter 36

Ronny talked Martha Q into taking Mr. Carleon to the hospital to see the new baby. Mr. Carleon didn't seem all that interested, but when Ronny said she needed to take a nap, the proper gentleman understood.

"There are some papers I need to go over with you when you feel up to it," he said.

"I'll call you when I wake," Ronny promised as she waved.

She moved into her apartment as they drove away. To her surprise, he seemed to enjoy Martha Q's company. He lived a very ordered life, and

Martha Q had never even organized her thoughts. Maybe opposites do attract.

Ronny looked around her place. Everything had been put back in order as if Marty had never been there. But she saw the little differences and she knew he'd always be with her. This time he hadn't left her; he'd gone on ahead.

Mr. Carleon had left a folder at the kitchen table where he often did his work. This was the first time he hadn't put every paper away in his case, and she had no doubt that the folder was for her.

Absently, she looked at it, knowing this was what he planned to talk to her about when she was ready.

On the top of a stack of papers was a plane ticket to Paris for September third. Scribbled in Marty's bold hand was a note. *You have to see Paris in the fall.*

She moved her thumb over the words he'd written before turning the page.

Next was a two-week cruise down the Rhine and another for the Mediterranean. Complete with luggage tags and agendas for each day.

Next, clipped together were all that was needed for traveling down the Nile.

Ronny turned over another ticket, then another, each dated, planned, organized.

Each trip moved into the next until finally, the last was a flight to New York for December twenty-third. *Promise you'll stay to ring in the New Year,* a note said.

Beneath the last ticket was a key and a final note. *My apartment in Manhattan. Stay as long as you like.*

Next, she noticed page after page of details. Tours, dinners, plays, concerts all marked paid in full on the agendas. *There is plenty to do in New York until spring. Walk in Central Park when the gardens start to green and feel my love walking with you.*

Ronny smiled. Marty was giving her the world. She would trade it all for one more day with him, but that wasn't possible, so he'd given her memories.

He'd also given her time to mourn. By the fall he wanted her traveling.

She pulled on her jacket and walked the blocks to the cemetery, loving the cool morning air. The tent was gone and hundreds of flowers now lay across his grave. Ronny didn't cry; she just sat in the grass beside him and remembered.

"In a perfect world, you'll be with me," he'd said, and someday she would be, but now wasn't her time to die. Now was the time to live so when they did meet again, they could compare notes on all they'd seen.

After a while, she stood and walked home, thinking of all the things she had to do to be ready to travel. She wanted to finish her last two classes online and get her degree. Marty would have liked that. She would have to train someone to take over at the post office. She'd have to shop for clothes.

Her mother was waiting in front of her house when she came back from the cemetery. Ronny walked past her window expecting to see Dallas race off at any moment to prove she still wasn't speaking to her child.

Only Dallas rolled down the window. "I won't come in," she said, as if she'd been invited. "I just came to tell you that you can come home. I hate the thought of everyone seeing you falling apart in public over some man who wouldn't marry you but came to live with you."

"He came to die." Ronny was surprised how calm she felt. Her mother's words didn't bother her at all. She could almost see Marty smiling at her from the front window.

"Well, what are you going to do with yourself? Never a wife, not a widow. He didn't leave you any money, did he?" She answered her own question. "Of course not. If he had money he wouldn't have moved in with you so you could be a free nurse to him."

"He didn't leave me a dime, but I've saved a little and I think I may travel for a while."

Dallas laughed. "You travel? You don't even know how to drive on the interstate. Except for that time your father insisted we go to Kansas, you've never even stayed in a hotel. You'll get as far as Dallas or Oklahoma City and turn around, crying all the way home."

"Maybe. I'll send you a postcard if I don't turn around."

"You always were a fool, Ronny. Why would you want to travel alone when you can come home and keep me company?"

Ronny turned away and was halfway up the steps before she looked back. "Good-bye, Mother."

Dallas gunned the car and drove off without a word.

Smiling, Ronny could almost see Dallas's reaction when a card from a different country arrived every week. She'd go on the trip Marty planned and, who knows, maybe she would stay in New York long after the new year.

# Chapter 37

Cord was in the air by ten, crossing back and forth over the land. Nevada wanted to go with him, but he knew she'd be safer with the sheriff. They all agreed that the shooter had wanted to kill.

He flew low, looking for a car that didn't belong, or even tracks in the pastures. The area where he'd been putting up fence last night bordered government land that was too rocky for much of anything. A man would have to know the land, know what he was doing, to track across that land. He'd also have to be a good shot to fire on them at night.

Nevada told him Bryce had been a hunter since he could tag along with his dad, but that wasn't exactly damning evidence. Many men in Texas could say the same.

Which left Cord with only one answer. The man trying to kill Nevada might be Bryce Galloway, but he didn't have the proof he needed. Bryce might threaten her now and have knocked her around when they were married, but Cord couldn't prove anything.

He kept his phone close, hoping Cameron would call in with facts.

Another piece of information kept rolling around in his head. Bryce spent his days building alibis. The kind of folks he was talking to wouldn't be able to remember if they talked to him on a certain day of the week by the time they were questioned. In a week he'd probably be able to produce someone who swore he was in town all day, every day. So far everything he'd done to try to harm Nevada had been at night, but he might have to act during the day if he wanted to get closer. Which would mean that he'd have to come on the ranch in daylight.

Cord had told the cowhands to search in

groups of two. They were all armed with rifles, standard for any man in the saddle. Cord guessed he was the only man on the ranch not armed. Nevada must have taken the Colt from the office drawer because it had been missing since the snakes visited.

The now-familiar feeling of trouble thundering in rattled through his body. He had to protect her. He had to do the right thing. He had to follow the law.

He crossed one more time over the place where he'd been working last night. His truck, with the windshield missing, looked abandoned. Knowing Nevada, she'd probably ordered him a new one. He'd never known anyone to spend money faster than she did.

As he circled back to his farm to refuel, he spotted the sheriff's cruiser parked near the field he used as his landing strip. Cord rolled to a stop and climbed out.

"Nothing?" she said.

"Nothing," he answered.

"I was afraid of that." She walked with him toward his old pickup. "I found your truck out in the south pasture earlier. It was shot up, just like you said. The crime team came over from Amarillo to work the evidence."

Cord pulled out two bottles of water from the cooler in the bed of his truck and offered her one. "They find anything?"

"Yeah, your truck was shot to hell."

Cord smiled because she'd used his exact words when he'd told her where to find the truck. "I should have gone into law enforcement."

"Something else. The bullets used were hollow point. Not as accurate from a distance, but if they'd hit one of you, they would have done some serious damage."

"Which means?"

"Which means whoever was firing at you wanted you dead, not just hurt."

Cord leaned against the old pickup. Between digging holes in hard earth all day and half the night and then sleeping on the sheriff's couch, he felt like a pretzel left out to dry.

Alex took a drink and added, "We're not dealing with just a mad ex-husband. If you're right and it is Bryce Galloway, he means to kill you both. Maybe he figures if he can't have Nevada, no one should."

"I figured that out up there." He pointed at the sky. "I think he tried to pay someone else to bother us, but when he got serious, he decided to do the dirty work himself. Nevada said that as far as she knows he'd always gotten everything and everyone he wanted until her."

Alex followed his logic. "Who stands to benefit from her dying?"

"Me, I guess. The lawyer asked us if we had wills, and we said we'd worry about it later. So if she dies, I inherit." He hardened. "That makes me a suspect."

Alex smiled. "You forgot one thing. Whoever was shooting last night was shooting at you both. I'd think that pretty well takes you out of the lineup."

Alex let her words sink in, then continued, "Nevada and you are both in danger. This isn't about the ranch, it's about you two."

"I'm not worried about me."

She smiled. "I could have guessed that, but *I* am. I don't like the idea of someone killing anyone in my town."

"Even me?" He wasn't sure he believed her.

"Even you." She laughed. "You're starting to grow on me. How about we go find Nevada?"

Cord tossed his empty water bottle in the bed of the pickup. "She's at the ranch house."

Alex straightened. "No. I was just there. I even tried her cell. No answer."

Without a word they both jumped into their vehicles and raced toward the ranch.

Five minutes later Cord hit the kitchen door first. Ora Mae looked up from pulling a pie from the oven and glared at him.

"Where's Nevada?" He didn't have time for her to remind him to wipe his feet or tell him what time it was. Any time he walked in early, that always seemed to be her first response.

Ora Mae nodded at the sheriff as Alex stepped

beside Cord. She answered formally as if testifying. "She got a call about twenty minutes ago saying one of her horses was acting sick."

"Who called?"

"I don't know, but Nevada took off in that old Jeep." She looked from Cord to the sheriff. "I'm sure she's safe. Her barn is not that far from the house and you've got an armed guard posted over there."

Alex didn't answer the housekeeper. She just lifted her phone and hit a number. "I need all deputies on the roads into the Boxed B. No one, and I mean no one, leaves this land unless I say so. Then ask the highway patrol to log all cars on county roads that border the ranch."

Cord walked beside her as she moved to her cruiser. "We may be overreacting—"

"We're not," he snapped.

Cord looked in the direction of the barn where Nevada kept her horses. He couldn't see it, but what he saw stopped his heart.

A few thin lines of smoke rose, widening in the air and disappearing.

Cord ran toward his truck.

# Chapter 38

Nevada stared at the fire growing in the center stall of her barn. She could hear the horses moving, kicking at their stalls, making low sounds of fear. They knew something was wrong; they could smell the fire.

"You can't do this!" she screamed toward the loft above her. "Leave me here, but get the horses out. Please don't kill them!" Hot tears rolled down her face. She fought against the rope binding her hands and feet.

"Why?" Bryce's angry voice came from above. "What do I care if they die—these pets of yours? You've made a fool of me, Nevada. I thought when you divorced me I'd go back to my life, but I couldn't. Not when you didn't get what you deserved."

He tossed a bale of hay on the fire he'd started a few minutes before. "My friends back home, even my family made fun of me. *Where's the little wife, Bryce? Lose her, did you?* I couldn't stand the jabs. Even when I tried dating, it never worked. They weren't as pretty as you. They didn't crumble as easily. I was treated like damaged goods. If you didn't want me, no one else seemed to. I finally figured out I'd have to deal with you before I could move on."

He glared down at her from above. "Only you messed it all up. I thought I could frighten you and you'd give in like you did when we were married, but you married someone else. You belong to me, Nevada. You have since I first saw you. After seeing the way your father and brother treated you, I knew you were made for me. I'd have no problem with control." He swore at her, then added, "Only you tricked me, and you'll pay by dying with the screams of your beloved horses in your head."

Bryce laughed. "Poor little unloved Nevada. Once you're gone I'll think of myself as a widower; after all, I will have lost the one woman I ever wanted."

Smoke began to fill the barn, and the horses' cries ripped at her mind. "Please," she said, knowing that he wasn't listening. "Please let the horses out."

Bryce started down the ladder at the far wall. He stopped to watch the fire as smoke fogged the air inside the barn. "I thought I could whip you into shape, but you were stronger than I thought. You didn't take the bit like you should have."

She struggled, wishing she could reach her duster only a few feet away. Deep in the pocket was her father's old Colt.

"You never cared for me," she said, more to herself than him. She'd known more love in the weeks married to Cord than she'd known all her life.

"You got that right, but I wanted you."

Nevada coughed. The smoke was getting thicker. "You'll never get away with it."

He laughed. "Who's going to stop me? The fire in your barn was an accident. I made sure it looked like the guard you left upstairs was smoking. He tossed a few cigars out the loft opening, and the fire department will find them and think one must have started the fire."

Nevada had been so shocked to see Bryce waiting for her in the barn, she hadn't thought of the guard. Johnson, the youngest of the brothers, was on duty today. "Where's the kid?"

"Oh, he's dead"—Bryce almost giggled—"or he will be soon. The smoke's getting thicker and thicker up there. I knocked him over the head and tossed the body in the back of the loft. They'll find his body during the cleanup. What a mess this place is going to be. In fact, I'd better hurry if I want to get out alive. I parked a bike out behind the barn, so I'll be miles away before anyone gets here."

Nevada steadied her voice. "You are really going to leave me here to burn to death?"

"Oh no, dear. I couldn't do that." He pulled her to her feet and shoved her toward the horse now going wild in the first stall. "I want you to be near your horse. You always worried more about them than you ever did me. I've even locked the barn door and plan to leave out the back. By the time anyone sees the fire and breaks in, it will be too late."

Nevada stumbled, unable to move her feet.

He jerked her forward, half dragging her with him. The ropes cut into her wrists, but she barely noticed.

"I'm going to let the horse kill you. Fitting, don't you think?"

He pulled her hands free of the ropes as he shoved her inside and pushed the bolt closed. "One more thing," he yelled above the horses' screams. "I shot this one full of a steroid. Even you won't be able to calm her, but don't worry, I'll wait until you stop screaming before I leave."

The mare shoved against Nevada, knocking her off her feet. She tried to reach the rope binding her feet, but the horse was too near, too threatening. All she could do was twist out of her way.

Nevada rolled against the stall as the animal raged, fighting to get out. A hoof slammed against her leg, snapping the bone just above the knee.

Nevada screamed and fought to press flat against the stall wall. She heard Bryce laugh as smoke blurred her sight.

If she couldn't see anything, neither could he. She clamped her mouth closed so tight she feared her teeth might crack, but she didn't make a sound. Let him think she was dead; she would be in seconds. If the horse didn't trample her, the smoke would suffocate her before the fire even reached her.

She waited for death, listening to the screams of her horses. She'd ride into the hereafter with them.

# Chapter 39

By the time Cord reached the barn, smoke was coming from the roof. He didn't slow the old pickup as he raced toward the barn door, closed and locked.

The Ford hit the huge doors hard and Cord hit the brakes as lumber tumbled around him. Bellows of smoke escaped with waves of heat that felt like opening an oven an inch from his face.

By the time he was out of the truck and running, his face felt sunburned.

He reached the first stall and threw the bolt. The horse almost ran over him.

As he ran for the second stall, he heard Alex yelling for everyone to stay away, but the cowboys came barging in, their bandannas around their faces, like bandits of old. One by one the stall doors were flung open and the horses were herded out. A few of the hands grabbed fire extinguishers and tried to fight the fire, but it had spread too far.

"Nevada!" Cord yelled, but there was no answer.

He moved to the next stall, where a mare was bleeding from fighting so hard to get out. When the horse ran past him, he saw a dark movement in the back of the stall. For a second, he thought it might be a colt, and then Nevada's blond hair brushed across the bloody floor.

Men were shouting all around him, but the world went silent. All he saw, all he could think about was the woman curled on the floor.

"Everyone get out now!" Galem shouted. "The roof is about to fall!"

Cord knelt, knowing he wouldn't leave her. Carefully, as if she were a newborn, he lifted her up. Her arm was bleeding and a gash on her head poured blood over her beautiful hair. One leg twisted at an odd angle. He knew it was broken. "Come on, Babe," he said as he pulled her against his chest. "Let's go home."

She cried out once as he moved her, but she never let go of him.

He carried her through the burning barn with fire flying around him. All the horses were gone, but the flames seemed to be laughing in victory.

Ten feet out of the barn he cleared the smoke, and a cheer went up. He knew they were safe.

A fire truck and an ambulance were pulling up as everyone backed away from the burning barn.

Medics ran toward Nevada. They both had packs of supplies and a stretcher balanced between them.

Cord slowly laid her on the stretcher. He looked up at the barn, now completely engulfed in flames. Only the charred outline of his truck showed at what had once been the opening. The cowboys were standing back several yards. Galem bandaged one man's hand and Ora Mae passed out water bottles.

The adrenaline slowly drained from Cord's body. Every man on the ranch must have seen the smoke and come running. Pickups and trucks were parked along the road and in the pasture like scattered toys.

"She's stable," a medic said. "Looks like we're dealing with a broken arm and a compound fracture of the leg. Got to have the doc check that head wound as well. We need to transport her. You coming along, sir?"

Cord didn't answer. He knelt beside Nevada and smiled when he saw her blue eyes open. "You all right, Babe?"

"I will be. Thanks to you."

He smiled. "We got an agreement; you have to sleep with me every night. I couldn't let you die and back out on that."

She tried a smile but couldn't manage one. He

had a feeling the shot the medic had given her was taking the edge off the pain. "Tell the sheriff it was Bryce who did this."

Alex moved closer. "You don't have to tell me. We found him behind the barn."

The medics moved in, lifting Nevada's stretcher. "Are you coming with her, sir?" he asked again.

"No." Cord looked at Nevada. "I'm going to stay here and end this now."

His wife nodded as if she understood. "I'll be waiting when you're finished."

When he leaned in to kiss her cheek, she added in a sleepy whisper, "I love you, you know."

He straightened. "I know."

As the ambulance pulled away, Cord followed the sheriff around the barn to the horse tank.

Johnson sat on the ground, while Dr. Freeman looked at his head. "I need to get to the horses and check on them, son. I don't have time to thump on you, but if you were a horse I'd say you're fine. Not too bright, of course, to drop out of a twenty-foot loft door."

Johnson grinned. "I had this guy to break my fall. I was coming to when I heard him say he was leaving out the back, so I held my breath and waited just above the little door. He didn't even look up, but he must have thought he was hit by a falling train."

Cord looked over at a man in handcuffs standing beside the sheriff's cruiser.

"If you're thinking of killing him, forget it." Alex walked up behind Cord.

"He tried to kill my wife," Cord said simply.

"He's going with me and he'll be locked away for a long time."

Cord smiled at the sheriff. "That's worse than anything I could do to him. I know. He's all yours, Sheriff." He took a few steps and added, "Remind him a few times on the drive in that Nevada is fine and she's with me."

"I'll do that, Cord."

Jackson and Jefferson straightened from where they'd been hovering over their brother. Jackson balled his fists. "He tried to kill my kid brother, Sheriff. Mind if I pound on him a little?"

"Sorry. I can't let you do that, but look at the bright side. Johnson had to get out of that barn. Bryce here saved him a broken bone or two by giving him something to land on."

Neither Jackson nor Jefferson looked happy about having to settle for nonviolence, but they respected the sheriff. "Would you let him know that if he ever gets out, one of us will be waiting for him?"

"Sure." Alex headed toward her car. "Johnson, if your boss has no objections, I'd like you to come on in and give a full statement. Then I'll get Nevada's as soon as the doctor gets finished with her."

As they moved around what was left of the barn,

Galem offered, "Boss, you might want to ride along with me. Your truck wasn't in too good of shape the last time I saw it. It appears trucks have a very short life around you. At this rate you might singlehandedly keep Ford in business."

Cord laughed. "Yeah, I keep parking them in the wrong spot."

# Chapter 40

Martha Q pulled into her drive, trying not to touch the steering wheel any more than necessary with wet fingernails. Looking up, she swore.

Two cowboys and a sheriff's deputy looking like they'd just had a run in with Smokey the Bear were sitting on her front porch.

"I'm going to chop that porch off and drag it into the creek bed." She climbed out of her car, forgetting all about her nails. As she headed up the walk, she yelled, "I'm full up, boys. No more room in the inn."

Amid all the dirt and soot, she recognized Cord McDowell. "And you, Cord, you need to go home to that wife of yours." She was at the steps when she added, "But take a bath first. You smell like a campfire."

"My wife is in the hospital with a few broken bones. She got trampled by a horse an hour ago." Nothing in Cord's tone was conversational. He was simply stating facts. "We're just coming along with the deputy. He's got a search warrant and we thought we'd give him a hand."

"Bryce Galloway in some kind of trouble?"

Phil Gentry stepped around Cord. "Galloway is under arrest for trying to kill Cord's wife."

Martha Q raised her eyebrow, surprised at being right.

Squeals came from just inside. The widows, if she were guessing.

Cord turned to Martha Q. "Would you mind if we went up?"

She wouldn't dream of saying no. This was the most exciting thing that had happened in months. While they tromped up the stairs, she called Anthony and told him to hurry over.

As he walked up to the porch, three gray-headed women rushed out, all chattering about there being too much excitement at the inn. Joni paused only long enough to give her notice of leaving to Martha Q.

"You've got a free night coming," Martha Q suggested.

"No, thanks," Joni said as she rushed away. "I'm going home."

Mr. Carleon stepped up beside Martha Q. "Is everything all right, dear?"

"Yes, Anthony, but we'd better step away from the door. I'll explain as they carry Bryce Galloway's things out. You won't have to worry about sharing a bathroom again."

He smiled as he took his chair on the porch. "Tell me all about it, dear."

They rocked in the porch chairs as the deputy and two cowboys carried out everything that had belonged to Bryce Galloway.

"I'm glad he's gone. I think Bryce was the one who grabbed Ronny the night before Marty died. Maybe he was just angry and wanted to take it out on someone, or maybe he knew she was Cord's friend and thought by hurting her, he'd get to Cord."

"Have you any proof?" Martha Q asked.

"No, just a hunch."

Martha Q shook her head. "Sometimes I'm afraid to be alone in this big old house."

She shivered, and he took her hand. "But you don't need to worry. I've decided to stay awhile, if the room's still available."

"It is for you, Anthony."

"Thank you, Martha," he added, without letting go of her hand. "I like it here."

"Here in Harmony, or here with me?"

He winked at her, and Martha Q giggled as if she were on her first date.

# Chapter 41

Cord cleaned up at the sheriff's office before going over to the hospital. He looked terrible, but he didn't care. His wife was going to be all right. Bryce was locked away, and this time there were plenty of witnesses who could back Cord up on exactly what happened. Thanks to Cameron, the sheriff found the rifles Bryce had used in the abandoned house behind the mall. No amount of family money would buy him out of this mess.

When Cord called to check on Nevada, the nurse on duty told him to come quick, she was throwing a fit wanting to get out.

He wasn't surprised. On a good day she didn't react well to stress. He had to get to her quick. Galem was waiting to drive him over, and then the cook said he needed to get back to the ranch. Cord knew he'd be back if needed, but it was a husband's place next to his wife now.

Five minutes later, she looked up from the forms she was filling out, Cord smiled down at her. "Hi, Babe."

"How are my horses?" she asked. "If one of them is hurt, I'll—"

"The horses are fine. Aren't you worried about me?"

"Why? You seem in one piece, except it looks like you've ruined another shirt."

"Sorry about that," he shrugged. "When are you getting out of that bed and coming home to sleep with me?"

Nevada frowned. "Are you crazy? What's not burned on you looks dirty."

"Well, if you'd stayed put in the house like I told you, I'd only be dirty and not burned."

The nurse darted from the room as if she thought a fight might break out any minute.

Cord and Nevada both laughed, and then Nevada cried in pain. He comforted her with his easy touch on the part of her arm not covered by a cast.

"She's out there telling everyone how mean we are to each other," Nevada said.

"I don't care."

"Me either. If I want to storm at my husband, I will."

He leaned so close she could feel his words against her cheek. "I love you, storms and all."

"I love you too," she answered. "Maybe even more than I love my horses, but don't you dare tell them that."

He grinned, knowing just how great a love that must be.

# Epilogue

## October 27

Cord worked until sunset worrying about winter coming on. They'd made a good profit on the cattle, but he'd kept quite a few head to increase the herd. The winter crops should have already been planted, so he'd have men working all weekend.

Any day the first frost would hit. For months he'd kept thinking that the work would slow down, but it never did. His list of things that needed to be done grew longer every day. He'd finished the rebuilding of the barn for Nevada's horses, but there were still things that needed doing and never enough hours in the day.

His mind was full of everyday problems when he stepped into his old farmhouse after dark. Nevada said she wanted to meet him there. He knew she'd been talking about remodeling the place, but Cord didn't have time to listen to all the details.

The doctor said it would give her something to do while she recovered. The arm healed quickly, but the leg had to have therapy. He'd slept beside her for more than a month before she'd begged him to touch her. Making love to her the day she got her cast off was like making love to her for the first time. He was afraid he'd hurt her and she was afraid he wouldn't be attracted to her, but in truth Cord didn't even see the scars. They didn't matter.

When he reached for the light switch just inside the kitchen door of his old place, he noticed candles on the table. For a moment, he just stood staring, thinking maybe he'd walked into the wrong house. The place looked nothing like it had. Like everything she did, Nevada must have rushed into decorating full steam ahead.

Nevada, wearing one of the cotton dresses he loved, stepped from the shadows with only a slight limp.

"Hi, Babe," he said. "What's this all about?"

"Our bargain is up. The weatherman says it'll come a hard freeze tonight." She held up the paper. "We made it all through the season."

He hadn't even had time to think about the bargain. Between work and getting her well, his days had been too full to count.

"I want you to move back to your place, so I fixed it up. Ora Mae and I even moved your clothes over this morning."

Cord couldn't seem to force air into his lungs. She couldn't be serious. They hadn't talked about the contract they'd signed the day they married since she'd been hurt. She'd told him she loved him a hundred times. Whispered it in his ear when others were near and screamed it out loud when they made love. He'd thought they'd go on forever.

She moved into the soft candlelight. "I don't have to sleep where you sleep anymore."

He nodded once. If he said a word, he was afraid he'd never stop. Maybe he hadn't made it plain how much he loved her, but it never crossed his mind that he would just be the next husband on her list to leave.

"So, since I'm free of that part of the bargain, I can sleep wherever I want." She took one more step, careful not to limp. "And from now on I'm sleeping with my husband in this house. In his house."

Kissing him softly, she whispered, "Because I love him dearly."

He pulled her against him as his tender kisses welcomed her and his heart started beating again. She was making it plain she wanted no bargain between them; only love would hold them together now.

Finally, he pulled back and smiled down at her. "I'm nothing but mean, you know. You might want to reconsider. I work too hard and I don't talk things over enough."

"There is nothing to reconsider. I found you,

Cord, and I'm not letting you go. Not ever."

"You sure you won't get mad one day and storm off down the road to your place?"

She smiled. "I gave the ranch house to Galem and Ora Mae today. If you don't keep me, I'll have to go live in Martha Q's inn."

"Oh, don't worry, Mrs. McDowell. I'm keeping you." He picked her up. "How about you show me the house, starting with our room."

"Don't you want to eat dinner first?"

He moved up the stairs. "Later. I want to see the stars through those skylights over our bed first, Babe."

She grinned. "I didn't think you were listening. I love you, Cord."

"And I love you."

# About the Author

Jodi Thomas is a certified marriage and family counselor, a fifth generation Texan, a Texas Tech graduate, and writer-in-residence at West Texas A&M University. She lives in Amarillo, Texas. Visit the author online at www.jodithomas.com. Or you can catch up with her postings on Facebook at facebook.com/JodiThomasAuthor or on Twitter at twitter.com/JodiThomas.

**Center Point Large Print**
600 Brooks Road / PO Box 1
Thorndike ME 04986-0001 USA

**(207) 568-3717**

**US & Canada:**
**1 800 929-9108**
**www.centerpointlargeprint.com**